LIMERICK BEYOND TIME

CAROL PEREIRA

LIMERICK BEYOND TIME

Alexandria - Canada — 2025

1st edition

@Carol Pereira 2025

Limerick beyond time

Author: Carol Pereira

Editing: Holly Cowman

Graphic Design: Jhean Ramos and João Vitor de Souza

Translation: Janaína Andrade and Carol Pereira

"To the city of Limerick, which welcomed me with open arms."

Sumário

Introduction _____ *11*
Time in Limerick _____ *19*
Other Times _____ *95*
New Times _____ *173*

Introduction

Olivia's long fingers were restless on the keyboard. She pressed F5 to refresh the page, but nothing happened. Everything remained static, even though the results should have been released ten minutes ago.

Every time she pressed the key, her heart seemed to stop for a moment. When nothing happened, she felt frustrated and convinced that her name would never appear on the screen.

She was once again anxiously awaiting the results of the Teachers of Brazil Award, a contest aimed at raising educational standards in Brazil and rewarding good teaching practices. The award was promoted by the Ministry of Education (MEC), the country's most important educational body, and was supported by CAPES, the Government scholarship agency, and other institutions. Olivia had won this competition twice before. The first time, many people thought it was beginner's luck, as if she had submitted her application and, like a lottery, had her name chosen. She felt like "no man is a prophet in his own country" and that people underestimated the importance of the award. Despite this, winning the competition had put the name of Alfredo Wagner, the small town where she was born and always lived, in the spotlight, as the project she created to record the history of the city was featured in the publicity about the competition. When she won the award for the second time, many people may have finally realized that it was not a matter of luck; maybe Olivia was really competent. But winning a third time seemed too much.

She kept pressing F5, but she didn't have high hopes. She had already gotten through the first stage of the contest, but if lightning never strikes in the same place twice, let alone three times, would it be possible to win again?

F5 again, and her hands were sweating. She didn't have anyone to share this moment with and didn't even know if she wanted to. If her name didn't appear, she would just close the page, take a deep breath, and move on with her life. She had already won two editions of the award; she didn't need one more, did she? She repeated this to convince herself, but of course, she wanted to win.

Olivia was a creative and fun teacher, a woman with shrewd intelligence and quick answers, but insecure from head to toe. She may have seemed to be a confident person, full of opinions, who defended everything she believed in, but only she knew how much the opinions of others affected her. It didn't match her persona, but the truth was that although she was much more than what many people thought of her, she was always concerned about their opinions.

One more F5, and there was her name: Olívia Walter Kalckmann, representing the south of Brazil in the Primary Education category.

She felt dizzy, a little disoriented, and it felt like her heart would burst with happiness. She opened the door and, to her surprise, there was no one in the hallways of the public building where she worked. She went down the stairs and, with long, hurried strides, crossed Anitápolis Street, the main street in the city center, and ran into the building where the Municipal Department of Education was located. Pale and breathless, she asked if the secretary was there. Seeing that she had rushed in, the Secretary of Education, Ana, replied:

"I'm here, Olivia. Come over to my room. What happened, girl?"

"Do you remember that award we were talking about? The one I had been approved for in the first stage."

"Yes, I remember. Did you get it?"

"Yes! The results just came out," Olivia said with tears in her eyes, visibly moved.

Olivia's explosion of joy caught the attention of the other employees, and when they realized what was happening, they also congratulated the young teacher.

"You're really lucky, Olivia! Won again?!" said Cláudio, one of the secretary's employees.

"It's not luck, Cláudio, it's competence. If it were luck, she should have played the lottery," said the secretary, knowing that this whole story about winning by luck bothered Olivia.

"And what is the prize?" asked another employee.

"There's a trophy, money, and a trip to Ireland."

"Ireland? Where's that?" said Cláudio, frowning, as if he had no idea where the country was geographically located.

"Ireland is the land of U2, Cláudio. How do you not know that?" replied the employee.

"That's right, it's in Europe. It's the land of U2 and also of The Cranberries, a band I've liked since I was a child. By the way, the prize will take us to their city, Limerick, where the band was formed. Oh my God, I can't believe I won!"

"The shift is almost over, go get your things. We need to celebrate," said the secretary, hugging Olivia again.

It was October 2017, and the trip would be in May 2018, but Olivia couldn't have been more anxious. It was a mix of feelings, and she didn't know what Limerick, that lost city in the middle of Ireland, meant. Yes, it was the hometown of one of the most important bands in her life, but what else did it represent? If it weren't for the award, she would probably never have gone there. Olivia loved to travel, but if she were going to visit Ireland, she would probably have stayed on the conventional tourist route, between Dublin, the capital, and the Cliffs of Moher, one of the country's most famous natural attractions. It was unlikely that she would ever have visited Limerick, but the city, without a rational explanation, had always fascinated her.

Time went by, and in January 2018, The Cranberries' frontwoman, Dolores O'Riordan, died. She was found submerged in the bathtub in her hotel room in London. The world felt her loss, and now Olivia's visit had even more meaning: getting to know the city where this band, which was very famous in the '90s, started their career. They already knew the trip's schedule, which involved technical visits to schools and universities, and tourist attractions, such as castles, the Cliffs of Moher, and many more places that would certainly make the trip unforgettable.

The young and dreamy teacher travelled with 29 other teachers. Everyone had already met at the awards ceremony, which had taken place in São Paulo in December 2017, and they were as excited as Olivia about the opportunity to get to know Ireland. From the plane, Olivia looked out the window, and her heart didn't seem to contain all the joy of seeing those varied shades of green, divided into countless rectangles that, seen from above, seemed to form a mosaic. That was Ireland.

Limerick, or Luimneach in Irish, is located in the Mid-West of the island and is the fourth largest city in Ireland, with approximately 94,000 inhabitants. It is 200 km from the capital.

When they arrived, they went straight to Courtbrack, the student accommodation where they stayed for seven days in the city. To welcome the Brazilian teachers, a dinner had been organized in one of the most famous pubs in town. There, they tasted Guinness, the iconic Irish stout, and listened to the country's traditional music. Olivia was delighted to hear that sound and taste Guinness for the first time in her life. She tried to explain to herself what she was feeling at that moment.

It felt like a homecoming. It was all so eerily familiar: the sounds, tastes, and atmosphere of the city as a whole. Olivia had never felt that way in any other place she had ever been.

Like so many other cities in Ireland, Limerick, a traditionally Catholic city, has dozens of churches scattered everywhere. Saint Mary's Cathedral is the most important of them, and a visit there was part of the teachers' itinerary. It's an all-stone church, built in 1168, located in the heart of the medieval city and on the banks of the River Shannon. Olivia marvelled at the church, an immense building made with ancient stones and beautifully decorated with colourful stained glass windows, full of details and meaning. She felt a strange and intense connection, like she had rarely felt in her life. The silence of that place seemed to bring back memories of something Olivia had never experienced before. There, she felt peace and a sense of safety, so she took the opportunity to pray.

Olivia was Catholic but not very religious. She had spent several years without going to church, as she believed that following God's commandments was more about her actions than anything else. She prayed every day to thank God for her life, but she was not accustomed to going to church. She had visited many churches around the world, but more as tourist attractions than for their spiritual significance. On one of these trips, she was told that when someone visits a church for the first time, they have the right to make three requests, and then they come true. Since that day, as a ritual, every time she visited a new church, Olivia always asked for three things: her grandmother's health, that her dreams would come true, and the love of Cristiano, the man she had loved for almost ten years.

Olivia harboured this one-sided passion for Cristiano. It was a complicated story that had made her stop drinking whiskey because she got very drunk the day the young man asked another woman to marry him. He had moved on with his life, but Olivia had not. She was stuck in a love that he had nurtured for a very long time, like someone who gives crumbs to fish and keeps them coming back for a little more. Olivia felt terrible, but like anyone trapped in a platonic crush, she believed that one day everything would change and, like in a fairy tale, they would live happily ever after. However, this unrequited love made her doubt the possibility that one day she would find someone who would make her happy and who would love her in the same way.

At least two-thirds of her three requests had come to pass. Her grandmother, who was the person she loved most in the whole world, was still healthy, and her dreams, the ones she believed in the most, were coming true. So, she took advantage of the silence and peace of the place to thank God for everything she was experiencing and for all the opportunities that life was giving her.

Olivia had dreamed of being a writer since she was a child. Her mother had taught her her first words and put a desk in her room so that her daughter could use it to write every day. Maybe Olivia's mother's dream was to be a writer as well, and as she couldn't achieve this dream, she projected it onto her daughter, not as a burden, but as a beautiful, pure incentive that made her take pleasure in words. The girl had started as a child writing a diary, then she created a blog in which she wrote about various subjects. The year before the trip, she had released her first book and was already scheduled to release her second. She was no best-selling writer, far from it, but she felt quite happy putting down on paper everything her vivid imagination had created.

When the group left the church, Olivia was trying to record the sound of the crows gathering over the trees. She had never seen crows before and thought of their sound as the soundtrack to Ireland. She took the camera and sneaked out so she wouldn't scare them and could get what she wanted. She recorded the sound and, before she knew it, she was on the graveyard side of the church. The Celtic crosses that adorned most of the tombs, many of them built more than a century ago, charmed her. She seemed to be hypnotized looking at the cemetery when the group called her, as they were leaving to visit King John's Castle.

Olivia shook her head as if coming out of a trance and followed the group. Outside the railings that bordered the church, she was still intrigued by the cemetery. She stopped again, looked around, and decided to take a picture, one of her best records of the trip.

Olivia spent another week in the city before returning to Brazil, and when she returned to her beloved Alfredo Wagner, the only thing she wanted was an opportunity to live in Limerick. There, she had met some students who had received scholarships to study at Mary I – as Mary Immaculate College was called by those who knew it well – and then she got it into her head that she would get one of those scholarships too. It wouldn't be easy, as she was convinced that her English was far below the required level, but she had to find a way to do it. This inexplicable desire became her life's goal and what she thought about all the time.

One day, while driving home, she started crying because everything she felt was so confusing. "Why did she feel this need to go to a place she barely knew? How could she be sure she wanted to go there when all the odds seemed against it?" The truth was that the girl felt her fate was in Limerick. Olivia had always been passionate about her city and had already turned down countless opportunities that offered better salaries and possibilities for professional growth because it had never been her plan to leave Alfredo Wagner. How had this crazy desire to change continents come to her mind? How was she so determined to move to a country where she barely spoke the language? She didn't have answers to all those questions she was asking herself incessantly, but she had already made up her mind. If she didn't get the scholarship, she would save money and do an English course in Limerick, and then, with greater English fluency, she would get the scholarship to fulfil her dream of studying at Mary I and living there. She talked to Bella, her best friend, several times in an attempt to express and understand this feeling. Neither she nor her friend came up with any explanations, but Bella encouraged her and said she was sure she could make this dream come true.

The fact was that perhaps the person who told the story of the three wishes was right, as the desire to fulfil her dreams had come true once again. Exactly one year after she had fallen in love with the Emerald Isle, she had applied for the scholarship. A couple of months later, Olivia received the news that she had been selected to be a Government of Ireland scholar.

The International Education Scholarship (GOI-IES) funding is an annual programme that distributes 60 scholarships to international undergraduate and postgraduate students across Ireland. Every year, thousands of students from around the world apply for these scholarships, and that year Mary Immaculate College received four spots. To Olivia's delight, she was selected by the Irish government to receive one of them.

In less than two months, she would be living in Limerick. She could finally cross the ocean and understand where her sense of connection to the city came from.

Time in Limerick

Leaving Alfredo Wagner had certainly been the hardest decision Olivia had ever made in her life. Knowing that she would spend a year far from the people she loved most in the world made her feel downhearted and overwhelmed, wondering if she really should make this life-changing decision.

Going to Limerick had undoubtedly been the fulfilment of a dream she had cherished for a long time, since returning to Brazil the year before, completely in love with that city. Olivia was a dreamer, but the kind who rolls up her sleeves and doesn't rest until her dreams come true. She had done everything in her power to compete and win the scholarship: studied a lot of English in online classes, taken the exam, carefully written her proposal, collected letters of recommendation, and finally she had received a positive response. However, when that answer came, she was filled with doubts. Olivia couldn't explain how she felt; it was a mix of emotions: first came the joy of having won the scholarship, but then came the uncertainty, embittering that moment of pure happiness.

Would she really cross the ocean? Could she leave her whole life behind to seize this opportunity? There were sleepless nights before she was able to decide. It was much harder than she had imagined, but she felt she had to go. Somehow, she felt strongly in her heart that Limerick was where she needed to be to live out the next chapter of her story.

Olivia looked at her packed bags and despaired, thinking that everything connecting her to her life in Brazil and her family was within them. When she finally arrived in Ireland, everything else would be new. She was boarding with her entire life packed into two small suitcases and armed with all the courage she could muster. After all, courage is almost always the main ingredient needed to make dreams come true.

While adapting to her new life in Limerick, she was still trying to understand where her need to move there and have a life so different from the one she had lived until then had come from. A time of lots of learning and profound transformation had begun for Olivia.

Even a few weeks after arriving in Limerick, she still felt like she was dreaming. In fact, this was more than she had ever dreamed of. When walking around town, she often thought that what she was experiencing wasn't even real. The way education was treated and respected, the cordiality of the people, and how friendly the Irish were... everything amazed her.

Living in a country so different from her own was certainly scary. She often joked that the only certainty she had in Limerick was that it would rain at some point during the day. That was a fact. Everything else was new and different: traffic, cooking, sports, personal relationships, weather. Even so, despite the many differences, Olivia constantly found similarities between Brazil and Ireland. Seeing the love that some people felt for Limerick reminded her of the same love and pride she felt for her homeland.

Mary Immaculate College, the university she had received the scholarship to study at, was a prestigious institution, responsible for training the best teachers in the country. These professionals were responsible for Ireland's significant improvement in international education rankings. In twenty years, the country had risen in the educational rankings, becoming a reference throughout the world. Olivia's lecturers were amazing and everyone involved with the Brazilians in Limerick was so attentive and willing to help that they made them feel welcomed, even though they were far from home.

Olivia was living with people she had never met before. They were people from all corners of Brazil, of different ages and with different accents and ways of living. They were there because of a programme sponsored by

CAPES, an agency of the Brazilian government that offered a professional development opportunity for school leaders in Brazil to specialize in Ireland. Although Olivia's scholarship was different, she would study alongside them.

Olivia was learning a lot in this diverse environment. However, she had some issues, of course. One of her issues, which she considered a bit silly, was that she was eating a lot of bread. This isn't a problem for most people, but it was for Olivia, who hated one of the most popular foods in the world. In her first two weeks in Ireland, she had probably eaten as much bread as she had in her entire life so far. But she justified it by asking herself "who in the world doesn't like bread?"

Another issue, which she considered really serious, concerned the language. Even though she understood everything people said, she still had a hard time speaking English fluently. Soon, the talkative Olivia became a great listener. But those who knew her well knew that this was a big challenge for her because she was Olivia! She loved talking, telling stories and interacting. She knew it was necessary to learn English right away to do all of that again and make the most of her classes.

Undoubtedly this was her biggest obstacle, but also her biggest goal. She felt very small not being able to express herself as she would like and told everyone that she felt uncomfortable and very limited by it. Olivia didn't like being wrong, but every time she spoke, she was corrected. It was important to be corrected so she wouldn't make the same mistake again. However, it just made her sad and frustrated, as she always seemed to be chasing perfection. One of her colleagues, Simone, seeing the girl's desperation, offered to help her by giving extra lessons so that she would feel more confident in following the regular classes. It felt like a blessing in her life.

If the English problem was being solved by Simone, the food problem was left to Rosa. This classmate, an excellent cook, was one of those people who liked to provide a cosy atmosphereand made everyone feel at home. It didn't take long for Olivia to form a partnership with her, because Rosa, with her big heart, wouldn't let her friend starve to death. The two were from the south of Brazil, so they shared a certain culinary familiarity and got along very well—in the kitchen, in classes and during leisure time.

They used to joke that they were participants in *Big Brother Brasil* (BBB), a famous Brazilian reality show where strangers were confined together to compete for a cash prize. They had never seen each other in their lives and now they were spending all their time together, both at university and at home. The house in question was Courtbrack Accommodation, the student accommodation at Mary Immaculate College, where Brazilian exchange students and 80 Irish first-year undergraduates lived.

Just like in *Big Brother*, cliques started to form right at the beginning, with groups formed by people who shared the most affinity. Simone, Rosa, Sofia, Marcos, Fabiana, and Ângela were part of Olivia's group of friends. They studied together and took advantage of their free time to explore some corners of the city.

With each passing day, she found herself even more in love with Limerick, though she couldn't quite say why, as it seemed like an ordinary city. Everything she had felt, all the desire to go back to that place was still a puzzle inside her head. She believed that there must be a stronger reason than just a schism, just a desire to change her life and go live in a place more than eight thousand kilometres away from home.

Limerick was an important city in Ireland. In fact, it was the third-largest city in the country, situated in the province of Munster in the midwest of the Republic. The city, which has a countryside atmosphere, is less than three hours from the capital, Dublin, a cosmopolitan hub, like most of the capitals of Europe.

The medieval city of Limerick was located on King's Island and was surrounded by the waters of the River Shannon and its tributaries, more specifically the Abbey River. The beautiful Saint Mary's Cathedral, built in 1168, reigned sovereign in the medieval city. The Cathedral was the oldest historic building in the city. It was an imposing building, with a tall tower adorned with beautiful stained-glass windows. Limerick's compact Medieval Quarter, the part of the city Olivia loved most, consisted primarily of the Cathedral and King John's Castle and was flanked by old Georgian villas built between 1714 and 1837. That was so Ireland! All the pictures of the country found on the internet had a certain profile: semi-detached houses in cheerful colours and the vivid green of nature as a contrast.

King John's Castle, built in the 13th Century, was one of the city's best-known tourist sites. It was also Olivia's favourite place to watch the sun set. As the building was on the banks of the River Shannon, at dusk, the scenery looked like a work of art: castle in the background, sky and water contrasting in shades of yellow, orange, and purple. It was a real spectacle that, at times, would even make Olivia emotional. She couldn't explain what she felt in the place. It was as if she was referring to a feeling she didn't remember well, but she felt it strongly inside her chest. Whenever she was there and saw the sun setting, she was overcome with uncontrollable emotion. Olivia had always been a sensitive person and although she didn't understand what was happening, she would always come back, as it was undoubtedly a beautiful sight. The entire region held a strong attraction for Olivia.

Thomondgate was the most important gateway to the city before the construction of John's Gate in 1494. This gate was used to ensure the safety of the city, controlling the entry and exit of people and goods. The neighbourhood was the gateway to the western part of Ireland and was well protected by the River Shannon and later King John's Castle. The traditionally Irish neighbourhood is also home to the Treaty Stone, the city's most important monument. The Treaty Stone, according to history, bears the signatures of a treaty dated to 1691, marking the surrender of the city. Limerick was then known as the Treaty City, and the stone keeps the record and memory of when the city exercised great influence on the ascension of William of Orange and his wife, Mary Stuart, to the English throne.

Limerick's history can be traced back to its establishment by the Vikings in the area that later became a walled city on King's Island—the island where the cathedral and castle are located, as well as the entire older area of the city. The island, an important site in the city, was the scene of Viking occupation in 812 and later of the granting of the city charter of Limerick in 1197, forming the city that Olivia would come to call home.

Before the Vikings settled in Ireland, the Celts had been dominant in that territory. Olivia wished she had more time so she could research and learn everything she could about Limerick and Ireland. She knew all about the historical importance of the Celts in that place, as well as the United Kingdom, because she grew up reading stories based on ancient Celtic legends, loaded with magic and superstitions. King Arthur, powerful Druids, Merlin himself, people who travelled through time across enigmatic and powerful stone circles, were all part of the books that the girl used to have in her hands.

Aside from all that, Limerick still represented a mixture of tradition and modernity. Despite the grey skies in winter and autumn, spring would bring different colours and scents. The smell of flowers mixed with the scent of potatoes and beer from the pubs. The slightest sign of sun was enough for everyone to get out onto the streets. And Olivia was sure it would be very difficult to find a country where the grass was greener or that had more rainbows than the land of leprechauns. Everyone probably spent hours (or, for that matter, a lot of money) mowing their lawns. The combination of rain and sun was much better than compost for making the grass grow, ensuring that Ireland's colour remained green.

The Irish were a special character of people: so kind, so helpful. They left behind any stereotypes one might have of Europeans, often seen by Brazilians as arrogant, unsympathetic and cold. Olivia saw the Irish as generous, easy-going people, always willing to help. After a Guinness or two, they would become friends with anyone. Guinness, by the way, is the country's symbolic drink and is to Ireland what caipirinha is to Brazil.

The city's main street, O'Connell Avenue, was named after Daniel O'Connell, who in the first half of the 19th century was considered by many people to be the liberator of Ireland. A statue in his honour can be found there. O'Connell was the nationalist leader who led the campaign for Catholic Emancipation, including the right of Catholics to sit in the Parliament of Westminster, thus having some voice in politics, something that had been denied for over 100 years. He also worked for the repeal of the Act of Union, which unified Great Britain and Ireland. The repeal of the act meant an Ireland free from the clutches of England.

If Brazil had Portugal as a great colonizing villain, Ireland had England as its counterpart. The English dominated the territory, imposed a new language and a new religion, made the life of Catholics miserable, and took great advantage of all the riches that the territory could offer. Besides, England played a leading role in worsening the Great Irish Famine in the 19th century, when it exported most of the food from the country, contributing to the death of more than 1.5 million Irish people.

One of the first times Olivia could remember hearing about Ireland was in the 1990s when she saw news on TV about constant conflicts between Catholics and Protestants in Northern Ireland. At that time, she didn't know that the island was divided and was bewildered by what she heard on the news about the I.R.A., the radical group that claimed hundreds of victims and left the world perplexed. Olivia was even more astonished when she visited the United Kingdom years later and discovered that, even in the 21st century, the city of Belfast, the main city in Northern Ireland, still had gates that were closed every night to avoid conflict between the two religious groups. How could this still happen? She knew it had to do with history, with religious fanaticism, and even with a certain influence and encouragement from England, but she couldn't understand how this still happened in a first-world country.

In the past, being Catholic in Ireland was not a sign of prosperity and meant bad luck. Olivia learned this long ago when she read Fred McCourt's novel *Angela's Ashes*. The book, which takes place in Limerick, recounts the suffering of Fred's family, involving their mother, father, and brothers. She had never forgotten one excerpt that said: "When I look back on my childhood I wonder how I survived at all. It was, of course, a miserable childhood: the happy childhood is hardly worth your while. Worse than the ordinary miserable childhood is the miserable Irish childhood, and worse yet is the miserable Irish Catholic childhood." In addition to having read the book, Olivia had also seen the film, produced in 1996 and shot in the city. She remembers that what had caught her attention was the misery of the city and the rain seen in practically every outdoor scene.

"How did this Limerick, portrayed in the book, in the movie, and so many other stories, become this beautiful city full of opportunities for everyone, including many foreigners?" Olivia wondered.

Some people would claim that the reason for this was a curse from the time when a friar was building St. Munchin's Church, located in front of the castle on the opposite bank of the River Shannon. The friar asked the townspeople for help in building the church, but no one helped him. The only person who complied with his request was an outsider, a man who was passing through Limerick. After that, the friar cast a curse on the city: those who were from there would not prosper, only those who came from outside would. Whether the curse came true or not, we will never know, but the fact is that the city seemed to be a good option for foreigners of all nationalities, especially Brazilians, who invaded this part of Ireland—there seemed to be no more space for them in Dublin—looking for English courses and job opportunities. Ireland had modernised and grown; it was even known to some as Europe's Silicon Valley, due to the sheer number of tech companies it housed. Google, Facebook, Airbnb, Twitter, Uber—all the tech giants were based on the island and attracted people from all over the world in search of good opportunities.

Limerick is a portrait of Ireland, with one foot in modernity and the other in ancient traditions. St. Munchin's, the church whose legend ensured success for foreigners, is just one of the town's churches; in its central area alone, there are more than twenty. But if the number of churches is impressive and makes you think that Limerick could be a colonial town in Minas Gerais, given the number of religious temples it has, it's only because nobody knows exactly how many pubs the city has.

The city has around 200 pubs, which reinforces the stereotype that the Irish are fond of liquor. Two hundred! This meant that the expression "there's a pub around every corner" is more than true in this case, as it's hard to find a block without pubs. There are pubs for all tastes and some of them, like JJ Bowles, The Locke Bar, Katie Daly's, and Mickey Martins, are between 200 and 300 years old. There are also those pubs that stay open late like 101, House, and the eccentric Nancy Blake's. A few others are more recent, but they also keep the local traditions, like Dolan's, Olivia's favourite pub. There you can hear the most traditional Irish music, played by ordinary people, who gather in pubs to spend happy moments. Pubs in Limerick, and probably all of Ireland, are like an institution: respected and loved by their regulars.

Regardless of the pub, Olivia had fallen in love with Guinness, the traditional Irish stout created in 1759 in Dublin. Olivia used to say that she didn't believe in love at first sight; a good example of this was Guinness, which gradually won her heart. Olivia felt like an Irishwoman, arriving at pubs and asking for her pint of Guinness.

The Milk Market was another very famous spot in the city. It's a large public market with everything you can imagine for sale: antiques, organic and artisanal products, various types of food, beers, etc. On Saturday mornings, the whole city seemed to get together to shop, meet friends, or eat. One of the most famous dishes at the market was a sandwich that looked like the hot dogs sold in Brazil, but with the typical Irish sausage freshly baked in front of the consumer. Perhaps because of this familiarity, the sandwich soon made its way onto the menu of the Brazilian group. Practically every Saturday morning, they went to the market just to eat that hot dog. It was on the first of these Saturdays that, among the stalls, Simone and Olivia found one with several silver pieces of jewellery for sale.

"Look, how beautiful this ring is."

"Oh, it's a Claddagh ring," Simone said.

"How beautiful! And what is this?"

"Do you want to try one?" asked the saleswoman.

"I do!" Olivia nodded, feeling a strange familiarity with the jewel.

"This ring has a meaning, doesn't it? I can't quite remember... could you explain it to me, please? How is it supposed to be worn?" Simone asked the saleswoman, who soon began to explain.

"Ah, it's the story of great love, and the way to wear it is: crown inward on the right hand means that the person's heart is available. She may be single or be wearing the ring as a symbol of friendship with someone. Crown outward on the right hand means that the person is committed, either dating or engaged. On the left hand, the crown outward means that the person has an infinite love for someone, and it is reciprocal, that is, he or she is probably married."

Olivia was lost in her thoughts and didn't know what she was feeling when she saw that ring. In order not to seem awkward, she tried to be funny by asking:

"What if the person wears the crown inward on the left hand?"

The saleswoman just laughed and replied:

"Well, then we'll have someone with a problem." The three laughed.

"I'll take the ring!" said the girl.

While Simone looked at rings with Celtic symbols, Olivia was still staring at her newest acquisition and placed it with the crown inward on her right hand. That ring seemed to have so much meaning, it seemed to be something important, but she convinced herself that it could just be the desire to buy something to put on her bare fingers. Her grandmother used to take her fingers and say that she had such a cute hand and that she should wear a ring. She always changed the subject, believing that her grandmother was worried that she still hadn't found a husband to put a ring on her finger. Despite this, she took a picture of the ring and sent it to her grandmother, who was happy that her granddaughter had finally followed her suggestion.

Occasionally Olivia would go out for a jog and on one of these days, running around town as she always did when she needed time to think and come up with ideas for her writing she ended up passing through the medieval area. Whenever she passed by the Cathedral, she used to feel something different, a kind of nostalgia, as if she had heard a call. As she never knew what to do, and as she always had her phone with her, she used to take photos of the place.

On that particular day, the photo looked even more beautiful. The sun was setting on the River Shannon and the light took on different shades. As she analysed the picture, she suddenly remembered another one she had taken the first time she had been in Ireland. Intrigued by the memory, she decided to find it.

When she got home, she turned on her computer, looked for the photo, and was quite impressed with what she saw. The only difference between the photo taken almost two years ago and the photo taken that day was the position of the sun; in the first photo, the sun had not set yet. She soon began to remember that every time she felt that sensation, she used to take pictures. When searching for these images, she was astonished to realise that all the photos were from precisely the same angle.

Olivia was astounded and shivering; the whole thing was very strange. She knew that whenever she took a picture of that place it was because she felt something she couldn't explain, but why did she feel it? As she always liked mysteries and was intrigued by the situation, she decided that she would go into the cemetery to see what could be catching her attention.

The next day she went for a walk and entered the empty cemetery. The tombs were between 100 and 200 years old. Olivia didn't have a goal or know what she was supposed to look for, so she just went around randomly looking at the graves and reading the names. In some, the letters carved into the stones were weathered and impossible to read, but even so, she kept trying. A lot of names didn't mean anything to her until one last name caught her eye: Crawford. She couldn't read the first name, but it appeared to be Janet. It was written: "Janet Crawford, beloved mother and wife, died in the year 1856." Next to it was the grave of Eugene Crawford, who had died in the year 1867, and right next to his grave was a grave that, Olivia knew, as soon as she clapped her eyes on it, was the one she was looking for: Catherine Crawford. Below the name was the phrase: "the light that lit up our days". Olivia was transfixed by that tomb. What was that? Who had that woman been? Why was she there, standing in front of that grave and feeling that mix of emotions? Once again, she felt her whole body shiver with a wave of chills.

When she returned home, she went straight to the computer to search and try to find out something about Catherine Crawford, but found nothing. It was all very strange, but knowing that she had a very fertile imagination and that she had probably created all these connections inside her head, she decided to forget about the subject. But things would change from then on.

A little over two months after arriving in Ireland, everything seemed to be going well, but suddenly the scenario changed and Olivia even thought about returning home. If Olivia left home looking for a change, this was where change really began. She was already almost adapted and despite all her insecurity, did the best she could. Then she was called into the international office for a casual conversation. An email had been sent to the office making a series of "accusations" against her. Another Brazilian student, very close to everyone in the group, questioned the intellectual capacity of Olivia and some of her classmates. He did it out of spite, arguing that she couldn't master the language. According to this colleague, having a student like her at the university would lower its standards. Olivia was called there to be informed about the situation. This Brazilian was always with the group and had probably done it out of envy because, until then, he was one of the only Brazilians who had received that scholarship.

Despite knowing that no one believed his words, it deeply wounded her. She arrived home desperate and went straight to tell Simone, who was outraged by the boy's attitude.

"Ah, but it can't be left at that," Simone said.

"Well, I've been told they'll be talking to him this week and that they're even thinking about cancelling his scholarship," Olivia replied.

"But that would be the least they could do; it shows that he has no character at all. These are very serious and unfounded accusations. Who is he to define whether a student would lower the level of an institution or not? Are you going to tell the others that he also mentioned their names?"

"No, I'm not going to talk to them. I think if it's going to make others feel as humiliated as I did, it's better not to know, since the lecturers don't agree," Olivia said.

"I respect your decision, but I think you should tell the others," Simone insisted.

"I am very ashamed," Olivia admitted.

"But why are you ashamed? Didn't they tell you that none of the lecturers agreed with what was written in the email?" Simone asked.

"Yes, I was told. But what image am I passing on to others?" Olivia wondered. "The image of someone weak? Dumb? Someone who is an embarrassment to the university?"

"No, you know they don't think that," Simone reassured her. "You are learning. Olivia, do you think everyone here woke up one day speaking English? No, it's years of learning and commitment. You are in the place where everyone else has been at some stage."

"But I'm a little naive, don't you think?" Olivia asked. "For exposing myself too much. I keep telling everyone that I can't speak English very well, I talk about my limitations, I point the finger at my mistakes."

"You are real. You are who you are and you are not ashamed to show it to others. I see no problem with that," Simone said.

"But I'm so ashamed. I was someone in Brazil. I had a job, a certain status in my city. I didn't need to prove to anyone that I was smart, that I deserved to be where I was. But here, it seems that every day I have to prove to my colleagues that I deserve this spot," Olivia lamented.

"Olivia, you are too worried about proving to yourself that you are competent. I don't think the others are that interested in whether you're good or not. It is you who feel pressured to demonstrate this, but you shouldn't. You need to stop being too hard on yourself and not pay attention to what others are thinking. You have no idea how you will grow with all this."

Simone had only known Olivia for a short time, but she was already saying what her long-standing friends used to say: that she needed to live her life without worrying about what others thought, that she had no obligation to prove anything to anyone, and that she was much better than she thought. Even so, the weeks that followed were full of sleepless nights, dominated by a feeling of shame and humiliation.

The truth was that Olivia seriously thought about returning to Brazil. She couldn't understand how being in Limerick could be better than being together with her family, whom she truly loved and to whom she didn't need to prove anything. The Brazilian in question had doubted her intellectual capacity, and that was very humiliating. However, what Simone had told her also didn't get out of her head: growing up wasn't easy. The thought of quitting should embarrass her more than her colleague's attitude.

It was around this time that Olivia received a rather unusual call, one that would be crucial to her decision to stay. One day, her phone was ringing and, to her surprise, it was Cristiano's name that appeared on the screen. He was calling to see how she was, to say he missed her so much and couldn't wait for her to return. Olivia was speechless listening to all this. The words she'd always dreamed of hearing were deliberately spouting from his mouth at that very moment.

The first question Olivia asked was whether Cristiano had finally broken up with his fiancée. He said he hadn't, but that he would find some way for them to be together. Olivia immediately hung up the phone. Everything Cristiano said was what every woman dreamed of hearing from the man she loved, but it was just more of the same, and she no longer had the time or patience to believe these things.

She decided that she was at a point where she should no longer think about her past or the things she had left behind. She was at a point where she should invest in herself to become a new person, someone with the potential to be better than the Olivia who had lived in Alfredo Wagner.

Olivia thus began a new stage in her life in Limerick. She put even more effort into learning English and decided that she should care less about what people thought. In a way, she wanted to show that she had potential and that Brazilian was wrong; she wasn't there by mere chance, but because she deserved it. She had worked all her life to make this happen, and now she was reaping the rewards of her hard work. She would enjoy this dream. From that moment, the Olivia of the past was, little by little, fading away.

But not everything would be a bed of roses.

Olivia decided to join the 'Language Exchange,' a group where people got together to exchange experiences in their native languages. There she met a Frenchman named Jean, with whom she started having a lot of fun, as he had a nice way of playing with words. But in the end, he proved to be a living example of the saying 'appearances can be deceiving.' As they got involved, Jean gradually conquered space in Olivia's life. She felt very needy at that time because she didn't know many people in the city (apart from her classmates) and wanted to get away from the home-college routine. She ended up finding in him a friend, someone different who could be good company, to show her a little more of the city of Limerick since he had lived there for some time.

Jean worked in the field of computers, was polite, seemed to be smart, and a good conversationalist. Also, he was patient to understand what Olivia was trying to say, but her English didn't allow for it to be fully understood. He was a good friend for a long time—until one day he kissed her. The kiss was nothing like the kisses she was used to in Brazil, full of passion and desire. It was a different kiss, but it felt full of tenderness, and that somehow made Olivia like it. He was very far from the stereotype of the conquering and charming Frenchman that we tend to create in our minds, based on passionate movie characters, but he seemed a good person who would do anything to please her.

At that time, Olivia had written her first short story in English, an amusing story about the origin of Ireland's crows. Since her first time in the country, the number of birds of that species, very unusual in her region of Brazil, had impressed her. The idea to write the tale emerged during a trip with her Brazilian colleagues to Belfast, the capital of Northern Ireland, which is part of the United Kingdom.

The story was really good, and those who had read it recommended that Olivia participate in a 'Short Stories' competition that was being promoted by another university in town. The tale won all the qualifying stages. Olivia was very happy and shared with a few more friends the first story she had written in English. She couldn't contain her joy when she received the news that the short story had been selected for the final stage of the competition. It seemed that everything was finally working out for her.

However, in Olivia's life, happiness sometimes had a limited term.

Little by little, her relationship with Jean became a bit odd. He didn't take the answer 'no' very well and acted like a spoiled child when he was annoyed. This started to intrigue Olivia, as it felt like their relationship was heading toward something that wasn't what she expected. After all, their dates were limited to a few pub trips to chat, strolls along the riverbank, and a warm kiss goodbye when he dropped her off at home. Now and then, Jean would get into some subjects that terrified Olivia.

"Olivia, do you like me?"

"Yes, of course, I enjoy your company, otherwise I wouldn't be seeing you."

"It's just that you're more than a friend to me."

"Yeah, you're not just a friend to me either. I don't kiss my friends."

"I just wanted to take you to the church tower to ask you something."

"What would you like to ask, Jean?" Olivia asked, wishing to run away. If he said something, she would have to make it very clear that she wasn't going to go through with it.

"In due time, you will know."

He was taking too long to get in touch. The plans to become a 'new Olivia' didn't seem to be going so well, as she needed to take the initiative to get out of this situation before he asked her on a date and complicated everything even more.

Things started to get even weirder when he started showing up in the places where the girl was. Jean always sneaked in, giving the impression that he was stalking her. The friends who lived with Olivia began to see him at night hiding in the garden as if trying to spy through the window. This situation forced her not to put off the decision to walk away from the guy any longer, but first, she wanted to talk to him.

"Jean, why are you doing these things? Showing up in the places where I am, in the place where I live? What's happening? I need an explanation."

"I think it's just a coincidence."

"Okay, you showing up at the same place as me, I can accept as a coincidence, but you were in my garden late at night. Would you say this is a coincidence?"

"Who told you that?"

"Everyone saw you there. I think if you're going to choose stalking as a career, you need to learn to be more discreet."

"Have you seen me there?"

"No, but my friends have."

"They just want to push us away."

"No, Jean, you're pushing us away with your attitudes. We won't meet anymore. We want different things, and now I still feel chased by you. I'm uncomfortable."

"Are you breaking up with me?"

"Breaking up? We never had anything. I'm telling you that we won't see each other again. Your attitudes are very strange, and you can't talk like an adult about it because you're telling me that it's a coincidence or even that my friends are fabricating the story. I don't feel comfortable with you anymore."

"Are you really going to do this? Breaking up with me?"

"Jean…" Olivia was interrupted by the abrupt reaction of the French guy, who stood up screaming, dropping his cup on the floor, and getting the attention of everyone in the cafe.

"You chose this, you'll regret it! You will regret it!"

What looked like a scene from a Mexican soap opera left Olivia speechless and unresponsive. For about 20 minutes, she sat in the cafe, thinking about how disproportionate the reaction had been. Then she tried to find the courage to get up and leave. Everyone was looking at her after the boy's rash attitude.

She returned home and told everyone what had happened. Then they started getting worried about Olivia's relationship with Jean.

"These events that have been happening lately and this reaction in the cafe just proves that he doesn't seem like a normal person. Olivia, you have to be careful," Rosa warned.

"But guys, he seemed like a normal person to me," Olivia replied.

"Oh, I agree with Rosa, you have to be careful. He may even look normal, Olivia, but it's worth remembering that no psychopath looks like one," Sofia said.

"Calm down, people. I don't think he's a psychopath; I think you're overreacting," Olivia commented.

"Look, whether we are overreacting or not, I think you should take care of yourself. Don't go out alone, especially at night, and be careful to notice if he accepts all this easily," advised the sensible Simone.

They had a few days without signs of Jean, but that only lasted until Saturday when they went to the Milk Market. They were almost back home when Marcos, one of Olivia's closest friends, warned her:

"Olivia, I don't want to scare you, but I just ran into Jean. He seemed to be watching you."

"Oh no, I can't believe it, this is just what I needed," Olivia said ironically, already disgusted by the situation.

Simone got to the market a little breathless and immediately asked:

"Olivia, what is happening?"

"What's this?" Olivia looked at the newspaper Simone was holding in her hands and realized that her story "Cailleach Aoife and the Crows of Ireland," which was in the final of the Short Stories competition, was published in the newspaper. But how? No one had asked for her permission. She couldn't believe it.

"How come your story is published in the newspaper?"

"I can't believe it! Who posted this? One of the contest rules is that the short story is unpublished; it cannot be published like that."

"You weren't the one who sent this, were you?"

"No, never! Do you think it could be someone from the contest?"

"No, look, it's in the classifieds section. Someone paid for this to be here. It is out of context; there is no reason for this text to be published here. It looks like…"

Olivia took a deep breath, took the newspaper from Simone's hand, and rolled it up. She looked at Marcos and asked:

"Where did you see Jean?"

"What are you going to do, Olivia?"

"I'm going to fix this situation."

Marcos said that he was on the upper floor of the market and that he would accompany her. She took the stairs two at a time and reached the top of it in one breath. Her friend pointed at Jean, and they went to him. Olivia felt like her eyes were burning. She had never felt so angry in her life, not even at the Brazilian who had sent that email to the college.

When Jean saw them coming toward him, he pretended he hadn't seen them. Olivia wanted to smack him in the face with the newspaper, but she held back. She just poked him in the back and said:

"Jean, why did you do this?"

"I told you you'd regret it."

"I sent you this because I trusted you as my friend. One thing has nothing to do with the other."

"Olivia, I gave you my heart, but you decided to throw it away."

"Throw it away? We weren't dating in the first place. Besides, what does my tale have to do with it? I will be disqualified!"

"I told you you would regret it."

"I don't regret wanting to stay away from a madman like you! You are sick!"

Olivia bit back her anger but couldn't hold back the tears that rolled down her face. It was unfair that her dream had gone down the drain because of Jean's cruelty. Maybe he was more dangerous than she had thought.

She even tried to appeal and did her best to keep her story from being disqualified, but the rule was clear: it could not have been published previously, either physically or virtually. To make matters worse, her text had also been published on several websites. Any search for the name of the tale would lead to hundreds of results that showed the full story.

Right after this episode, Olivia started having several problems with emails and social networks as she realised she had been hacked. Even her blog was down for a few days. She had registered it with the Gardaí, the Irish police, but she had no proof that Jean had made all that mess.

However, it seemed that he was exposing himself more and more because he started to be seen sneaking around the place where the Brazilians lived. He first began to follow her on the street during the day, and one night he was seen in the garden of the accommodation. He was there spying on her, but as Olivia had told him the day they broke up, he needed to learn to be more discreet because everyone could see him. After Olivia made a new complaint, the police decided to arrest him.

A Garda officer went to Courtbrack the next day to say that Jean had autism and schizophrenia and was taking strong medication so he could live a normal life. However, as he was having a crisis, the family decided to take him to continue his treatment in France. Olivia was saddened by the situation and couldn't wait to call Bella and tell her what had happened.

"Of course, I had to date a nutty guy, right?"

"Stop being silly, Olivia. How could you have guessed?"

"No, it's not a matter of guessing; it's a matter of being me. I will never find anyone. My love life will always be this Greek tragedy, this thing where I don't know whether to laugh or cry. One day, when I'm older, I'll be able to write a book just about all the crazy guys I've met in my life and how I died alone, surrounded by cats."

"Oh my God, you are so dramatic!"

"It's not drama. It's not drama! He was crazy! Almost a psychopath."

"Dramatic and over-the-top."

"It's not like that! When they said he could be a psychopath, I also thought it was too much, an exaggeration, but he premeditated things and ended my chances in the contest. Why do you think he was spying on me? He could be planning to kill me."

"Olivia, stop exaggerating. He was sick, but now he's in another country. You're safe."

"I'm safe, but seriously… I'm not getting involved with anyone else here. How will I feel safe after this?"

"Is everyone crazy now?"

"I don't know, and because I don't know, I'd rather stay away."

"Where's the new Olivia? Will you keep doing what you've done your whole life? Hiding your heart so you don't get hurt? Keeping away from people for fear of getting hurt? If so, I agree with you. You'll die alone, surrounded by cats, because you don't give people a chance."

"That's not true, Bella. I gave Jean a chance, but look what happened. Now that's enough."

Olivia knew not everyone was crazy, but the truth was, she was a bit lazy about the idea of going out and meeting someone to the point of getting intimate. This whole relationship thing took a long time to develop into something serious. She wasn't willing to waste time on it anymore. After all, she hadn't gone to Ireland to find a boyfriend, but to study, so she would focus on that.

The end of the year was approaching, and Olivia stuck with her intention of not getting close to anyone. She spent most of her time at the university, and on Fridays, she and her friends used to go out just to dance, have some Guinness, and have a little fun. She already had a pretty set routine. In the mornings, she attended Simone's English classes, followed by college lectures with her colleagues. In the afternoons, she studied in the library. In the evenings, she would go home for dinner. She helped Rosa prepare dinner, and she was responsible for the dishes. Now she was used to her daily life, and she loved it!

Olivia had a teenage cousin who, influenced by her, loved The Cranberries. The girl wanted to do a presentation about the band for a school art project, so she asked Olivia to take pictures of some places that might have been memorable for the band. Pictures like the school where Dolores studied, the place where they used to meet to rehearse, the place of their first show… As the other members of the band still lived in Limerick, maybe even a photo with them or something like that.

By coincidence, Olivia's English teacher, Ilona Costelloe, had gone to school with Dolores and commented, while Olivia was presenting a project that referred to the band, on how the vocalist had been discovered by the three boys to form the quartet.

"I was in school with Dolores. The boys, who were already my friends at that time, were looking for a singer for their band. Then one of our other friends asked if his girlfriend could audition. When he said that, I almost didn't believe him. Dolores was a shy, introspective girl who had recently arrived from Ballybricken."

"She went to the same school as you?"

"She was in the same class as me. I knew her; I know everyone in the band."

"Tell us more, teacher," asked Marcos.

"So…" said the teacher, coming to the front of the board and starting to speak. "Dolores was already playing the piano. I think she used to sing in church, and when her boyfriend mentioned this opportunity, she was excited, but I don't know if the boys were very convinced of her talent. She didn't look like a singer, let alone a rock star. However, as soon as she opened her mouth, everything changed. Dolores was simply amazing! She had a soft voice, but at the same time firm, strong, powerful, and full of emotion. Well… from there you already know the story."

"Oh, but we want to know more. How was it when they started to become a success?" Olivia asked.

"It was amazing; we couldn't be more proud of them. They made Limerick known all over the world. You, Olivia, are an example of this, by saying that even before you understood a word in English, you were already in love with them. Their sound is more than that; they can touch people's souls without words."

"I agree," said Olivia.

"That's it, guys."

"No, no, wait, I have one more question. How was it when she died? How did people react?"

"It was horrible, not just here in Limerick, but across the country. But here… here it was as if people had lost a loved one, someone from their own family. It was a general commotion. You would walk down the street and see people crying, inconsolable. It was very sad, even more so because it was not known exactly how she had died."

"How did she die?" Marcos asked again, as excited about the subject as Olivia was.

"Well, from what I've read, she drank a lot of alcohol, got intoxicated, and drowned in her bathtub," Olivia replied.

"Very sad and shocking. She had so much ahead of her. I was also very shaken. It's always difficult when someone close to you, and who is the same age as you, dies," concluded the teacher.

When her cousin asked her about the band, Olivia immediately remembered that conversation. She asked the teacher for tips on interesting places that could be photographed, and she was very helpful. She invited Marcos to accompany her on this photoshoot since he seemed to be quite interested. On a Saturday afternoon, the two went out to take the pictures. It was raining and the photos were the worst. It all looked kind of sad and very grey, but as they only had one more address on the list, they decided to go. Supposedly it was the house where the band used to rehearse and it would have also been one of the first places where they played "Linger," one of their best-known songs. This was the song responsible for making Olivia fall in love with the band in the early 90s when she was just a child.

It was a big house and it seemed to be very old. As soon as Olivia saw the house, her heart raced.

"Come on Olivia, what's up, is everything okay?" asked Marcos.

"I don't know, my heart raced. It's as if I remember this place," Olivia said, looking at the house. "The door, the windows, the whole architecture of the house seemed to bring back memories and a feeling of inexplicable nostalgia."

"What do you mean, have you been here before?"

"Not in this lifetime, at least not that I can remember," Olivia said with a nervous laugh.

"How then?"

"I don't know how to explain it, I feel like I've been here before, but I know that's not true. It's as if I even know what I'm going to find if I open the door."

Olivia was aware that everything she was saying sounded crazy, but it was the truth.

"Stop! You are scaring me."

"Let's get closer."

"Are you sure?"

"Yes, I have to remember where I know this place from."

"You might have seen a picture of the house in something related to the band, you know? Newspapers, magazines… stuff like that."

"Yes, that could be it."

She agreed with her friend but didn't seem convinced. What she was feeling was stronger than the mere impression that she had already seen the picture of that place before. She felt some connection to that house. It felt like, somehow, the place was very important, although it just didn't make any sense.

An elderly man approached the two friends who were standing across the street, talking and watching the house.

"Hello folks, are you enjoying the rainy afternoon?"

"Yes, we're just walking around town."

"Where are you from?"

"We are from Brazil."

"No chance of you being from Brazil. I would say you are from Germany and you... from some Middle Eastern country," he said, a little hesitantly, referring to Marcos, but with complete certainty about Olivia's nationality.

"Oh, we're used to stereotypes, nobody thinks we're Brazilians," Olivia said.

"Yeah, we also suffer from the stereotype that every Irish is an alcoholic. I haven't even had 10 pints of Guinness today," joked the old man, laughing out loud and patting Marcos on the back.

"But tell me why you guys are taking pictures of the Crawfords' old house?"

"Crawford? Crawford?"

Olivia had heard that name before; she just couldn't remember where. While Marcos was talking to the old man, she struggled to remember. She nearly lost her breath when she realised where she had already seen that name. At the cemetery. Crawford was the last name of that Catherine woman whose grave she had seen, but she hadn't discovered anything when she searched the internet.

Olivia felt dizzy and leaned against the wall, completely pale.

"Olivia, Olivia, are you okay?" asked Marcos.

"I'm a little dizzy, I think I need to sit down."

"Come on, let's go to the pub. I'll buy you a Guinness and we'll get the girl some water," said the friendly old man.

While she was drinking water, Marcos said goodbye to the old man, who said he needed to go home. When he returned, Olivia asked:

"Where is the old man?"

"He's very nice, isn't he? So kind and cute…"

"Yes, yes, very nice, but where is he?"

"He had to go; he was late."

"Oh no, I wanted to talk to him! I wanted to ask some questions about the Crawfords."

"You were thrown by that, weren't you?"

"Yes, I think I was just impressed by the building. I must have had a drop in blood pressure, I don't know."

"Are you okay now? I guess I'd better call a taxi so we can leave."

Olivia was planning to return to the cemetery the next day. This was very strange. Why did this family keep crossing her path? Why did she feel these things every time they happened? It was too strong and she needed to understand why.

The next day, she returned to the cemetery and wrote down everything she could, determined this time to find more information than she already had. Janet Crawford, beloved mother and wife, died in the year 1856. Eugene Crawford, who was probably the father, had died in the year 1867, and Catherine Crawford. The name was the only information she had. She decided to make a note of that and the names of other Crawfords she had encountered there as well.

She bent down to take a closer look and see if she could get any more information out of the stone but was interrupted by a voice calling her name from across the street.

"Olivia, Oliviaaaaaaaaaaaa"

She looked over and saw Lucio, another one of her college classmates, across the street.

"What are you doing there, girl?"

"Nothing, I just came to see the cemetery more closely. I thought it was interesting," she said without saying too much. Lucio was just an acquaintance, not a close friend with whom she would share information.

"Let's go to The Locke for a Guinness?" Lucio invited. The Locke was another charming and traditional pub in the city, located next to the cathedral, also on the banks of the River Shannon.

"Drink at this time?" asked the girl, smiling.

"There's a party going on there. Classes are ending and a lot of international students are returning home, so the farewells have started."

"And who will be there?"

"Let's stop talking and start moving. It's just a pint. Nobody can refuse a Guinness, right?"

Olivia accepted the invitation. After all, she didn't have much else to discover there in the graveyard. Still, she was determined to find out more information about Catherine Crawford.

"I will, but just for one Guinness. Today we will have dinner with our teacher at my house. Then we're planning to go to Nancy's. I think it's going to be a lot of fun."

"I know, this will be my warm-up for the night," said Lucio.

The two left and joined the others at the bar.

Back home, she and her friends had a fun night drinking, laughing, and chatting with the teacher in the kitchen. Afterwards, some of them called taxis and went to the pub. Nancy Blake's is a traditional pub located in the central area of the city, next to the Milk Market. In one part, there is a normal pub, similar to other pubs in town, but in another area, there is a dance floor. The DJ at Nancy's had very different musical tastes and Olivia had never heard music like that played at any common party in Brazil. She would probably only have heard it at some retro party, and maybe that was what made her find Nancy's so appealing. The place was a favorite among Brazilians who lived in the city.

That was just another crazy night at Nancy's. It felt like half of Limerick was there, dancing. Olivia loved the place for its eccentricity, but on this particular night, the pub was more wild than ever.

Olivia thought that all the holiday parties, groups of friends, companies, hurling teams, Gaelic football teams, golf buddies, neighbours, everyone, absolutely everyone, had ended up in the same place that night. Olivia was a bit annoyed by the loud noise, the cigarette smoke, and the shoving, so she decided to keep dancing and drinking Guinness to forget about it. She was trying to unwind because she had studied a lot in the last few weeks and still felt a bit shaken by the whole thing involving the crazy Frenchman.

So, there was nothing better than the typical Irish drink to erase unpleasant memories from her head, even if only for a short moment.

Olivia's friends thought she should move on, stop being silly, and enjoy life more; the story with Jean had been an isolated incident. She was trying to do just that when the DJ started playing "Sweet Dreams" by Eurythmics, and the pub practically collapsed. Their circle closed more and more, and each one began to dance differently, without worrying about what the others might think. They were at Nancy's and they were allowed to dance in absurd ways.

Suddenly, Sofia took Olivia's arm and said, "My God, look at those two guys coming in, they're the kind of men you like."

Olivia looked back and didn't even need to confirm with Sofia who her friend was talking about. It was evident. Then, to the rhythm of "Sweet Dreams," they got closer. Olivia knew there were two of them, but her eyes focused on the first one, a tall redhead with strong arms. Olivia felt her heart race when she saw him. She didn't know how to explain that feeling, and she even thought it could be the effect of the Guinness. The boy didn't look at her, but she continued to stare at him. Then, she realized that the other guy, a tall blonde and quite strong too, had noticed that Olivia was looking in their direction. At that moment, she blushed. She stopped staring at them and started talking to Sofia.

"Okay, we can define that as the meaning of 'whatever'."

"Yes, whatever... Either of them... Are they brothers? If so, what good genes, huh-?"

As soon as Sofia finished saying that, Olivia turned around and bumped into the tall blonde.

"Hi."

"Hi."

"How are you? What are you doing here?"

Then Olivia answered, but without paying much attention, as she wasn't prepared to talk like that. She just didn't know how to do it. It seemed kind of forced, and the place, crowded and noisy, along with her English, which was still far from good, contributed to the conversation stalling. When the blond boy left, Olivia was almost beaten up by her friends and her teacher for turning the handsome guy down. During their quick conversation, she had discovered that he was Austrian and studying at a university of technology in the city.

"But you're really stupid, Olivia. I can't believe that you gave that ridiculous Frenchman a chance and now you rejected such an incredible man!" said Angela, another friend in the group. The teacher agreed with Angela and decided to buy Olivia another Guinness, as the student would certainly need more help to think better.

That night, it seemed that all the problems in the world could be solved with the most traditional drink in Ireland, and Olivia could do nothing but accept it. She pretended not to pay attention to her friends' jokes, but she knew they were right. What did she have to lose? It certainly wouldn't be a waste to spend a few minutes kissing that man. Half the girls in the pub would love to have the chance to kiss the Austrian guy.

A few pints of Guinness later, the Austrian passed inside the circle formed by the group and, again, was dancing and facing Olivia. When he returned from the bar, he excused himself, walking past her once more.

"Oh no, Olivia, if you don't kiss this guy, I will," Sofia said.

"Well, do it, no one is stopping you from kissing him," Olivia said, laughing at her friend.

"But seriously, aren't you going to hook up with him?"

"Okay, if he stops by again, I'll try," Olivia promised, feeling like she was twelve years old.

The girl didn't even have time to finish her sentence before the boy came back. Angela, who was already tired of Olivia's indecision, stopped him and asked, "Do you want to kiss my friend?"

He didn't understand anything, so he asked Olivia what the other girl had said. Olivia, encouraged by Guinness, replied, "She asked if you want to kiss me."

"Why?"

"Because you should!"

Olivia finished talking, and the boy kissed her. It hadn't been that difficult after all and was far from a bad experience. She had practically forgotten what it was like to get a real kiss. After that first kiss, the Austrian invited her to smoke in a quieter place. Olivia had never put a cigarette in her mouth and hadn't intended to do so that day, but she understood that he wanted to go somewhere with less noise to talk and went with him.

Between kisses, Olivia opened her eyes just in time to see her friends leaving.

"Where are you going?"

"We're leaving."

"No, wait for me, I'll go with you."

"Stay with me, let's go to my house. Wait here; I'll just get my coat from my friend." The Austrian said that without even giving Olivia time to answer and left to find his friend.

"Guys, I'm leaving with you. Wait for me here, and I'll let him know."

Her friends stood at the door waiting for the taxi while she returned to Nancy's to speak with her admirer. She found him talking to the redhead she had seen him enter with. Again, when she saw him, she felt her heart race. He was kissing another girl and didn't even notice her. The Austrian insisted that Olivia should go to sleep at his house, but she refused. She said she couldn't, he asked for her number, and then they said goodbye. Before leaving, she took one more look at the redhead and inwardly felt jealous of the girl he was kissing. She immediately felt terrible for thinking that.

When she got into the taxi, she had to listen to her friends laughing at her:

"Wow, for someone who didn't want to kiss, you had a lot of fun, huh?" said one.

"Olivia, have you already looked at yourself in the mirror? Your hair is messy," said another.

"Where are your earrings? My God, she even lost her earrings!" exclaimed Sofia.

Olivia found the situation very funny, and without a doubt, the night had been a lot of fun. It had served to ease the tensions she was feeling and even to make her feel safer, as a handsome man like that had spent all night intent on kissing her.

The following week, as they were already on vacation from college, they would have time to do a lot of things they always wanted to do but had never had time for, due to the strenuous study routine. Olivia took advantage of this free time to return to the cemetery and search the town library for more information. In the cemetery, she found a few more graves with the surname Crawford. She wrote down everyone's data to help her in her search. She had no idea where the quest would take her, but it was making her very excited.

As a child, before choosing to finally accept her vocation and become a teacher, she had thought a lot about becoming a journalist. She wanted to pursue a career in investigative journalism or perhaps be a correspondent sent to war sites. Maybe those were just childish ideas, but she thought she still had a little bit of the journalist she had dreamed of being inside her. So, she had the perfect task for that afternoon.

She went to the city library and asked the librarian for help. The librarian showed her some books and old newspapers and pointed her to some websites where Olivia could get information. That afternoon, she discovered a few things.

Catherine Crawford was the daughter of Eugene Crawford and Janet Crawford. The couple had many children, and four of them died in infancy. The girl, Catherine, had died after giving birth to a baby. Olivia had even found a picture of Catherine, a portrait taken on the day of her engagement to Fred Stafford who, according to the paper, was one of the most important men in town. Unfortunately, she couldn't see the bride and groom's faces clearly, but he was holding her hand as if he were showing the ring. Olivia felt sad to see the photo. It was an inexplicable sadness. She thought it might be related to the fact that poor Catherine had married a good man who could have given her a good life. They had probably waited a long time for their son, but a tragedy like this had happened. She tried to find information about the beautiful couple's son, with no success. He could have died in childbirth too, but inwardly Olivia wished he hadn't.

Unfortunately, that was the only information she had been able to find. She struggled to find more information, as many documents were written in Irish and some of the scanned documents available online were in Latin, so everything she found that day just proved that the Crawford's and her had no connection, and it was just a coincidence.

Olivia had enjoyed researching her new friend Catherine; it was nice to see what Limerick was like almost 150 years ago. She found many pictures of the city and some records in books that compared Limerick to Vienna due to its architecture. Olivia knew the places where some of those old buildings were located and could hardly believe that those beautiful structures had given way to buildings that, in the pretence of being modern, had abandoned all charm.

But if, on the one hand, architecture had been lost, the social side had improved in recent times. The city had changed a lot after recent recessions, becoming more prosperous again and full of opportunities for everyone.

Olivia left the library relieved, as she had been convinced that she would find something there that would intrigue her. She had this fixed idea that all the trips to the cemetery, the story with all the photos in the same place, what she felt when she saw the grave with that name, and the old Crawford house… It was all related and had happened for some reason as if to show her something. Soon, she was quite pleased to have seen that it had just been her imagination. It had just been a sad story, but in no way could it be related to her story, through, let's say, a past life.

Since she was very young, she used to think about past lives. This interest began when she watched a soap opera called "A Viagem (The Voyage)", in which Diná and Otávio met in many lives and loved each other in all of them. Although she was Catholic and had never studied the subject deeply, she believed that the soul could be reincarnated many times and that souls could find each other again in the next life. But Olivia was going too far with all these daydreams.

That week, some of Olivia's classmates began to return home while others travelled around Europe. She was going to take advantage of the ease of being on the Old Continent, as Europe was known in Brazil, to visit some countries in the United Kingdom and others further east, rather than going back to Brazil.

Gradually, the student accommodation where they lived began to empty out and Olivia felt a mix of enthusiasm for her trip and envy of those who were returning to Brazil to see their families during the holidays. Olivia didn't know what else to do with the longing she felt in her chest. She had never spent so much time away from her city or her family, and certainly, the proximity to Christmas only increased this feeling.

By the end of the week, there were only a few people left. So, as she had nothing else to do, she and Sofia decided to go to Nancy's for the last time before travelling. Yes, everyone believed that this was the reason and not because they would never miss a chance to go to Nancy's.

The two went alone and on foot. Both Olivia and Sofia found it very funny because they would never, under any circumstances in Brazil, walk such a long distance on foot, at night, to go to a party. This was even more absurd for Sofia, who lived in Rio de Janeiro and had never felt safe doing this in her hometown. Life seemed simpler and more pleasant in Limerick. Olivia couldn't explain it, but it seemed that people there still preserved some of their innocence. Not that they were naive or that they could easily be made a fool of, it wasn't that. She saw a purity that was hard to find in Brazil. It seemed that there was still some magic there, the kind of magic one would only find in fairy tales. She loved being there.

When they arrived in the city centre, they went first to another pub, called the Old Quarter, which always had a rock band playing on weekends. The highlight, as always, was when they played "Zombie" by the local and world-famous band, The Cranberries. It seemed that Irish people learned this song in school, and that day it was sung almost like an anthem. As soon as the first chords played, everyone got ready to start singing.

The girls had already arrived at Nancy's and the first thing they did before heading to their favourite place in the pub was to go to the bar to get something to drink. When they arrived there, Sofia took her friend's arm and said: "Look over there, the handsome brothers."

"My God, let's get out of here."

"Hey, don't you want to hook up with him again?"

Olivia didn't know if she wanted to kiss him again, but what she did know for sure was that she didn't want to be around him early in the night since she liked to go to Nancy's to dance. Based on her previous experience, she knew he preferred kissing over dancing. But it looked like she wouldn't escape, and soon she heard him saying: "Olivia??"

She was friendly and her heart raced again when she saw the redhead who always accompanied him. He asked if the girls had cigarettes and as Sofia used to smoke on such occasions, she said 'yes' and they went together to the smoking room.

Apparently, in Europe, it was very common for people to buy tobacco and roll their own cigarettes. In her town, Olivia had seen people doing the same, but usually older people, wrapping their straw, which had a very characteristic smell. However, in Limerick, it was quite common for people to roll their own cigarettes. Of course, they didn't use straw but silk. The girl found the whole ritual very strange and was impressed by the dexterity with which they did it. And she also understood that the act of smoking in this situation was much more than just inhaling and exhaling smoke; it was practically an act of socialisation. It was one more way to start a conversation. Olivia already felt like a passive smoker since many of her friends smoked.

There in the smoking room, they discovered that the two were not brothers, just college friends, and the redhead, whose name was Matt, despite having an Irish face, was from Canada. Olivia had to watch herself not to act silly when looking at him. He was even more handsome up close, but she couldn't expect anything; after all, she would probably kiss the Austrian that night. Then, Sofia decided to ask the boy what he had done with her friend's earrings, and he whispered in Olivia's ear:

"It's just that I usually take off with my mouth the earrings of the women I'm going to take to bed."

Olivia felt quite disgusted when he said that. If the intention was to seduce, the plan backfired. The only feeling he managed to elicit was revulsion. After that, she invited Sofia to leave and go to the place where they usually stayed, leaving the two of them there.

"Aren't you going to kiss him, Olivia?"

"I don't know, I thought he was very cocky when you asked about my earrings."

"Oh, I don't think that was the intention, he was trying to seduce you."

"Maybe, but let's avoid being around them for now, let's enjoy dancing."

The girls went to the place, near a staircase where they used to stay. It was in the back of the bar, and from there they could see everything that was going on. They were already well acquainted with the place and were starting to become known there, to the point of feeling part of the pub. They were practically friends with the security guard who was watching from the top of the stairs, they were known to the 80-year-old man who sat nearby, and they knew some of the other Brazilians who also frequented the pub. Olivia commented that she thought going to Nancy's was an anthropological experience because she observed many socially interesting interactions there. The place contained an eclectic mix of people of different ages and backgrounds; it was a place for families, it was a place to drink, it was a place to dance, it was Ireland itself.

As time went on, the two handsome men came over and the Austrian tried to kiss Olivia. She was playing hard to get but had already convinced herself, with the help of some Guinness — which in Olivia's case was a maximum of four, as she had a low tolerance for drinks — that by the end of the night, she would accept his attempts. She and Sofia had even made a deal: Olivia would hook up with the Austrian and Sofia would make the sacrifice to hook up with Matt, his Canadian friend. Inwardly, Olivia was jealous of her friend, as she had found Matt much nicer than the Austrian, not to mention that she was attracted to him from the first moment she saw him.

Suddenly, Matt seemed to have been abandoned by his friend, and as he stayed in the company of the two, they had the opportunity to talk and dance together. The Canadian was fun, he danced differently and Sofia and Olivia agreed that he could dance whatever way he wanted, that he would still be awesome.

Olivia wanted to kill herself, as she had ended all chances with Matt when she kissed his friend the previous week. But she began to notice that he was also looking at her. Sofia also realised this and because she didn't want to be in the middle of this story, she said she would go to the bathroom. At that moment, Matt approached Olivia and the two kept dancing and laughing. It was as if they had already known each other, as if they had been friends for a long time. It was good because the unpleasant atmosphere Olivia felt — which maybe existed only inside her head because she was attracted to the friend of the boy she had kissed the previous week — was broken. When Sofia came back, they continued dancing and having fun, recording videos and taking pictures.

Olivia couldn't look at Matt. She felt his whole body tremble as their eyes met. It was something so inexplicable that it even scared her.

A man went to talk to Sofia and left the way free for Matt who, looking a little embarrassed, went to Olivia and invited her to dance. The DJ was playing "Sweet Caroline," a slow, romantic song by Neil Diamond, one of the most popular songs played at Nancy's and she had no choice but to accept his invitation.

He was leading the dance, and poor Olivia felt a little ridiculous as she didn't know how to dance. Matt was probably aware of that, but he didn't seem to care and was willing to teach her. He held her very close to his body, and Olivia could feel her heart race as she felt his heartbeat race as well. Then, looking up, she found his eyes looking down at her tenderly.

They stared at each other and he kissed her. As corny as it may sound, Olivia felt like she was having her first kiss again. It felt like her body was floating and that it was watching the two of them kiss from above. It seemed that everyone who was in the pub had just disappeared and there were just the two of them, in the middle of that kiss. She didn't know how long the kiss lasted, whether it was a long, movie-like kiss or a quick kiss. She knew it lasted long enough to make her smile every time she thought back on it. When the kiss ended, they realised that the lights had been turned on and that the security guard, as he always did, was asking people to leave, because the night was over. Matt looked at Olivia and asked for her contact information.

He took Olivia's hand and the two, accompanied by Sofia, headed towards the exit. Halfway there, Matt let go of Olivia's hand as they passed the Austrian who was kissing another girl in the same place he'd kissed Olivia the previous week. She saw the scene and wondered if the girl still had the earrings, or if he had already taken them off indicating that he wanted to take her to bed.

Outside the pub, the two said goodbye with another kiss that almost made Olivia lose her breath. When she got into the taxi, she kept looking at him. She couldn't believe she had kissed that man. The truth was, Olivia had never really been involved with a man like him, so big, so strong, so handsome. She sighed inside the car, and Sofia laughed at her friend's silly expression.

They had barely reached O'Connell Street when Olivia received a message from Matt.

"Loved the night with you, it was amazing!"

"Oh my God, Sofia, look at the message he just sent me!"

"Wow, how cute. He's so sweet, Olivia!"

"Yes, he is... very sweet, polite, very different from that Austrian."

"I think you should meet him again."

Olivia agreed with the idea, but when she got home and checked the guy's social media, she realised that he wasn't just friends with the Austrian, but that they lived together, in the same student accommodation. Since Matt had even let go of her hand when they passed his friend, he probably didn't want to get involved with Olivia. But it was okay, Olivia didn't believe in those overwhelming passions that only happen in movies.

The days went by and they didn't exchange messages, since they didn't have much to talk about. Olivia was already completely convinced that this was just another fun story that happened at Nancy's, like so many others she and her friends had experienced there. One day, while scrolling through her social mediafeed, she saw a photo of the Austrian with Matt and another friend, drinking the Austrian's last beer in Ireland, according to what the image caption said. It took less than an hour for her to get a message from Matt, asking if she would like to have dinner sometime that week.

They even tried to match their schedules, but as the two had their holiday trips scheduled, they didn't have the opportunity to meet again that year, which helped keep the flame burning inside Olivia's heart. She didn't believe in love at first sight, but she believed Matt was much more than a guy she'd kissed after a few pints of Guinness in an Irish pub.

Olivia spent almost 30 days traveling and during all those days there wasn't a single day that she didn't think about Matt. She felt so silly, she wasn't a teenager anymore to indulge in passions like that, but what should she do? Although she felt too old for it, she could now dream of a life where love finally worked out easily and without pain. This was unlike the kind of love she had experienced, a love in which she had always had to beg for attention. A love that brought nothing good, only suffering and pain. A love she needed to remove from her heart. She was referring to Cristiano. It was Cristiano's birthday that day and after receiving a cold message to thank her for the message she had sent, she wanted to forget about him once and for all. She took advantage of being alone in Scotland to do something she should have done a long time ago - erase Cristiano and all traces of him from her life.

"Freedom & Whiskey"

She couldn't drink whiskey anymore.

Whiskey was the distilled flavour of her "defeat."

Whiskey reminded her of a hangover from the early 2000s.

A hangover she got in an attempt to forget the loss of her great love.

Everything should have ended with that engagement proposal.

It should all have ended with those three shots of crappy Wild West whiskey.

It should all have ended with that "no," disguised in the middle of some "yes."

But no, it wasn't over.

The suffering spread, renewed itself, had several endings, but also countless beginnings.

Cowardice, self-indulgence, insistence, stubbornness, stupidity.

The only thing that had ended that night was the dream of having a library in her house,

Where she would spend hours reading, writing, talking with friends, and enjoying a good whiskey.

She felt that it was about time to put an end to it.

The feeling that, in fact, the endpoint had already arrived was a reality for her;

Distance and indifference had taken care of that, but she still worried, after all,

they were above all — and only — friends.

She, too good as always, on a special date, sent a sweet message.

She received a cold thank you, with a full stop.

The penny dropped.

That endpoint was indeed the endpoint.

Finally.

She felt free, light, and confident.

So, to get rid of the ghost once and for all, she decided that she wanted that dream again, wanted to drink whiskey, to smell it without her stomach twisting. She wouldn't let him take that away from her anymore.

She was in Scotland; there couldn't be a better place to settle this. She plucked up her courage, went into a tavern near the castle, and went to the counter: "Give me a single malt, please."

The waiter served her; she paid and stared at the glass. Drinking it all in one go would only seem like a lack of courage, so she savoured the first sip and smelled it too. It tasted and smelled like freedom! She drank the rest. She slammed her glass down on the counter. She nodded to the waiter, who returned the gesture. She was free.

She opened the door, felt the crisp December air, walked out of the tavern and let the door slam behind her. She left everything behind. After all, as the Scottish poet, Robert Burns, would say, "Freedom and whisky go together."

She published the text on her blog, knowing that many people would be able to decipher that she was referring to Cristiano. That gesture ended a cycle that had lasted much longer than she would have liked it to. She had wasted nearly a decade of her life chasing a love that never gave her anything in return. It was time to move on, and her heart was free to receive all the love someone wanted to give her. It might not even be Matt, but she was ready to open up to new opportunities.

The trip was wonderful, and she loved every country she visited. But when she finally landed on Irish soil, her heart felt at home again. She knew she was going to spend a few days alone, for until school resumed, there would be two long weeks where she would be completely by herself at Courtbrack.

Matt and Olivia had been texting each other throughout the holidays. As he was also back in Limerick, he asked her if she would like to do anything that week. Olivia accepted because it was all she had ever wanted, but she was nervous. What if he didn't like her anymore? What if it had been a momentary thing, and now he saw that he was wrong? And the worst fear of all: how could she be interesting, funny, and captivating using a limited vocabulary? It's one thing to do all this in your native language; it's quite another to be able to do the same in English.

When she arrived at the restaurant, she couldn't believe he looked even more handsome than the night they'd met. Olivia had already been so unlucky in her life... It seemed that the game was finally changing. During dinner, they talked a lot, and in a few hours, they already knew everything about each other's lives: family, dreams, experiences, passion for dogs, and childhood. Both were from small towns, and although there was a great geographical distance between them, they seemed to have a huge connection. They left the restaurant and went to the Mickey Martin's pub, one of the oldest in Limerick, which was turning 200 years old that year.

Along the way, Olivia didn't know whether to take his hand or just walk beside him. Matt was very considerate, always concerned about how comfortable she was, and always wanted to know what would make her happy. He also appeared to be a little nervous and unsure of how to act. The connection was so strong that even the usual awkwardness between people who still don't have much intimacy had passed. They walked the streets of Limerick side by side, talking, laughing, and looking into each other's eyes.

They could have kept talking all night, but it was getting late. He offered to walk her home and worked up the courage to ask her out again. They were still in the middle of a date, and he was already asking about the next one. Sometime later, Matt confessed that he found his own attitude strange.

"You told me you like sushi, right?"

"Yes, I love it."

"Would you like to go with me on Sunday to a great sushi restaurant on O'Connell Street?"

"Yes, I would." Of course, she would. Like him, she was already thinking about when she would meet him again.

As they got closer to home, the kiss she'd been waiting for all night finally happened. There was no mistake; she felt something very special for him. He was so big, his arms wrapped all the way around her, and although he was slightly cold, his body was warm. As they said goodbye, Matt hugged her, and as she rested her head on his chest, Olivia heard his heart pounding.

The next day, Olivia went to the teacher's husband's cafe with the only friend who was already in town, Fabiana. There, both the teacher and her friend noticed that she seemed to be in love with the ginger—as redheads are called in Ireland. Olivia just smiled and said that they would get married someday.

Fabiana and she agreed to go to Nancy's that night, after all, they had already missed the place. She decided to send a message to Matt. It might have sounded strange, after all, they had scheduled a date for the next day, and she knew that he would be home with some friends that night. Still, to her surprise, he decided to join them. They met, enjoyed their time together, and couldn't wait to see each other again the next day.

Once again, the date was perfect in every way. They went to the sushi restaurant and then listened to typical Irish bands at The Locke Bar and Dolan's. They spent hours holding hands, looking into each other's eyes, without saying anything. It reminded her of scenes from the light-hearted movies Olivia grew up watching; it didn't seem real. As usual, they talked about many subjects, including the cultures of Canada and Brazil.

"Olivia, do you like living in Brazil? I have a Brazilian friend who said she will never go back there because it's too violent."

"Well, I think some parts of Brazil are violent, but I'm very lucky because my city is far from them."

"Do you feel safe living there?"

"Yeah! It's been about 10 years since we lost the house keys and never found them again."

"Oh, I can't believe you live in Brazil."

"Yes, I do. The world has to end this stereotype that the country follows a pattern that only includes violence, football, black women with sculpted bodies, corruption, and bad people. Brazil may have all of that, but not only that. Our country is immense and has a huge and rich culture, but I have the impression that only this part is shown to the rest of the world."

"I understand you, most people who live in the United States think that we Canadians live in igloos."

"Do you?" Olivia asked, teasing the boy, who answered with a wonderful smile.

"Yes, just like you are Black. In fact, if I had to guess your nationality, I would never say you are Brazilian. I'd guess you're German, maybe French, but never Brazilian."

"And I'd say you're Irish because you fit the stereotype here too."

"Well, I'm of Scottish descent on both sides of my family, so I'm very close."

"And I'm of German descent, so you did well in your guess too. But wait a minute, don't tell me you wear a kilt..?"

"Yes, I do. I have some in my clan's colours."

"Oh Matt, one day you'll have to wear one for me."

"I can wear it to our wedding," he said jokingly, but Olivia couldn't help imagining the scene and secretly, involuntarily, wishing it would happen.

He said his dream was to visit the Isle of Skye in Scotland because the McLeod clan was from there, and he would very much like to know the land of his ancestors. Olivia told him about her visit to Scotland and said she would certainly like to return one day. It seemed very crazy, but she was sure that one day she would return with him.

The next day, she had to call Bella to tell her she was in love.

"I'm in love."

"What do you mean in love, where did that come from?"

"Do you remember that handsome guy I kissed last year at the pub I always go to?"

"The Austrian?"

"No, the Canadian."

"There are more than 190 countries in the world, and you want me to remember the nationality of everyone you kissed?"

"Stop being silly and pay attention to me."

"Okay, go on… the Canadian."

"Yes, the tall, strong, red-haired Canadian. I felt my heart stop when I saw him walk into the pub the day I kissed the Austrian."

"Then I'm the silly one…"

"Stop! We've had three dates in the last three days, and I can't even explain how I feel. Every time I see him, I get butterflies in my stomach. We can spend hours talking and never finish things. He can make my day perfect just by holding my hand."

"And what are the Canadian's flaws?"

"What do you mean…?"

"The flaws, because whenever you meet someone, you talk about all their traits, all their qualities, but then you pour out a lot of problems and kind of predict what will make your relationship fall apart. You start what your psychologist used to call 'Olivia's self-sabotage.'"

"Today, I will disappoint you and my psychologist. Of course, he must have some flaws, but I still haven't been able to find any."

"What? No flaws? Oh my god, seriously?"

"He's human, so he must have some, but they seem to be very inconspicuous. So far, I have nothing to complain about. It feels like I'm living in a movie."

"Oh, you've got to be kidding! Is Cristiano's era over for good?"

"Who is Cristiano?" Olivia joked.

"Oh, speaking of him, you should learn from the Canadian and be more discreet too, because your post made many people, including Cristiano, think the message was for him. He even came to talk to me."

"What do you mean?"

"Oh Olivia, everyone could understand the message."

"I want to know why Cristiano went to talk to you. I don't care if they understood the message or not."

"What? This isn't you. Where is my friend who always worries about what others think of her?"

"Spill it!"

"But weren't you the one who closed the pub door and left the past behind, as we read in your text?"

"My goodness, today you are unbearable. I'm losing my patience. Tell me!" Olivia asked, laughing. But she was really getting annoyed with her friend for not telling her what had happened.

"Okay, okay, I was just kidding. Well, first he came for a little chat asking how you were, if everything was okay, and if you had already settled down."

"Wow, how concerned," said Olivia sarcastically.

"That's it… worried! Then he asked me what had happened with your social networks because he had tried to talk to you recently but couldn't."

"I deleted them and blocked him."

"Yes, I think he understood. Then he told me that he had tried to talk to you because he thought you exposed him with that text."

"Oh, poor thing!" said Olivia once again with sarcasm.

"Then I said it was the least he deserved. That you should have put his name and ID in the text so everyone could know that he is a jerk. Cristiano said he understood and could see your position, but he also thought it was very unfair for this to happen right now, especially without you even giving him a chance to talk and explain why he had responded the way he did to your birthday wishes. He believes you would have understood."

"I wouldn't, because thank God that Olivia, who accepted all this humiliation for 10 years, doesn't exist anymore. That's enough. I can't understand how I got stuck in this monotonous, sad, repetitive story all this time. I begged for this man's love. He made me believe that love was really about suffering. I believed that love was indeed a pain, as in Camões' poem," said Olivia with a nervous laugh.

"My goodness, you reciting that poem is like a throwback to our 8th grade. Please spare me. And love doesn't have to be about pain unless it's not love. And it's about time you found someone who can give you back all the love you have to offer in the same proportion. I'm telling you this story just so you know he knows that you've blocked him and that you've put an end to this. I even showed him a photo of you with one of your foreign admirers. I hope it's the right one."

"Shut up! Which one did you show him?"

"I think I showed him the right one, with you and the redhead!"

"That's it! That's the right one." And they both laughed.

"Did you see? The moment you opened your heart, someone showed up. You should have done that a long time ago."

"It seems I was waiting for Matt."

"Who's Matt? My God, another one?"

"Stop, Bella. Matt is the Canadian!" They spoke for a while longer, amid much laughter, as always happened when they called each other.

When Olivia hung up the phone, she thought about what her friend had said. It was good to know that Cristiano knew she had blocked him and that, even though he no longer had contact with her on social media, he continued to visit her blog. But she didn't want to know what he had to say. She knew that vicious cycle and had no desire to enter it again. She didn't feel anger, hate, or anything like that. What she felt was worse than all that; it was apathy. He didn't mean anything to her anymore. She thought even the chance of being friends with him again was unlikely. It was all over.

Things with Matt followed a natural flow. They would meet whenever they could, and the encounters were more and more special. In the most unexpected moments, he would send her cute messages, saying that he was thinking about her, or that he heard a song that made him think of them— things that made her feel like the most special person in the world. They watched movies, went to many restaurants, and listened to a lot of traditional music together. They were passionate about the rhythm of Ireland and could spend hours listening to those songs. They walked hand in hand through the streets and stared at each other with silly faces. When they finally spent the night together, Olivia was sure she was lost.

When she arrived at his house, he was already waiting for her at the gate with the biggest smile in the world—a smile that would warm any heart. After entering, Matt took off her coat. Inwardly, she already knew what was going to happen and wanted it more than anything else. He hugged her around the waist, and Olivia could feel Matt's entire body in contact with hers. He lifted Olivia, who entwined her legs around his body. His breath on her neck and his hands running over her body had her delirious with pleasure before it even started. No words were needed; just the exchange of looks was enough to express all her desires.

She had never felt such a connection with anyone. As clichéd as it may seem, she felt that they were one, that their bodies had been created only to find each other again in moments like these. Matt was different from the other men Olivia had dated. All of them seemed to have learned about relationships by reading the same manual, as if they had a degree in: "Being into it, but not showing it", "Wishing one thing and doing another", "Not showing interest in maintaining a relationship", and a few more topics that only make life difficult for women, especially insecure women like Olivia. But Matt wasn't like that; he didn't seem to be playing any games.

Since their relationship started, he seemed to be more in love with Olivia than she was with him. He always made it clear how charming he found her, how much he enjoyed spending time with her, and that from the moment he met her, he wasn't looking for anyone else. This made Olivia gradually become a version of herself that had never existed in a relationship. A more confident, secure, freer version.

She could spend hours lying with her head on his chest, with him stroking her hair and telling her stories. He didn't mind repeating the same story in different ways because of her difficulty with English. He wanted to hear about her dreams, paid attention to details, and supported her in everything. He loved hearing about the books she was writing, what she was studying, and the stories she wanted to tell. Loving him was inevitable. However, she was scared...

"Great, Olivia, now you love this guy! So now what? What if he doesn't love you back? 10 more years? Congratulations, Olivia, congratulations!" she said to herself, returning home and realising that she loved him.

But fate was on her side, as the 'Olivia's self-sabotage' mode had been frustrated once again. They had gone to Nancy's with a few more friends, and it was there that he said 'I love you' for the first time.

"Olivia, I really, really like you," Matt said, which gave Olivia the courage to take the initiative to tell him that she loved him, but first, she wanted to say she was in love. After all, she didn't want to scare him. She still wasn't sure he hadn't read that manual.

"I like you a lot too, actually I think that I..." Before finishing the sentence, she saw her courage vanishing. How could she tell him that she was in love, that she had been in love since the first kiss? It seemed too soon.

"That you love me?"

"What? No, no, no!" He had misunderstood. That's not what she wanted to say. In fact, it was, but she wanted to go step by step and he had skipped one. She decided to use it to her advantage.

"Why? Do you love me?"

"Yes, I love you. I love you. I've loved you since the first time we kissed."

"I love you too." They shared a passionate kiss. Olivia thought she had never kissed someone with such passion and love in her life. He loved her! He loved her! She was full of joy.

He asked her to be his girlfriend to the sound of 'You Had Me at Hello' by the band A Day to Remember, a song that Matt said translated everything he felt for Olivia. He said she had conquered him with the first 'hello', for he felt exactly the same way, in love since their eyes met for the first time. The Cranberries, of course, were the soundtrack of their relationship, but according to Matt, they would dance to 'You Had Me at Hello' at their wedding, as there was no way they could choose just one song by the Irish band.

They had a week off, so they booked their first trip together. They went to Scotland because since childhood, Matt had wanted to know about the land of his ancestors, more specifically the Isle of Skye. Olivia was very excited to travel and was sure it would be perfect to do so with the man she loved.

They flew from Dublin to Edinburgh. They would enjoy the city for a while before renting a car to go to the island. The city was the same place that had stolen Olivia's heart months ago when she'd first visited. Olivia used to fall in love with cities far more than with people, and Edinburgh had been a maddening passion. She loved the castle and all those medieval streets, and she was thrilled to see Matt's joy.

"It's impressive, it feels like I've been here before," he said.

"How so?"

"I don't know how to explain it. I feel almost nostalgic, as if everything once meant something very important to me."

"Don't worry, I know exactly how you're feeling."

"How do you know?"

"I know because I felt the same way when I was in Limerick for the first time; it felt like home to me."

"Well, that's exactly what I'm feeling. It's as if I know every corner of this city without ever having set foot here."

"It's scary, isn't it?"

"Not scary, but I think we need to have a whisky!"

"I agree, especially now that I can!" She had updated him about her story with Cristiano, and Matt was happy because he also wanted to drink whisky with Olivia in the library they would have in their house.

They stayed two more days in Edinburgh before heading to Inverness, the largest and most important city in the Highlands, and then went to the island where Matt's ancestors once lived. Olivia couldn't get enough of admiring the Highlands; the scenic beauty was jaw-dropping. The brown against the green, the outline of the mountains, the sinuosity of the relief—everything was so perfect. Apart from the historical part, the records of the struggle of its people against English oppression, the determination of its men and women—with all this, it was easy to understand why this part of Scotland was so fascinating.

The Isle of Skye, linked to Scotland's northwest coast by a bridge, is known for its rugged landscapes, picturesque seaside villages, and medieval castles. It is a place with a spectacular landscape where everything exudes strength and magnificence. It is the largest island in the Inner Hebrides archipelago and has an indented coastline with peninsulas and narrow lochs, which radiate from the mountainous interior. The town of Portree was their base to explore the island. There were many pubs and boutiques next to the port, but as they were tired, they ate something quickly and went up to the room, where Matt said to his girlfriend:

"My love, I feel something here too. As if I know this place."

"I think you might be overwhelmed, having so much related to your last name here. You practically own the island!" Olivia said, mocking her boyfriend.

"No, I'm serious. It seems to be even stronger than in Edinburgh."

"Are you happy to be here?"

"Yes, a lot! Tomorrow I have to take lots of pictures to send to my father and uncles. Some of our family members have already been here and signed a book. We will sign it tomorrow."

"You will sign, not me, because I'm not a McLeod."

"You will sign too. You might not be a McLeod yet, but soon you will be!"

"Are you asking me to marry you, Matt McLeod?"

"On our third date, I told you that we were going to get married. Don't you remember?"

"Of course, I remember. I just didn't know if you were serious or not. And you promised me you'd be wearing a kilt!"

"I've never wanted something so badly in my life. And as for the kilt, wait and see!" He said that and kissed his girlfriend, who was swooning over him.

The next day, they went to Dunvegan Castle, where the entire history of the McLeod clan was kept.

Olivia was taken by surprise that morning when she saw Matt wearing the kilt in his family colours: yellow, with three black stripes and a small red line.

"You look handsome, my love."

"Do you like it? You better like it because, as I promised you, I'll be wearing one of these at our wedding."

"Of course, I love it. However, I have a question for you..."

"Ask me."

"Is it true that you wear the kilt with nothing underneath, without underwear?"

"Of course, it's true."

Olivia smiled and kissed him. She'd gotten a lot of ideas from that information, but they were late leaving.

They made their way to the castle that had been the clan's headquarters, and there they found a book that many McLeod descendants from around the world had signed, saying that they had returned to their ancestral land. The place also had some records of the older McLeods and stories about their lives.

"Matt John McLeod," he wrote, and "Olivia Walter Kalckmann McLeod," she signed, as he photographed the first time his girlfriend signed her last name. He couldn't hide how happy and proud he was.

While Matt was talking to someone who seemed to be a very distant relative who lived in the States, Olivia was lost among the exhibits that told the stories of her boyfriend's ancestors. She was getting more and more amazed as she read. If she had a heart condition, she would think she was having a heart attack because her heart raced remarkably when she found a report about a McLeod who had lived and died in Limerick. She was approaching the exhibit when Matt walked up to her and asked:

"What happened, dear?"

"Look, this man, this Ian Alexander McLeod, lived in Limerick."

"Wow, looks like I wasn't the first of my clan to end up there then. It's so weird, I seem to have heard that name before."

"Are you serious? I wonder if he was important in Limerick's history. I also had a strange sense of recognition when I read this. I feel like I've heard of him."

The two started looking for more information but hadn't found anything very significant until they saw an old newspaper clipping with the following note:

"My beloved Ian Alexander McLeod

Eight months of missing the one who will always be my great love.

C.C.M."

The two were intrigued by that, so Olivia started to make some guesses about who those initials could belong to, but nothing made sense. No one in the history she knew of Limerick had those initials. They probably didn't know anything about that woman. Matt then went to talk to the person who was taking care of the place.

"Sir, do you happen to have any more information about Ian Alexander McLeod, this man here in the newspaper?"

"Oh yeah, I think it talks about him in one of those books. Let me see if I can find it," said the man while looking for the book.

"Well, young Ian went to Ireland, to this city, Limerick, in 1867, intending to set up a whiskey distillery in partnership with a cousin, but unfortunately, he was killed under unclear circumstances. At first, he just disappeared, but after a few years, a Reverend friend of the family found out what had happened. He said that Ian got involved with a girl engaged to someone very powerful in the city, and it all ended up turning into a very big tragedy. Many people died, and from what the Reverend said, Ian was shot and stabbed, and his body was thrown into the River Shannon."

Matt and Olivia were completely caught up in the story. Olivia couldn't hold back the tears, even though the man was just reading the records, without expressing any emotion. They never thought they would find anything that mentioned a place they knew so well.

"And the girl?" Olivia asked.

"It doesn't say much about her, just that she was the one who wrote that note in the newspaper and that, not long after that, Catherine died."

"Catherine," Olivia said, looking a little scared.

"Yes, Catherine Crawford."

Olivia stared at the man with her mouth open, unsure of how to react.

"What's the matter? Is everything okay?"

"You will not believe it. Remember that story I told you, about the cemetery photos, that I always felt an inexplicable urge to stop and, not knowing what to do, I always took a photo until one day I realised that I had more than five photos, all taken from exactly the same location?"

"Yes, I remember when you told me about it."

"Do you know whose grave it was?"

"It cannot be!"

"Yes, it was Catherine Crawford's grave."

"Do you have any more information about this woman?" asked Matt.

"No, only that this love story was a real tragedy," said the man.

"It's very confusing, because if this is the same woman I researched, she ended up marrying her fiancé, Fred Stafford, and even had a child with him. I don't know if the baby survived, but Catherine died during childbirth."

"Yeah, unfortunately, I don't have more information about that. But your connection to this story definitely seems like a coincidence."

They left the castle and Olivia was quiet, thoughtful.

"You were enthralled by the story, weren't you?"

"Yes, a lot!"

"I was intrigued as well, this is very surreal."

"Seriously, I'm scared. I saw this woman's grave there and now I find her name here again? There must be something else behind this story."

"When I read the name 'Ian Alexander McLeod,' I felt a tightness in my chest. I can't explain it."

"I think we're very bewildered by it all. When we get back to Limerick, we can go to the newspaper and the church. I'm sure we'll find out a few more things."

"Yes, we will. We will find out who killed my ancestor. But for now, I have some other ideas," he said to his girlfriend in a seductive tone.

"What ideas?" Olivia asked, as if she were getting into the seduction game.

"Well, this morning I noticed you were very interested when you heard that I don't wear anything under my kilt."

They went home and that night they made love as they had never done before. If Olivia always thought it was fantastic, she couldn't find the words to describe what they had done that night. Rita Lee, a Brazilian singer, had managed in one of her songs to separate sex from love, but that night everything was mixed in perfect harmony: love and desire, passion and tenderness, voracity and sweetness. As they made love Matt said:

"I want to have a child with you."

That was it! She was sure that he would be her children's father and that she would stay with him forever. What she didn't know was the world was about to go through an unprecedented event, which started in China, but didn't take long to affect all countries. Covid-19, a flu-like illness that affects patients much more severely than the common flu, was arriving in Ireland. Many people had already died in China, Italy, and Spain, and it was starting to spread alarmingly across Germany and the United Kingdom. They were still on the plane when they read the news about border closures and the suspension of classes at their universities, as measures to prevent the spread of the virus.

They didn't know it yet, but this pandemic would affect not only their lives but the lives of billions of people around the globe. The entire world suffered terrible consequences, millions of lives were lost, an immeasurable pain for families and entire nations. The consequences were less severe in countries that took Covid-19 more seriously and prioritised the lives of their inhabitants, which is what Ireland did as soon as the authorities realised the gravity of the situation. Classes were suspended, pubs were closed, big festivities such as Saint Patrick's Day were cancelled, and the Prime Minister, in one of his speeches, said a phrase that was heard and spread by almost all Irish people: "We are asking people to come together as a nation by staying apart from each other."

After arriving in Limerick, the quarantine began. They faced several restrictions, such as staying at home. Several countries were asking their international students to return home. As all of Olivia's colleagues had come to Ireland through a Brazilian government programme, they were given the option to return home or stay in Ireland. Most of them decided to go home. As Olivia was there for an Irish government programme, she did not receive an official offer, but she knew that she would be fully supported to return, if necessary.

"I can't go," she said to Simone.

"Why can't you go?"

"I can't go back like that. I no longer have a job in Brazil, and my English is not at a satisfactory level. If I go back, I'll have to look for a job. How will I have time for my studies? The email said that from now on, everything will be online."

"I agree. If I were you, I would stay too. It's different for us because we have families that depend on us back home. You're free."

"I think the same, but I cannot pretend that it's an easy decision."

"What about Matt?"

"Well, he said he'll stay as long as he can, but I don't know if it's possible."

The girl had to say goodbye to her friends who returned to Brazil. She was very sad as all the plans, all the things they dreamed of doing just became impossible in a matter of days. They all had the feeling that they still had a lot of living to do in Limerick, but unfortunately, the course that the pandemic took didn't leave many options. Courtbrack, once so full of people, was now practically empty, as the Irish students had also returned home. The empty spaces seemed to be filled with the fear and uncertainties that the virus brought to everyone. Dark times were approaching.

Olivia couldn't even think about the possibility of losing Matt. He promised that he would do everything possible to stay. But things got complicated when he received an email from the Canadian Embassy saying that it was recommended that all international students return because the borders would be closed and, after this, people would no longer be allowed to return home.

Olivia couldn't believe this was happening. Things were getting worse; she had never imagined that she would face such a situation in her lifetime. Being forced to separate from the man she loved and having no power to prevent it from happening was terrible. She thought she was the unluckiest person in the world to have found her great love and lost him in such an absurd way, for a reason that neither she nor anyone else in the world had any control over.

"This is the kind of thing that only happens to me, Bella. It takes me a lifetime to find someone I love and who loves me back, and what happens? A pandemic arrives to destroy everything."

"Olivia, don't be so arrogant as to think that the pandemic arrived to end your romance."

"No, Bella, of course not, but you have to agree that it's very bad luck."

"Yes, it's bad luck, but he's not dying. He's just moving, and I'm sure you'll meet him again."

"How will we meet again? Everything is uncertain now. When is it going to happen?"

"We don't know, Olivia. Everything will end well, and you know you can always count on me. We'll find a way; you won't miss the chance to live out this great love."

Olivia knew that she could count on Bella for everything and knew that her friend, if necessary, would move heaven and earth to make her happy. Now it wasn't a matter of effort, it wasn't a matter of isolated actions. In fact, it was more a matter of time, of waiting and of believing that everything would end well.

Matt was also trying to comfort his girlfriend.

"My love, don't cry like that."

"But what am I going to do without you? How am I going to give up what I feel for you?"

"You don't have to. We'll find a way to be together. This situation will be over someday."

"But how?"

"I don't have the answer, but I know I can't lose you. I love you so much."

"I can't lose you either."

"When I see you, I have to control myself not to stare at you because you're so beautiful."

"Your smile lights up my days, lights up all the places where we are. Your kiss stole my heart; it was as if I was yours before I even tasted it. I came from a small town in Canada, you from a small town in Brazil. We met in Limerick, a small town in Ireland. We had to cross the ocean to find each other. There's no way we won't be together. We'll be together."

"Promise me?"

"I promise, I'll do everything for us to be together because you are the love of my life, my future wife, and you will be the mother of my children."

"I want to give you a present."

"What is it, my love?"

"I want to give you my Claddagh ring," she said, taking the ring off her finger.

"Are you sure? Since I met you, you've always had it on your finger."

"Did you know that when I got home from our first date, I turned the crown outward? I wanted to signal that my heart was already taken and that I was no longer available. On the day of our second date, I turned the crown inward again, afraid you'd think my gesture was crazy, but the fact is, my heart is yours, and I want you to take my ring as a reminder."

"You are so sweet, my love. My heart is also all yours, and I promise that we will be together," Matt said, kissing his girlfriend.

None of Matt's promises could ease the pain Olivia was feeling. It took her so long to find someone, and now that she had finally learned what love was, it would be so unfair to lose it.

In another conversation with her best friend, she even said that she would rather have never met him, just to avoid the terrible pain of living apart from her love, but soon she regretted saying that. How could she die without feeling what true love was? How could she go through life without knowing this breath-taking love that warmed her heart at the mere memory of a hug?

She believed in the strength of the love they felt for each other but knew that there would be difficult times when they were living in different countries.

They spent the entire week together before Matt's departure. For a few moments, she forgot that these were their last days together. He cooked for her, they watched movies and studied together because they were finishing their courses. Olivia wanted to memorise every feature of the man she loved. When he studied, he always listened to heavy, upbeat music, and with every paragraph he wrote and approved, he nodded in front of the computer. The dexterity with which he cut food to prepare meals, the glass of milk he drank while he had lunch and dinner, the way he hugged her before bed, and all the comfort she felt, despite sleeping in a small single bed. She wanted to capture it all and keep it forever in her memory, but she didn't want to and couldn't let this love turn into just a beautiful memory. She was determined to do whatever it took to fight for this love after this damn pandemic was over.

On the day of the farewell, Olivia felt like one of those women who say goodbye to her man before he goes to war. She knew the situation wasn't the same, far from it, but the pain she was feeling was comparable. She was saying goodbye to her love, not knowing when she would see him again or what their future would be like. A future that seemed to be taking shape in a way she hadn't imagined, not even in her wildest dreams, but which now seemed like a tragedy, a story that could be in the pages of a poorly written novel.

They kissed, declared their love once more and he got on the bus. Would that be the last time she would hug him? If it were, she would like to live in that embrace. She wanted to keep that feeling forever, the smell of his hair and the taste of his mouth.

She stood by the stop, waiting for the bus to leave, holding back tears and feeling the cold air of Limerick entering her lungs.

From inside the bus, he sent a message:

"Goodbye, my love. I will always love you, I will never forget you, and we will definitely see each other again because I love you so, so much. I'm so glad I woke up with you in my arms these past few days! You are the best thing that has happened in my life. I'm glad that in our first kiss you bit my lip and stole my heart. I love you. Your smile will continue to brighten my days."

When she read that, she didn't even try, because she knew it would be impossible to hold back the tears. She started to cry and looked at him, as he watched the scene from the window. That last week, although she'd had many good and unforgettable moments, had also been a painful week, as Olivia was unable to talk about it without bursting into tears. The bus left for Dublin, from where he would take the plane back to Canada.

On the way home, it started to rain, and Olivia felt as if she carried all the weight of the world on her back. The tears mixed with the rain, and in a silent cry, she walked the almost 2 miles that separated her house from the bus and train station from which her lover had left.

At home, she changed rooms to carry out a two-week quarantine, since she couldn't put anyone at risk, having spent a week away. She knew these would be two of the loneliest weeks of her life. She would have to share that room only with the pain of having lost her love, the uncertainty about the coronavirus, and the concern for her family in Brazil, a country which, at that point, did not seem to be taking the pandemic seriously and had a completely unprepared, incompetent man running the nation.

To make matters worse, in the middle of those two weeks, she would have a very special day that had already been planned. It was Olivia's birthday, and she and Matt were going to spend a weekend in Dingle, on the coast of Ireland. She knew it would have been another perfect weekend, but now it would only exist in her imagination. The reality was different: she would spend her birthday without even receiving a hug. The girls who stayed with her at the accommodation even made a cake and a special dinner, and the day was much better than she expected it to be, but this birthday would be forever marked in her biography. Olivia had always loved having birthdays and the expressions of love she usually received on that day, but on this one, she had very little of that.

She and Matt used to talk every day, and although they were far apart, she didn't feel that the love they had for each other had diminished. As soon as he returned to Canada, Matt had all the symptoms of Covid-19. At the hospital, they recommended that he take the test, which, to his relief, came back negative. It would have been terrible if one of them had caught the coronavirus; it would have made this story even more dramatic.

However, fate was willing to shake Olivia's life one more time. After a week, she had left quarantine and returned to her room when one of the girls started feeling Covid symptoms, and it didn't take long for Olivia to start feeling ill too. By the irony of fate—yes, fate again—the girl who showed symptoms first was the one who was most paranoid about the whole situation, the one who hardly ever left her room and was always wearing gloves.

Everything happened very fast. Olivia began to experience fever, tiredness, and a dry cough, and in the evening of the same day, she began to experience difficulty breathing.

She texted her family and Matt to tell them she thought she had Covid-19 right before the ambulance arrived to take her to the hospital. It was so difficult to breathe that she couldn't even walk. Her friends hurriedly put her Irish visa in a plastic bag and handed it to the paramedics, as no one could accompany her in the ambulance. Olivia handed her phone to a friend and asked her to keep in touch with her family and Matt.

Everything was happening at breakneck speed. She was put on oxygen as soon as she got into the ambulance. Just a few minutes after leaving the accommodation, she felt a thud. The ambulance appeared to have crashed into another car. There had been a problem with another ambulance, which made it stop in the middle of the lane. Another car crashed at high speed, causing a serious accident, and the ambulance that Olivia was in almost crashed into this car. The driver managed to swerve in time but was forced to stop to help his colleagues. They would be able to continue without problems, but the first ambulance was also taking a patient with respiratory difficulties and symptoms of Covid to the hospital. In addition, the patient from the first ambulance had been injured in the accident, so they put her in the ambulance with Olivia before heading to the hospital.

Shortness of breath must be one of the worst feelings anyone can experience in life. Breathing is such a common and automatic action that no one is grateful for being able to do it. Olivia started to regret not having appreciated it her whole life at the exact moment she started having trouble getting air into her lungs. She felt like her heart was going to burst in an attempt to get all the oxygen it could from her blood. She felt lightheaded, as if her head were a balloon, and suddenly everything went grey, a dark grey, like an oil slick in the ocean. She just heard a small hiss in the background.

The next day, Olivia's friends called the university staff to ask for support because they couldn't get any information from the hospital. The Director of the International Office personally went to the hospital. When she arrived, she couldn't believe what she found.

Olivia had died.

They said the ambulance that was bringing her had some setbacks, and when she arrived at the hospital, she was already in a very complicated situation. They intubated her, but she couldn't survive.

"No, that can't be true, she was conscious before getting here."

"Yes, but unfortunately, her condition worsened after the accident the ambulance was involved in."

"There's not much to do. You need to notify the family, but they won't be able to repatriate the body. It will have to be buried here, with a closed coffin, as these are the measures recommended by the WHO. Furthermore, it is not safe for anyone to come from there for the burial, which, by the way, is recommended to take place as soon as possible to prevent the risk of contamination."

The director was desolate when she left the hospital. How would she call the girl's parents and deliver this news? She decided that she would go to the accommodation first and talk to her friends before deciding how she was going to approach Olivia's family. When she told them, no one could believe it. They were all in shock and, more than that, afraid of what could happen to them.

Fabiana, the friend who had kept the phone, had the sad task of talking to her family and also to Matt. Olivia's mother, who had been in contact with Fabiana since the night before, couldn't have received worse news. As soon as Fabiana spoke, she heard a silence followed by a desperate cry, which could only be compared to the cries of other mothers who had also lost their children. She realized that someone was helping the woman, but soon that person started to cry too. Fabiana had to wait a few moments until they calmed down. She explained that the funeral would have to be immediate and that it would not be possible for anyone to come to say goodbye to Olivia. The friend promised to pack Olivia's belongings and send them to Brazil as soon as it was all over.

With every sentence that Fabiana said, she felt as if she were putting another knife into the heart of that mother, who had just lost one of the most precious things in her life.

"How? How am I going to live without even being able to say goodbye to my daughter?"

"I know, but you need to be strong. You need to be strong."

"I don't want to be strong; I just want my daughter here with me."

That had been one of the worst experiences Fabiana had ever had, and she still needed to complete the task and call Matt. She called him from Olivia's phone, and he answered with a happy voice.

"Hello, my love."

"Hi Matt, this is Fabiana. How are you?"

"I'm okay. What's up? Did something happen?" Fabiana then began to cry and said:

"Yes Matt, something terrible has happened."

"What happened, Fabiana? Tell me."

"Olivia is dead."

"No, it can't be true. No!" he said, crying, mixing despair and disbelief.

"Please calm down, Matt."

"No, that can't be true. She's the love of my life; she can't leave me alone here. I shouldn't have left her in Ireland. My God, this is my fault."

"No, Matt, this is nobody's fault. It's this damn virus's fault."

"But she was young and healthy. My God, I talked to her all day yesterday. This can't be real; this can't be real."

"Unfortunately, this is real, Matt. You have to accept it; you have to understand."

"No, I can't understand. I'm going to Ireland today; I need to say goodbye to her."

"You will not have time for this. Her burial will take place in a few hours, after receiving the Reverendpriests blessing."

"I want to die. I want to die too; I can't bear it. I was going to marry her; she was going to be the mother of my children. No, Fabiana, please tell me this isn't happening."

"Unfortunately, this is happening, Matt."

Matt hung up the phone and couldn't believe what he had heard. All of a sudden, his future dreams with Olivia were shattered. Everything he dreamed of living was no longer possible, and he wondered how he would live in a world without her smile to light up everywhere he was.

Her friends kept their distance from the hospital as recommended, following the protocol. They entered her room and packed everything: her books, her clothes, her computer, and her phone. All Olivia had left of her personal belongings fit into two suitcases, but her friends' memories were filled with beautiful moments they had lived together.

The news soon spread in the small town where the girl had lived until then. Former classmates and students all left tributes on social media and mourned the death of Olivia. Fate has no limits, and it was once again messing with people's lives, as Olivia was still alive but in very serious condition in the hospital in Limerick.

Everything happened very fast. After being admitted to the hospital, Olivia soon lost consciousness and needed to be intubated. The other woman who came along in the ambulance was in a similar situation, but her condition was worsened by the accident after hitting her head. She was intubated as well, but she couldn't survive.

As the two arrived at the same time and only one of them had documents, the dead woman had been registered as Olivia Walter Klauckmann, and the real owner of the documents was lying on a bed unidentified. The photo on the Irish immigration card, the document that Olivia had, and the state of the victim's face, added to the urgency to close the coffin due to the virus, all contributed to this terrible mistake.

Olivia, the real one, was struggling to survive. While unconscious, she had strange dreams about Matt, her family in Brazil, old movies, books she'd read, and a kiss from a man who was Matt, but at the same time, she knew it wasn't him. These dreams made her very agitated, and that same night her condition worsened even more. The lack of oxygen was triggering reactions in her heart, which had to work very hard to pump blood.

Olivia could hear from afar all the machines that were attached to her body going off, with a series of beeps, flashing red lights, and a panel showing her desperate heart, beating very quickly. She started to hear the agitated nurses calling for doctors, and she also heard when a doctor arrived.

The next thing she heard was the doctor asking for the defibrillator so he could perform CPR on Olivia in an attempt to revive her.

Biiiiiiiiiiiiiiiiiiiiiiiiiiiiiiiiiiiiiiiiiiiiiiiiiiiiiiii

Olivia heard that sound, and everything went dark again.

Other times

Catherine was sitting on one of the cathedral's pews while her father talked to Reverend John. She wasn't sure whether she liked it or not, but since she was a child, she had accompanied her mother to church. Her family had always been very religious, and her father was a great supporter of the church. The Reverend used to visit the family home every week.

Since her mother died, Catherine had followed the same routine of going to services at the cathedral every week and praying daily at home. She had six siblings still alive, but her mother had had ten children, three of whom had died before they were two years old. Her father thought it was the loss of the children that ended up killing his wife, who had died nine years previously. After losing his wife, Eugene never thought about getting married again, despite having several admirers. He was a good catch, rich and very handsome, as it was broadly agreed, but it seemed he had no interest in getting another wife. He devoted himself to business and to arranging good marriages for his daughters, as the four boys, who were the oldest, were already engaged.

Since their mother died, the father had become the daughters' best friend, raising the three girls to be good wives, but giving them everything they wished and doing what they wanted. Despite this, they had not grown up spoiled girls, but responsible girls instead, adored by all.

Margaret was two years older than Catherine and had married within the last year. She lived in nearby Cork and was already expecting her first child. The two were never very close, but Catherine had always admired her. Margaret's voice was the most beautiful in the whole world. If angels could sing, they would surely sound like her. She always caught everyone's attention when she sang in church and also at frequent dinner parties at her father's house. Now that she was married, all eyes were on Catherine, who would get married next spring.

Catherine was adored by everyone, always very friendly and helpful. She had friends of all ages and in many parts of the city, as she used to accompany her father was well-connected with many people. Also, she had always had a lot of interest in Limerick history. She loved hearing stories from elders who travelled around the city, stories of what life was like centuries ago. Stories about Vikings and the Celts who once occupied that territory. Despite being very young, Catherine was one of the people who knew the most about the history of the place. She used to write all this down in her notebooks and had a huge fascination with all the mysticism and stories about the druids who, according to reports, had inhabited that region. Her father always said he didn't like her reading about it and that it was just nonsense, paganism, but whenever he travelled and found a book that talked about the topic, he would bring it as a gift to his daughter.

The girl was engaged to Fred Stafford, heir to one of Limerick's most powerful families. Fred studied in London, and when he returned home, prepared to take over his father's business, he became the most sought-after bachelor by the local young ladies. In fact, not only by the young ladies but also by their parents, who wanted to ensure their daughters married well.

It was at a service that Fred first saw Catherine, who, at the time, had just turned 18 years old. It is said that the man fell in love at first sight and went to talk to her father on that same night, who almost exploded with happiness. He immediately accepted that the man would have dinner with the family that same week.

Eugene saw the rich heir as an eligible bachelor, but he hadn't entered the race to introduce his daughter. However, it seemed that luck was on his side: without having done anything, his daughter had won the heir's heart.

Catherine thought Fred was elegant, polite, and very intelligent. His always neatly-trimmed moustache tickled when he kissed her hand. He didn't like to talk about music or books or painting, but he would spend hours talking to Catherine about the family business and how much money they'd made that week. Catherine, like the good would-be wife she should be, would just smile. It was all she could do. At first, she even tried to give some opinion, but soon she heard:

"Don't worry, my dear, this is too complex for you to understand."

Those words really enraged her. She wanted to make it clear that if he didn't care about her opinion, then he shouldn't spend hours talking about his damn business. However, her mother, and later her father, had always said that a woman needed to hear and fulfil her husband's requests, so she decided that she would just listen, agree, and smile back when it was convenient. After all, all her friends envied her for dating that man.

The envy of her friends reached a climax when Catherine was given an engagement ring with a diamond the size of which probably no one from Limerick had ever seen before. It was something magnificent! Her father's eyes shone brighter than the diamond itself on the day of the proposal.

Eugene's youngest daughter was called Emily. She was only two years younger than Catherine but they were very different. Although she was against some rules entrenched in marriage, such as the fact that a woman had to be subordinate to her husband and do whatever he wanted, Emily was fascinated by her sister's engagement ring and would often ask to wear it. She also didn't believe women should be doomed to live the rest of their lives with a man they didn't love just to live up to society's expectations. At the same time, she felt like most young ladies at her age and dreamed of soon finding a good match whom she loved, and of having the same luck as her sister, to get an engagement ring as beautiful as the one she had. To her, Catherine was very lucky, as she had found beauty and love in the same man.

However, Catherine herself didn't know if she felt that way.

Surely she had been lucky to have found a man with all those qualities: handsome; charming; intelligent and wealthy. But she hadn't found the most important: love. She had been told all her life that love wasn't that essential to marriage. Her eldest sister didn't love her husband as soon as she got married, but she was living a very happy life. The important thing was to be a good wife and hope to have many children, she knew that. But it seemed that deep down she wanted something more. She wanted to feel the passion she saw in the housekeeper's eyes when she waved at her husband through the window or the same passion her old teacher showed when she met her fiancé at the end of each school day. She wanted to feel those butterflies in her stomach, the same felt by the protagonists in romance novels. She didn't know if she would ever feel that as it seemed just a literary invention that would never happen in real life. She had to settle and thank God that she had found a good man to marry and that would have to be enough.

That's what she was doing when her father called her. He was talking to the Reverend about the dinner they were having that week and called his daughter to check some details. When Catherine came to them, another man was also entering the church and was introduced to them.

"Come here, my son, I want to introduce you to my friends. These are Catherine and Eugene Crawford. This is Ian."

Catherine blushed as soon as she saw the young man. He was a red-haired man, tall and strong. He first greeted his father, then greeted Catherine with a kiss on her hand.

"Nice to meet you, Miss," he said with a heavy accent and looking into her eyes. Catherine felt as if there was a magnet making their eyes stare at each other. She was frightened and unsure of how to act, so she snatched her hand away.

"My pleasure, sir," she replied to the young man.

"He's the son of some friends of mine in Scotland. He arrived just a week ago with the idea of setting up a whiskey distillery. He's my guest, and for now, he's helping me with some church renovations," said the Reverend.

"Yes, I arrived earlier, but my cousin is arriving with his family in a few weeks. For now, I'm happy to help you."

"He is a very good man and plays the bagpipes and guitar like few others, you have to hear him."

"Since he is your guest, he's also invited to have dinner at our house," Eugene said.

"Very well, it will be a great opportunity for Ian to make some contacts that could be important in the future. Very good, my friend," said the Reverend.

"Yes! We'll have very important people there."

"Thank you very much for the invitation, sir. I would be very happy to attend."

"I'm looking forward to seeing you play and tasting your Scotch. I bet you must already have something for your friends to taste."

"I do, I will bring the drink with me then."

"No, no, my son. I know my guests, they drink a lot. I don't want to cause you a financial loss before your business starts. We're still going to discuss the drink; if it meets my approval, I will buy some barrels from you."

"I have no doubt it will meet your approval, sir. My whisky is guaranteed quality."

"Ah, that's true, my friend," said the Reverend.

"Oh, then we'll do business."

While they were talking, Catherine couldn't take her eyes off the young man. He was wearing a white shirt with the sleeves rolled up and a few buttons were undone; he was sweaty from work, making his muscles stand out even more. The young woman blushed again and excused herself to go out into the street and take a breath.

She didn't know what she was feeling, and she looked like she was feeling sick. A fine drizzle was falling, and she felt like going underwater to get rid of her thoughts. That's when she heard Ian's voice asking:

"Does it always rain like this here?"

With her heart racing, she turned around and replied:

"No, it's just the season. In spring, we have beautiful days."

"Since I arrived, I still haven't had a day without rain."

"They say it's the only certainty that anyone born in Limerick has, that it will rain, at some point in the day, it will rain."

"I know how it is, in my country we also have many days like this."

"Where are you from?"

"I'm from the Isle of Skye, but I was living in Edinburgh..."

"Catherine, let's go, my daughter. See you then on Friday, Ian. Don't forget the whisky," Eugene said, holding his daughter and putting up the umbrella.

Catherine just turned around and nodded. Ian stared at the two of them and said that Eugene didn't have to worry, as he was going to taste the best whisky of his life. He was selling himself, after all, the Crawfords would likely become his customers.

When they got home, Catherine went to her room and there she thought about Ian. Where had that man come from? His eyes were so piercing! When he touched her hand, she shivered. The Isle of Skye, Isle of Skye in Scotland. What would his family be like? What would his tartan colours be? Did he wear a kilt?

She didn't know much about Scotland, but she knew that each family had a pattern of stripes and colours, called tartan, which was usually seen on kilts, the kind of skirt that the Scots wore. Once, when she went to Dublin with her father, she saw some Scotsmen wearing those kilts. She found it strange to see men in skirts, but she knew they were proud to wear them because they represented their families.

Emily burst into the room.

"So, we're having another guest for dinner, then?"

"Yes, did Father tell you?"

"Is he handsome?"

"Who told you he's handsome?"

"Nobody told me; I want to know. We never have anyone different here at home. I hope he's good-looking. You'll be with your fiancé, but I still need to find one."

"He's ugly. Just another red-haired man."

"Oh no, but… what could I expect from a Scotsman, right?"

"Well, he's not a man for you," Catherine said, unable to control her words. She was disdaining the man who had taken her breath away. It looked like she was jealous of her sister for being interested in Ian. She couldn't recognise herself; she was ashamed to have these thoughts.

"Of course not. Father said he must be a lowly fellow. I want a man who will give me a ring just the same as yours or even bigger. Speaking of which, let me wear it one more time."

Catherine handed the ring to her sister, who put it on her finger and started acting as she always did, saying, "Yes, I will marry you, my love," pretending that a man was kneeling at her feet.

The girl went to the window and there she started daydreaming: "Did Ian have a fiancée? A girlfriend?" Yes, he really did look like a pauper, not even close to her fiancé, who was always well-dressed and well-groomed. But enough was enough; she didn't want to think about this anymore.

"That's enough, Emily. Give me back my ring. If you want one for yourself, find a fiancé," she said, taking the ring and gently pushing her sister onto the bed.

Everyone in the house was working on the dinner. All the important people in Limerick would be there. The father followed the tradition of holding a service and dinner every March in honour of his wife, whose birthday was that month. It was a way to bring family and friends together and, in some way, honour the memory of the mother of his seven children. Eugene always invited all his friends to this celebration, and the daughters were excited about it. Despite their mother's absence, they were never sad because it was a special moment.

Margaret would arrive the next day, and the four brothers were to arrive with their families the day before the dinner. Catherine had seven nieces and nephews, and the house would be in chaos. She loved it, but Fred hated it. Whenever they were at the house, he would find a way to leave early because he just couldn't stand the kids. Even the noise coming from the backyard, where the little ones usually played, bothered him.

They had a lot of work ahead of them. The maids arranged everything, but the father always said that the last word in the organisation was his daughters'. Since they didn't want to disappoint their father, this dinner became the most important thing in their lives for the entire month.

The dinner day arrived, and just before the appointed time, an errand boy appeared at the front of the house, bringing a message from Fred:

"My dear father-in-law, I'm very sorry, but I won't be able to attend tonight. I don't feel well, I have a fever and I feel sick. I wish you all a wonderful night."

Eugene read the note to Catherine, who was disappointed to hear that her fiancé wouldn't come to the dinner.

"Wouldn't it be better for you to go over there with one of your brothers and see how he is?"

"Father, I don't see the need. He certainly has someone to take care of him. Besides, my whole family is here, and this is where I want to stay. This dinner is in memory of my mother, and I want to enjoy every moment."

"But he's your fiancé; he has to feel supported by you."

"But he won't die in one night, Father. Tomorrow morning I can go there, but today I'll stay here. Besides, I need to be here to help you. After all, you want to impress your friends, don't you?"

"You're right, my daughter, you can go tomorrow morning."

"That is just what I need!" thought Catherine. "Having to go to Fred's house just to see how he's doing… let him wait until tomorrow."

They went to the church to attend the service, and from there they would go home. The girls were well-groomed; they always got new dresses for the service in honour of their mother. Catherine looked to every corner of the church as if she were looking for someone.

"What's going on? Who are you looking for?" asked Emily.

"Nobody, I'm just watching who's in the service," replied Catherine. But the fact was that she wanted to know where Ian was. Would he really go to dinner at her house? It didn't look like it, as he definitely wasn't inside the church.

The Reverend, as always, spoke beautiful words about the girls' mother, highlighting how generous, altruistic, and committed she had been to the less fortunate. From a very young age, she had worked for social causes and she had helped many during the Great Famine.

When the service was over, Catherine took one more look around for Ian but didn't see him. What had happened? And she couldn't even ask yet; she'd have to wait for the Reverend to drink a few beers.

When they got home, Catherine went straight to the kitchen to see if everything was going well. To her surprise, she bumped into Ian.

"What are you doing here?"

"Waiting for you."

"Why didn't you go to the service?"

"I did."

"No, you didn't."

"How do you know that? Were you looking for me?"

"Of course not."

"But it looked like you were looking for someone," Ian said, placing the barrel of whisky on top of a kitchen counter.

At that moment, Emily ran into the kitchen, euphoric:

"Did you see it? Mr. McNamara's son looks so handsome, and he certainly feels something for me. I saw; he turned around three times during the service just to keep looking at me."

Catherine, to warn her sister of the young man's presence in the kitchen, said:

"This is Ian, the Reverend's friend!"

Emily looked at him and whispered in her sister's ear:

"He's not as ugly as you said."

She turned to him and said:

"Very nice to meet you! My sister told me that you're from Scotland, and you really are because you're even wearing your kilt."

Catherine had already noticed that he was wearing a yellow kilt with a checked pattern formed by three black stripes and a red crossed thread.

"Emily, don't be rude. Let's go back to the room. We'll talk later, Ian."

Catherine pulled her sister's arm and Emily asked, "Why are you doing this? Why did you lie about him? He's handsome and strong!"

"Emily, stop! He's not for you; he's poor."

"And not for you either. He's poor, and you are engaged."

"My God, have you lost your mind? I'm not interested in him. Where did you get that idea? Did you forget that I'm engaged to the best catch in town?"

"So take it easy and let me admire him."

"Emily, grow up." She said that and left her sister talking to herself to see if her father needed anything.

She started questioning herself. Was she jealous? What was happening? Ever since she walked into the church for the service, the only thing she wanted was to see him. When she walked into the kitchen and saw him, she thought she wouldn't be able to hide her smile. Ian looked so handsome, wearing his kilt and a waistcoat with a white shirt underneath, his hair cut and shaved, which set off his eyes. Oh no, she could never think of him that way. She should think these things about her fiancé and not that damn Scotsman. What was happening?

As always, right before dinner, the father used to raise a toast to her mother that touched everyone, leaving them full of longing. The heart was almost caressed by the beautiful memories that came to mind with the words full of tenderness spoken by the father.

Catherine spent the entire dinner trying not to look at Ian, but it was hard. His accent was so beautiful, and the way he spoke and expressed himself was too. He stayed up all night talking to one of her brothers, and they seemed to have gotten along well. It was easy for Ian to fall in favor of the guests, as he was Reverend John's friend and produced excellent scotch enjoyed by everyone at the table.

When dinner was over, the men went to the living room where they would talk and drink until late. Margaret called Catherine to a corner of the room.

"Where did this Scotsman come from and why doesn't he take his eyes off you?"

"Doesn't he take his eyes off me? What do you mean by that?"

"I mean what I said; don't play dumb. He hasn't stopped looking at you for a second. I think Father even noticed."

"But it's not my fault."

"It's a good thing Fred wasn't here to see it; he would surely die of jealousy."

"It was just your impression," said Catherine, sneaking away from her sister and barely able to hide her happiness. "He looked at me all night long," she thought and sighed.

She went to the kitchen and when she got there she found Ian with a knife, trying to open another barrel of scotch. When he saw Catherine, he got scared and the knife slipped, landing on his finger.

"Iosa Crìosd," said the man in Scottish Gaelic. Catherine knew a little of the language and knew it meant "Jesus Christ."

"My goodness, are you okay?" said Catherine, going towards the guy and holding his bloody hand.

"It was nothing, it's fine."

"It was nothing!? It looks deep!" she said, raising her eyes, which, once again, were locked on his. At that moment she felt her heart race and realised that his breathing had also changed.

"Catherine..."

He couldn't finish what he was going to say as one of the maids entered the kitchen. Catherine, as if recovering from a trance, asked the girl to get a clean cloth and help with a bandage. Ian said that he didn't need to, that he would wash his hands and that surely everything would be fine.

The maid's name was Eileen, and she'd been working in the house for a long time. She was a little older than the ladies of the house, but they had grown up together, and being one of Catherine's best friends, she knew her better than anyone. She saw the way Catherine was behaving when she was around Ian and just smiled, surprised at her friend's reaction, as she had never seen her behave like this before.

As expected, the night was long and full of drinks. The Reverend, as usual, was the last guest to leave. It was common for the Reverend to sleep over on nights like this, but since Ian was staying at his house and was sober, Catherine's brothers took him to the carriage that would take him home. They had some trouble getting him into the carriage, as the Reverend had acquired a certain corpulence, and that night he was drunker than ever. He blamed it on the whisky being so good, but it wasn't news to anyone that the Reverend needed no excuses to get that way.

Catherine saw the Reverend's hat on the chair and ran out into the street to give it to the Scotsman.

"Mister McLeod, the Reverend's hat."

"Is he always like this?"

"Occasionally."

"Thank you so much for dinner; it was very good."

"I'm glad you enjoyed it, have a good night."

"Have a nice night, Miss Crawford."

Catherine turned towards the house, smiling because she couldn't contain her joy every time she spoke to him.

That night, Catherine dreamed of Ian. She had a weird dream where Ian had a sword and spoke to her in a strange language. She didn't remember the dream very well, but she remembered that the two of them couldn't stop looking at each other. It was a different dream, but she woke up smiling. However, real-life was waiting for her and early in the morning, her father knocked on her door to ask if she was ready to go with her brother to her fiancé's house and see if he was feeling better.

"Father, is it really necessary for me to visit him?"

"Of course it is; you need to play your role as his betrothed and look out for his well-being."

"But I'm still not his wife."

"But you will be, and it's good to get used to what that will mean. Come on, hurry up."

"Then Emily will go with us."

"So be it, but I hope she's ready. Hurry up!"

Soon they left the house and set out on their way to Fred's house, but they did not find him there. One of the maids said that he had left the day before for Galway, a neighbouring city, and that he should be back in a few days.

"But wasn't he going to warn me?" asked the bride.

"Yes, he asked me to send you this letter today. We were about to send the errand boy to deliver it to you."

Catherine was intrigued by the message because it seemed that Fred had made up the story of being sick just to avoid attending the dinner at his father-in-law's house. She wouldn't mind, but she thought her father would be very sad. Her brother also found the situation very strange but said that his future brother-in-law must have had urgent matters to deal with in Galway and that he must know what he was doing.

On the way back, her brother stayed in the city centre to talk with an old friend while the two sisters went back home. To their surprise, they bumped into Ian on one of the corners.

"What a surprise to find you here."

"Oh yes, we're coming from the..." Emily was interrupted by a stomp on her foot.

"Where are you going?" asked Catherine.

"I'm kind of lost. The Reverend gave me this address and asked me to get some documents, but apparently it's not around here."

"Let me see. Oh no, it's not actually right here; it's further down the road. But come on, we can take you there," said Catherine.

"But..." Emily started to speak but gave up when she saw the look on her sister's face.

They were walking through the city streets and talking. Catherine asked about his finger, and he repeated that it was nothing and that he was fine. They talked about the Reverend, who had woken up with a hangover, about the weather, and the rain that never stopped. They found the house and collected the documents, their conversation never stopping for even a minute. Emily hid a small smile on her lips. She had never seen her sister behave like that. She saw a friend from school and went to talk to her, while the other two said goodbye.

When they had said their goodbyes and Catherine was leaving, Ian finally took heart:

"Catherine, would you like…"

She turned around, and before he could say anything else, she replied:

"Yes, I would!"

"What?" The two smiled at each other, and it was evident that he was thinking about something, but he still didn't know exactly what it was.

"Um… um… perhaps to do something tomorrow…"

"We can… we can fish on the Shannon, you and I, and the Reverend and my sister."

"Of course…" said the young man, not understanding the suggestion.

"Don't say anything to my brothers."

"Alright, will I see you tomorrow at church after lunch?"

"Yes, wait for me there."

To fish? To fish? Couldn't you have thought of anything better? And what was it like to accept such an invitation? She had a fiancé! What if he found out that she accepted an invitation from another man? She just might have lost her mind. She needed to tell her sister, and as soon as she returned she said:

"Emily…"

"What is it? Why do you look so scared?"

"I need to tell you something."

"I bet it won't be a surprise for me."

"I can't stop thinking about the Scotsman, and tomorrow we have a date with him."

"I already knew that you couldn't stop thinking about him; you look like a fool when you look at him…"

"The truth is, I was really jealous of you. I haven't been able to stop thinking about him since the day I met him at church, and today I found myself in an inexplicable mood just because of hearing his voice..."

"Catherine, explain the date part to me..."

"Tomorrow we go fishing with him and the Reverend."

"And Fred, have you forgotten about him?"

"No, I haven't, but what's wrong with going fishing?"

"Nothing, there's nothing wrong with going fishing. The problem is when you say you can't stop thinking about him and that tomorrow you'll go fishing," she said, making fun of her sister.

"Could you support me for once in your lifetime?"

"You know I'll support you in anything, but do you really think this is right? You are engaged and accepted an invitation from a man who isn't your fiancé, a man you can't stop thinking about..."

"The Reverend and you will come along."

"Okay, and what are you going to say to Father?"

"Father doesn't need to know."

"And that's the problem. If Father can't know, it's because it's not right."

"Since when does my little baby sister give me advice, huh?" asked Catherine as she messed with her sister's hair.

"From the moment you started showing that you need an even bigger diamond on your finger to remind you that you're engaged! By the way, where's your ring?"

"It's here in the bag; I'm afraid of losing it."

"Did you take the ring off, Catherine? Did you take the ring off when you met the Scotsman?"

"Don't be silly, I was just afraid of losing it," lied Catherine to her sister.

Emily was right, and that said a lot. She had always been dazzled, passionate, reckless, and much more spontaneous than Catherine, but the two had been best friends ever since their mother's death, which happened when Catherine was just six years old, and became even closer after that. Their older sister, Margaret, wasn't very close to them, so they grew up always having each other to count on. Emily had always seen her sister Catherine as an example, a role model. The two looked alike; both were blonde and had blue eyes, while Margaret had red hair and green eyes. The youngest had always had an issue with Margaret, and that's why she said she didn't like anyone with red hair.

Catherine couldn't sleep that night. She was excited to meet Ian the next day, and she felt so bad about it; after all, she had a fiancé. In fact, she was trying to convince herself that just fishing wouldn't hurt anyone, but deep down she knew she wanted to meet him because she felt something she'd never felt before.

The brothers were still at the family home and would stay there until the next day, as they would take the opportunity to spend more time with their father.

Emily agreed to accompany Catherine on this fishing trip, but that would come with a price: she would have to let her wear her engagement ring for a week. Catherine agreed without bargaining, as all she wanted was for her sister to accompany her.

At the scheduled time, they went to the church, and Ian was waiting for them.

"Hello, I'm glad you came."

"Yes, how have you been?"

"I am well. And how did you spend the night?"

"Fine too. Where's the Reverend?"

"Well, I guess he won't be able to join us as he's not feeling very well."

"Headache again," Emily said, laughing.

"And what will we do?" asked Catherine, distressed at the possibility of having to cancel the meeting.

"Can we go without him?" asked the boy, visibly nervous.

"Oh, let's go at once!" replied Emily.

They were walking towards the River Shannon, and Catherine was afraid someone would see her. Without the Reverend, she knew there might be some gossip, but they were fortunate because the city was empty that day. The fishing expedition itself was doomed to be a failure. The young man had only found one fishing rod at the Reverend's house, and the young ladies hadn't even thought to take some from their house. Ian hadn't found enough equipment necessary for fishing but he had taken his guitar instead.

Emily understood her sister's intention and kept the only fishing rod while the two sat on the riverbank.

They spent hours chatting by the Shannon River. Ian told Catherine how he missed his father who, like her mother, had died when he was a little child. Even though he had little contact with his father, it was he who had taught him to produce the scotch that carried the family name: McLeod. It was a tradition passed down from father to son for generations and his brothers and cousins had also learned how to make it. Catherine became emotional when she told him about her mother and how much she missed her.

Ian gently wiped the tears from Catherine's face and said he didn't want to see her sad. He said he learned to play the bagpipes and guitar when he was still a child and that he could play for Catherine if she wanted him to.

Of course, she wouldn't miss a chance to see him playing the instrument. It was amazing to see such a big and strong man showing all his sensitivity and playing beautiful songs, and how his strong hands gently strummed the guitar strings. It was impossible not to be delighted.

When he stopped playing, they continued the conversation and Catherine told him how much she loved living in Limerick, despite the constant rain and how much she would like to visit London.

"You have to visit Edinburgh, it's better than London."

"Is it better? I doubt it!"

"Scotland is far better than England in every way and that shouldn't be news to you. The Highlands are far more beautiful than any part of Europe. And Edinburgh has the most beautiful castle I've ever seen in my life."

"Tell me more about it," said Catherine, delighted by the way he told the stories.

"It's on top of a rock! To this day I wonder how they could have built anything there. In fact, it looks like it was carved out of the rock. The sun setting behind it is a real spectacle."

"Speaking of sunset, we need to go... the sun is already setting."

"Stay a little longer and watch the sunset with me."

She looked into his eyes and didn't have to say anything else; the answer was evident. They sat there, the two of them, watching the sun go down and dye the waters of the Shannon, making the sky take on shades of orange, purple, and lilac. Ian gently placed his hand on hers and her heart skipped a beat.

"Catherine, we need to go! Father must already be missing us," said Emily, interrupting the moment.

"Yes, I really need to go," said Catherine, getting up hurriedly.

"Will I see you again?"

"Yes!" said the girl, smiling as her sister pulled her by the arm.

It was only when the two of them were out of his sight that Emily began to speak:

"See you again? You must be insane! I've been observing you two. You seem to be in love with this man!"

"In love? Don't be silly! He's just different from other men. He's different from Fred; he seems to listen to my opinion. He actually listens to what I'm saying. I feel like I'm somebody when I'm with him, whereas when I'm with Fred I'm no different than a vase."

"A vase? What do you mean?" asked her sister, trying to hold back her laughter.

"That's right, a decorative object that is just there, taking up space, but no one really cares. Everyone wants a nice vase in their house and Fred found his."

"And only now that you've met the handsome Scotsman do you come to the sense that you're just a vase?"

"Emily, it's becoming impossible to talk to you!"

"No, I'm just asking to understand. Up until last week, you seemed pretty satisfied and happy with your fiancé. Now you feel meaningless when you're with him."

"I don't understand why you keep putting Fred in this story since it has nothing to do with him."

"Oh, really? So you're going to tell him you spent the whole afternoon fishing with Ian?"

"Of course not, he would never understand!"

"So bringing Fred into your story with Ian might make some sense, no?"

"Hush now and let's go home, that's enough!"

The sisters returned home. Neither their father nor anyone else was surprised by their absence during the afternoon. Since they were little, they had often gone out to play or ride horses, so their absence was quite common.

While trying to sleep, Catherine couldn't get a sentence out of her head: "you're in love." Was she really in love? Was it passion? She couldn't get Ian out of her head; all her thoughts were of him. She'd never thought of Fred like that, not even when she had first met him and thought he was one of the most elegant men she'd ever seen in her life.

In the morning, as the sun began to rise, she heard something banging on her window. When she opened it, she noticed a flower and a note on the doorstep.

"I can't stop thinking about you!
Our afternoon was wonderful. I hope to see you at church today!
Your smile lights up my days.
Ian Alexander McLeod"

"Emily, Emily, wake up, check this out!" said Catherine, showing the flower and the note to her sister who, still trying to open her eyes, read and spoke:

"Great, he's in love with you too."

"Do you think so? Oh my God!!!"

"Catherine..."

"Hush! I'm not asking your opinion! Isn't it enough for you to know I'm happy?"

"It is, but..."

"Then be quiet and get up! It is late and today is going to be a wonderful day!"

Everyone was getting ready to go to church. Life would finally get back to normal at the Crawford house, but before they left, they would all go to church. Catherine was dressing as best she could because she knew Ian would be there waiting for her.

She wore a green dress, one of her favourites because it had belonged to her mother. She asked her sister to braid her hair and she put on the pearl earrings her father had given her when she turned 15. Her sister said she looked like a princess, and even her father was surprised; his daughter usually didn't dress up like this to go to church.

"You look so beautiful! Is your fiancé coming back today?"

"My fiancé?"

"Yes, or are you now trying to tell your father that you forgot you have one?"

"Oh yes, yes, I hope he is well and returns soon."

"I hope he is recovering well in Galway."

"Father, do you really think he went there to recover? Aren't you angry that he didn't come to your dinner?"

"What are you saying, my daughter? It is not your role to doubt your future husband's motives."

"Father! I can't believe you're going to side with him in this situation," Emily intervened on her sister's behalf.

"Ahh Emily, Father will have a hard time finding you a husband! No one will be interested in you!" said Margaret, scolding her sister.

"Oh my God, are you two unable to stop arguing for a minute? Come on Emily, let's go ahead," said Catherine, holding her sister's hand.

As they were heading to the Cathedral, Catherine was reflecting... Her sister was right, what was she thinking? There was no way to take a situation like this forward, no way to hide Ian from Fred. She was definitely in love with the Scotsman, but it was no use fantasizing. She was going to be married in a few months and nothing between heaven and earth would stop that marriage from happening. She was completely convinced to forget all this nonsense; until she saw Ian standing by the Cathedral. Her heart instantly raced, and she went weak at the knees. Once again she found herself completely mesmerized by him.

"Hello, good to see you!" said Ian, handing a flower to Catherine.

"Yeah, good to see you too. I missed you."

"Sorry to interrupt again, but Father is coming," said Emily, taking the flower from her sister's hand.

"Yes, yes, let's go inside."

Once inside the Cathedral, Emily spoke to her sister:

"It's okay if you don't intend to mention Ian to Fred, but I think it would be nice to tell Ian that you have a fiancé. You're being unfair, my sister. He's involved and he'll suffer when he finds out you're just doing this not to feel like a vase."

"I hate to admit it, but you're right. I need to stop this and kill my feelings for Ian."

"Oh, so you admit you have feelings for him?"

"Yes, of course. I think I'm completely in love. I feel something I thought only existed in books, not in real life."

"So live it! Who said you have to marry Fred? Tell Father. He wouldn't want you to be unhappy."

"Emily, that's not how things are. Father would never let me call off my engagement with Fred. It would embarrass our whole family and you would never get a husband."

"I think that's very unfair. And I really shouldn't pay for your mess," said Emily, being visibly facetious with her sister.

During the whole service, Catherine stared at Ian, who was sitting a few pews ahead and occasionally glanced at her out of the corner of his eye. Every time she did that, her heart raced. If her father asked her anything about the Reverend's sermon, she wouldn't have been able to say a word. She didn't pay attention to anything but Ian, all the quirks of his face and hair, his broad back and the way his muscles were evident even though he was wearing at least two layers of clothing. It was as if in the church, at that moment, it was just the two of them and the world slowly revolved around them. However, they were not alone, and at the end of the service, Margaret approached and said:

"You seem to have forgotten that you have a fiancé who, by the way, hasn't been around for the last few days and is leaving the way clear for this scheming. I'll tell Father."

"Margaret, please don't do such a thing. The poor man isn't doing anything wrong, I think it's just your imagination."

"He might not be doing anything wrong, but you haven't stopped looking at him."

"He was between me and the altar, where else would I look?"

"I know I'm not our mother, but if she were here, she would tell you that a woman of respect is not carried away by carnal desires. He's handsome, but you're committed, and you can't embarrass your family."

After Margaret finished her speech, she went to accompany her husband, while Catherine found Emily and took her by the arm. At the Cathedral door, Ian was waiting for them.

"Beautiful celebration, don't you think?"

"Yes, extraordinary."

"Catherine, you look very beautiful today. I confess I didn't pay attention to anything in the service, just you."

"I didn't either."

"Catherine, I'm going to talk to your father."

"No, you can't."

"But why can't I?"

At that moment, Emily pulled Catherine and took her away from Ian, as Margaret was heading for the Cathedral door, where the three were standing.

"You have lost your mind for good. You held his hand!"

"I need to tell him that I'm engaged. He wants to talk to Father about the two of us, certainly to ask permission to court me. What should I do?"

"Oh, that's a concern I pray every night to have, having to decide between the millionaire or the most handsome Scotsman I've ever seen. Please Catherine, don't humiliate your sister who is about to be a spinster for the rest of her life, thanks to you."

There followed another night in which Catherine didn't sleep, thinking about how much she was in love and how much she needed to be able to kill that feeling inside her chest. As the sun was about to rise, anxiety took hold of her. She waited for Ian to act as the day before, putting something on her window. She was very disappointed when she realised he would not show up. What had happened? Had he forgotten about her?

Catherine and her sister went to Potato Market, a popular market in town, to see if they could see Ian, but he wasn't there. She thought about going to the Reverend's house to ask for him, but it would be too risky. Why would she be looking for the Scotsman? Catherine was starting to get worried.

She could barely sleep that night, thinking he might be angry that he found out she had a fiancé. She should have already told him. What could have happened? Had he gone back to Scotland? Had Fred found out that they had met? There were too many questions plaguing her head and keeping her from sleeping.

However, she almost had a heart attack when she heard the noise at the window again. She hurried but couldn't see him, only the flower and the note he left:

"I had to go to Lahinch yesterday for the Reverend.

I miss you so much, can we talk this afternoon near the castle?

Your smile brightens my days.

I'll be waiting for you, my love."

My love? My looooove! Catherine repeated it as if she had never heard it before. Her heart was bursting with happiness! For almost a second she forgot that she couldn't go through with it, but when she remembered, she started crying. It was so unfair. Emily woke up and saw her sister's despair. She understood the situation and suggested that she should tell their father. Surely there would be a solution. He always stood by his daughters and always said that his biggest dream was for them to be happy.

"No, I can't tell Father about this."

"Then you need to talk to Ian."

"I know, I'll meet him today to talk about it. I don't think he'll ever want to look me in the eye again; he'll think I'm an adulteress."

"My sister, you are far from an adulteress. You have done nothing wrong, you have not promised him anything. Come on, you will clear everything up and everything will be fine."

"Everything is going to be fine, but not I. I won't be fine. I'd rather have never met him than feel all this and not know how to deal with it. It feels like my heart is falling apart inside my chest. I feel a mixture of shame, guilt, and immense sadness."

"Catherine, as our mother always told us: the truth may not solve everything the way we expect, but it sets us free. You'll feel better after you tell him everything," said Emily, affectionately hugging her crying sister.

Catherine walked as if she were going to the gallows. She wasn't going to die, but it felt like she was going to kill something: her love. The purest love, the only one she had ever felt in her life. That was very hard. How could one kill something so beautiful? Her sister's embrace gave her strength and led her to do what was right, if not right, at least necessary. She couldn't take this any further. However, all her conviction faded the moment she saw Ian near the castle, wearing his kilt and flashing his best smile. It was as if that smile lit up the whole city, which was experiencing one of its grey days.

"I cannot do it, Emily, I shan't be able to talk to him," Catherine said to her sister just before they reached Ian.

"Yes, you can, and it has to be now."

"Hi, my love, seeing you makes my day happier."

"Mine too! Can we go for a walk? I think we have much to talk about."

"Catherine? My beautiful fiancée, what a surprise to find you here." The owner of the voice was Fred who, without ceremony, took Catherine by the waist and, taking advantage of her father's absence, kissed her.

Emily didn't know what to do or say, and neither did Ian. He looked at her sister and asked, almost whispering, "Fiancée?"

"What are you doing around here at this hour?"

"We came, we came..."

"We came to buy tea," Emily intervened, realising that her sister was failing to come up with an adequate answer.

"And who is this?"

"Oh Fred, this is Ian. He is the Reverend's guest, he's a whisky maker. He's the one who provided the drink for dinner."

"Nice to meet you," said Fred, completely ignoring Ian. "My dear, please excuse me, it was impossible for me to attend that dinner, but now I have completely recovered and I intend to make up for my absence," he said, taking the hands of his visibly embarrassed fiancée. As he held her hands, he missed the ring and asked, "Where's your ring?"

"It's with me!" replied Emily quickly. "I'm sorry, I just asked to wear it for a moment."

"My sister-in-law, I told you, you need to find a fiancé who will be able to give you a ring like this one. But apparently, you'll have to choose better," said Fred, looking at Ian with disdain.

It looked like Catherine's fiancé had understood that there was something between Emily and Ian and, by realising the mistake, she decided that this was the best solution.

"My brother-in-law, it's Father's job to find me a fiancé, not yours, but that's not the case... excuse me," she said, motioning to Ian to walk with her towards the river.

"My dear, your sister cannot get involved with a man like that. He doesn't have a pot to piss in."

"Fred, she's not involved with him. Ian is the Reverend's guest and we're being nice to him, that's all."

"Well, I'm going to talk to your father. It's not appropriate for my sister-in-law to be seen around with that man."

"No, please, don't say anything to Father."

"Of course, I will. Speaking of him, let's take the opportunity that he's not here. Give me one more kiss."

The girl, before kissing him, peeked out of the corner of her eye and could no longer see Ian and her sister; they had crossed the bridge.

"Emily, please, tell me what's happening. What's going on?"

"I'm not the one who should tell you that, Ian."

"But you must, otherwise I'll go there and ask in person."

"No, stay here. She was going to tell you everything today, she was determined. I'm sorry it all turned out this way, that you found out like this. They're engaged."

"And why was she doing this to me?"

"Because she's been in love with you since she saw you for the first time and she didn't know how to deal with her feelings, she didn't know what to do."

"Well, so tell her I'll never see her again. I'm disappointed, she should have told me, she was reckless."

"Ian, I won't let you talk or think those things about my sister. As far as I know, she never promised you anything and she didn't choose to fall in love with you. Come back here…" said the girl, screaming as he walked away.

He continued walking along the riverbank as Emily watched him, also feeling very sad that it had all turned out this way. She needed to go back to check on her sister, who must also be very nervous about this whole situation.

Emily found them near to where she had left them. Things with Fredseemed to be fine and she returned home with her sister. As soon as they arrived, they locked themselves in the room, and Catherine cried profusely, shedding all the tears she had been holding back since Fredfound them.

"He'll never want to see me again. I should never have let it go this far, my God, what have I done? Help me, Emily, help me. I can't breathe…"

"Calm down, Catherine, everything will be fine," she said, hugging her sister.

"Do you promise me?"

"Let's pray."

"Let's pray? At this point, praying is useless. You can't imagine how much I prayed not to have feelings for Ian. It didn't help, and now this has happened."

They were interrupted by their father's knock on the door, followed by the command:

"You two come to my office right now!"

The sisters looked at each other without understanding what was happening, but from the tone of their father's voice, it didn't seem to be good at all.

Catherine tried to wipe away her tears and the two went to the office.

"Yes, Papa," said the youngest daughter.

"You are the one I want to talk to. I want to know what you were thinking when you got involved with a man like that?"

"What are you talking about, Papa?"

"Don't play innocent. Your brother-in-law came here and told me he caught you being courtedby the Reverend's friend today by the river. Do you want to shame me to death? Do you want to throw our family name in the mud?"

"Father..."

"Hush, Catherine. I'm also furious with you for covering up your sister's shamelessness. You should set an example! I didn't raise a daughter to be a nobody. I'm so ashamed."

Their father was out of control, red as they had never seen him, mad enough to spit after this mess.

"Father..."

"Hush, Catherine! It's the last time I'll warn you."

"What did Fredsay, Father? Nothing is going on between Ian and I."

"Father..." On the third attempt, the man grabbed his daughter's arm, and she felt her wrist almost break.

"You have no shame! One will never find a good catch, and the other will lose the one she has!"

"He's certainly not a good catch. If he were, he wouldn't have made up what he told you. I don't know what he said, but I can assure you it didn't happen. And I don't know why you are so angry! Fredis nothing but a cretin and you are an ambitious man who wants to sell your own daughters."

The man slapped the youngest one in the face. He had never raised a hand to either of his daughters and Catherine knew that slap should have been on her.

"Father!"

"Stop, Catherine..." said the sister.

"Get out of my sight... now!"

Back in the room, Catherine apologised to her sister.

"You should have let me tell Father; he needed to know it's my fault and not yours."

"He would have killed you, my sister. I don't know what your fiancé said, but it just proves what a horrible man he is."

"What could he have said to make Father angry like that?"

"I don't know, but I never expected Father to hit me like that. He didn't even let me explain what happened."

"I will never forgive myself for letting this happen to you, my sister."

The days passed and the atmosphere in Catherine's house was terrible. Their father didn't let the sisters step outside the house and didn't even talk to them. They ate their meals together, without exchanging a word. He couldn't even look them in the eye. The sisters were surprised when their father told them on Saturday night not to be late for the service.

Church, service... Catherine wasn't sure she was ready to meet Ian; he would be there for sure. But how would she look into his eyes now that he thought she was a liar? And how would she manage to talk, now that her father would keep his eyes wide open, thinking the Scottish outsider was making advances on her sister?

It was a very complicated situation. She even thought about pretending that she was sick to try to avoid going to church, but that would be too cowardly. She already felt like a coward for letting her sister take the blame for her involvement with Ian. Also, she wished she could see him, at least one more time, and say that what she felt wasn't a lie.

When they arrived at the church, Fredwas waiting for them at the door.

"My dear, how beautiful you are, and so are you, my sister-in-law."

"I'm disgusted with you," Emily said to her brother-in-law.

"Your sister needs discipline, my dear."

"What did you say to Father? What did you make up? He hit Emily; he was very angry and for no reason because I told him my sister has nothing to do with Ian.

"If he hit her, it was because she deserved it. Do you want your sister to throw your family name in the mud? How am I going to marry someone with such a scandal in the family?"

"What are you talking about?"

"Evil is nipped in the bud. I doubt that disqualified Scotsman will ever mess with your sister again."

"What did you do, Fred?"

"Don't worry, he just got what he deserved. Surely now he's going to learn not to mess with people who aren't his ilk."

The subject was interrupted by her father, who arrived to speak with his future son-in-law. Catherine went to talk to her sister, who was sitting in one of the church pews.

"What happened, my sister? You look pale."

"I'm afraid Fred did something to Ian. He said he gave Ian what he deserved and that the 'disqualified Scotsman' will never mess with us again."

"What do you think he might have done?"

"I don't know, I don't think we know Fred. I think he might be capable of terrible things."

The service began and, once again, Catherine couldn't concentrate. She searched for Ian with her eyes, but he wasn't there. What could Fred have done to him? There was only one solution: ask the Reverend.

At the end of the service, she asked her sister:

"Distract Father and Fred. I'll ask the Reverend what happened to Ian."

"Are you crazy?"

"My sister, whatever has happened was my fault and I need to know about it."

"But what if the Reverend tells Father?"

"If he does, I'll take the consequences."

Emily didn't have time to try to hold on to her sister, who walked out towards the Reverend.

"Good evening, Reverend, it was a great celebration."

"I'm glad you enjoyed it, my daughter."

"Reverend, don't tell Father, but I need to know what happened to Ian."

"I knew this had to do with one of you."

"Please, tell me!"

"He is very injured. Now he is recovering, but he has at least a couple of broken ribs. He was beaten by at least five men. I don't know how they didn't kill him."

Catherine's eyes immediately filled with tears. "And where is he now?"

"He's fine. I believe your father was wrong. It wasn't your sister he was interested in, was it?"

"Reverend, please, I need to see him."

"My daughter," said the Reverend, taking the girl's hands, "I am taking care of him. You can't do anything, and seeing him will make the situation even worse, which is already worse than I thought. I thought he had feelings for your sister, but for you... it's even worse. You are engaged to a powerful man."

"Do you think it was my father who ordered Ian to be beaten up?"

"No, I don't think your father would do this."

"So who was it?"

"I think you have the answer, my daughter. That's why you need to stay away from Ian," said the Reverend, looking at Fred, who was approaching them.

"Reverend, we look forward to having you at my father-in-law's house tomorrow to play cards and have a nice chat."

"Of course, Fred. As always, I'll be there."

Catherine went to meet Emily with a plan already set in her head. She told her sister about what had happened to Ian and about the Reverend's suspicion that the beating had been ordered by her fiancé. She knew the Reverend wouldn't tell her father that she was the one involved with the Scotsman, and she would take advantage of the Reverend being at her house until very late to check on Ian.

"You're really out of your mind, aren't you?"

"No, I'm not. This is my only chance. He could have died because of me. And he would have died thinking I never loved him, that I only deceived him."

"How do you intend to do this?"

"We both know these game nights at the house usually go on until dawn. Father, Fred, and the Reverend will be here, so I'll have time to go to the Reverend's house and talk to Ian."

"You make it sound very simple."

"I know it's not simple, but I can go out through the window, put on Father's cloak, and go there without being seen."

"And you want me to come along?"

"No, I don't want to get you involved in this anymore. I'll go alone. If I get caught, it will be only me. I need to have this conversation alone with him."

"Are you sure you're going to do this?"

"Yes, I am."

The next day, after dinner, the men went into the living room, as usual. After making sure that everything was alright, the girls retired to their room. They always did that, therefore they knew no one would suspect.

In the bedroom, they started putting the plan into action. They waited until midnight, as they knew the street would be deserted at that time. Emily had taken a cloak from her father and helped put it on her sister, covering her hair so that anyone who saw her would think she were a man. The window was opened and the young lady jumped out, launching herself into the street.

"Good luck, sister," said Emily.

"Thank you."

The girl walked through the dark streets of Limerick and the only sound she could hear was the noise of the wind, her footsteps, and the rain that fell softly that night. She was afraid, not afraid of walking alone at night, but afraid of not knowing how she would be received by Ian. Would he want to talk to her? How would it be?

Arriving at the Reverend's house, she took the key that he always left in the same hiding place. The sisters had gone to the Reverend's house many times, at his request, to get something while he was at the family home. So she knew this place very well, and she thought she even knew the room where Ian would be staying. She walked in, walked down the hall and when she opened the bedroom door, he was sitting on the bed, looking scared.

"Who's there?"

"It's me, Ian."

"You? What are you doing here?"

"I think we need to talk."

"No, I don't think we have anything to talk about. We could have had this conversation before, but you preferred not to say anything to me."

"No, we need to talk. My God, what happened to your face?" The girl was shocked when she got closer to him and saw that his face and part of his back were covered in bruises.

"I think it was at your future husband's orders. That coward!"

"How are you so sure it was him?"

"I recognised one of the men who beat me. He is your fiancé's employee; I saw the two of them together in the afternoon."

"Did you report him? He can't get away with this."

"Catherine, what fairytale do you live in? Your fiancé is untouchable here in this city. The Reverend advised me not to file any complaints, as it would likely be dismissed and further increase his anger against me."

"I'll talk to him. He shouldn't have done this to you."

"No, you won't do any of that. The Reverend also told me that it would stain your sister's honour forever. I don't want to do that to her, after all, she was more honest with me than you were."

"Ian..."

"Please go away. I don't want to have any more problems because of you. Get out of here," he said without looking the girl in the eye.

She didn't know what to do, so she started walking towards the door. When she got there, she couldn't move. That wasn't what she'd risked herself for, so she turned around and sat on the bed where he was.

"I came here to talk to you and that's what I'll do."

"No, you came here to cause me even more trouble. You're getting married and you love someone else."

"I don't love him, I love you."

After Catherine said that, their eyes, which had been missing each other since this whole mess started, finally met again. She could feel that his feelings were also still alive. When she realised this, she didn't think twice and kissed him.

She was taken by this impulse and it was certainly the feeling that she carried throughout her life that made her sigh whenever she remembered. A feeling of surrender, of finally feeling complete, connected to a heart that beat inside another chest. With that kiss, she was sure that she loved him and that she couldn't marry Fred. That was true love. She felt as if she and Ian were one, yet inhabiting different bodies.

"What are you doing?" said Ian, pushing her away.

"I'm saying that I love you. That I wasn't fooling you, and that I think I loved you from the first second I saw you, that day the Reverend introduced us. Since that moment, I can't get you out of my mind. At first, I didn't know what to do with what I felt. Things aren't as simple as they seem, and I didn't choose to feel that way for you, especially because I'm engaged to another man. I didn't want to go through this." She started to cry and he took her hands.

"My love, I have felt the same way about you since that moment. It was like I had waited my whole life to find you, and when I saw you, somehow I knew it was you I was looking for."

"I don't know what I'll do, but I can't marry Fred loving you."

"Let's run away! Let's go to Scotland, let's go to London, let's go wherever we can live out our love!"

"But... but..."

"I can support us. I couldn't afford to provide you with all the luxury you would have if you were married to Fred, but I'm a strong man, I have a profession. I'll do anything to give you the best life I can."

"And I can work too. It has been my dream to work as a teacher; I studied for that, but Fred said his wife would never work outside the home, and my father does everything Fred wants."

"We can be happy."

"Yes, we will."

They kissed again and Catherine had a feeling she could stay there all night, but she knew she needed to go home before things got out of hand. She said she would return the following week, while the Reverend was at her house, so they could work out how to run away. When she was at the door, Ian called her back.

"Wait, my love... there's something I need to give you," he said, opening the nightstand drawer and taking out a small leather bag

"What is it, my love?"

"This is the ring that belonged to my mother. Shortly before my father asked her to marry him, he had come to Ireland and heard the story of this ring. It is called the Claddagh ring. It was created by a fisherman who had been kidnapped by pirates, but who had left his beloved in Ireland. He learned to work with gold and silver and created this ring to symbolize the love he hoped to find again. At the time, my father had also left my mother in Scotland and hoped to find her again so they could get married. My father asked them to make this ring, hoping to give it to my mother. It's two hands holding a heart with a crown on top. The hands represent friendship, the heart means love, and the crown, loyalty. This is the ring my father gave my mother when he asked her to marry him, and now I want to give it to you."

The girl took the ring in her hand and stared at the object.

"I know it's nothing compared to that diamond Fred gave you. But this ring symbolises that you have all of me: love, loyalty, and friendship."

"It's beautiful! I don't need any diamonds, all I need is love."

And the two shared one more passionate kiss before the girl left.

When she arrived back at her house, her sister was waiting at the window, distressed, hoping that everything had gone well. She couldn't wait to tell her everything that had happened. They sat on the bed and talked until daybreak.

Emily thought running away with him would be too risky, but she was willing to help with whatever was needed. It wasn't just a question of her sister seeking happiness alongside the man she loved, but also of preventing her from marrying a dangerous person, as Fred was turning out to be.

Catherine showed her the Claddagh ring and said her sister could have her diamond ring.

"No, you're going to keep it. It's a way to start your life. You can sell it and get some money. I think Father will be really angry at you for a few years, but then he'll accept it."

"My sister, you know that when I run away it will be very difficult for you to get married."

"We don't have to worry about that right now, Catherine. As a last resort, when you've settled down, I'll move in with you and Ian can introduce me to some handsome cousin. It's impossible that all the beauty in the family was bestowed upon him alone."

The two sisters laughed, hugged each other and went to sleep.

Catherine spent the week sighing in the corners, remembering the kisses exchanged with her lover and counting the days until her next encounter with Ian. She couldn't wait to feel the warm touch of his lips again.

On Sunday, after the service, everyone went to her house, including Fred. Lunch was about to be served when he walked into the kitchen holding the ring Ian had given Catherine.

"Look at this, Father-in-law, it seems that the Scotsman hasn't learned his lesson."

"Fred, what are you doing with that?" asked Catherine, visibly terrified.

"I found this in your room. Your sister is still seeing that miserable wretch."

"Stop being silly, Fred. How am I going to be meeting him if you almost killed him?"

"That's a very serious accusation. Can you prove it?"

"I know it was you."

"How do you know that? See, I told you, she's still seeing him."

"Emily, explain to me what you're doing with that ring."

"Dad, I swear I can explain, but please, you need to listen to me."

"Father-in-law, she needs to be punished to learn. I think that's what your daughters need."

"My dear friend Fred, you know that I really appreciate your friendship and you also know how much I respect you, but within my house and regarding my daughters' education, the last word is mine. Please, I apologise, but let's deal with this just the two of us, Emily."

"I apologise, Father-in-law, I didn't mean to interfere."

"But you were. Emily, let's go to the office."

"Father, no, please."

"Catherine, calm down, I'll go alone, everything will be fine," said Emily with tears in her eyes.

"You have no right to break into our room and go through our things. Who do you think you are?"

"I am your owner," he said, holding Catherine close to his body, kissing her while he pushed her against the wall.

"What are you doing, Fred? You're insane!"

"Insane for you, it's about time you were mine."

"Stop it! What are you doing? I'm going to scream!"

"Don't do that, otherwise I'll end your sister's life. We're getting married, it won't be a sin."

"Stop it, stop it!" He was lifting her dress and trying to get his underwear off.

"Today you will be mine. Today I will be your man."

"Stop!" She said that and managed to reach for a candlestick to hit him on the head so she could escape. But he came after her and knocked her to the living room floor. At that moment, Eileen came running and kicked him, and Catherine could escape again.

"Get out of here, Fred! Get out!"

"Get out, Mr. Stafford, are you possessed? I'll call Mr. Eugene, get out!"

He stood up and punched Eileen in the face, knocking her to the ground. The commotion in the room ended up catching the father's attention who finally got there.

"What's going on here?"

"Father-in-law, I beg your pardon. I went too far with your daughter; I dishonoured her. But I will fulfill my obligations; I'll bring forward the wedding."

"Father, no. It wasn't my fault! He went after me. I couldn't defend myself!"

"Eileen, what happened?"

"I don't know, sir. When I got here, he was on top of her like an animal! I tried to help her, and look what he did to me!"

"Fred, get out of my house, please."

The father was perplexed by everything that was happening. How could Fred have done such a thing to his daughter under his roof?

"Father, please, it's not my fault. I don't know what happened! As soon as you left, he attacked me, forced me to kiss him, and tried to get my skirt off!"

"Stop, stop, I don't want to hear any of this! I'm ruined! What a terrible father I am. I had to punish your sister while you were losing your honour in the room."

"Father, did you hit Emily? I can't believe it!"

"Yes, I did! How could someone accept a present from a man like that? How could the Reverend put a fellow like him under our roof? He's come to bring ruin to our family! I had never hit any of my children like I did today, but I did it to teach her a lesson."

It was enough for Catherine, she couldn't take it any further. It wasn't fair for her sister to be punished because of her.

"Father, it's not her fault. The ring is mine; Ian gave it to me. I was the one he was meeting with when Fred saw us. Emily took all the blame to defend me."

"I can't believe it! My daughter is a whore!" The man said this and slapped Catherine in the face. She fell to her knees on the floor, and her father kept beating her while she tried to explain herself.

"An engaged woman getting involved with another man, accepting gifts from another man is outrageous. We'll have to thank Fred if he still wants to marry you, as nothing can guarantee that you were still a virgin when he took you to bed! Whore, you whore!"

Emily ran into the office, accompanied by Eileen, to get her father off her sister, who was already covered in blood.

"Get this adulteress out of here before I kill her!"

While they were helping her, the Reverend was arriving and was perplexed by the scene.

"My good Lord, what is this?"

"My father has gone mad, Reverend! He almost killed Catherine!"

The Reverend looked at the girl and went to the office to try to calm his friend.

In the bedroom, Catherine looked disoriented, not quite understanding what had happened. It was all so fast! Fred's attack, getting beaten up by her father. It felt like she was having a nightmare, a bad dream that she couldn't wake up from.

"My sister, I can't believe he did this to you. I had already been beaten; you shouldn't have said anything."

"I couldn't let him believe it was you."

"Let's take your clothes off, my dear, and give you a bath," said Eileen.

As Eileen undressed Catherine, the girl she'd watched grow up, one thing caught her eye: her underwear was clean, with no sign that she had lost her virginity.

"My dear, I know I'm not your mother, but I watched you grow up and I need to ask you something. Weren't you a virgin anymore?"

"Of course I was! I've never done any of this before."

"But why do I see no mark of your honour?"

"Mark of honour?" Emily asked.

"Yes, when a man takes away a woman's honour, there is a sign. She bleeds."

"But why does she bleed?" asked Emily.

Eileen was visibly embarrassed by the question, but now she had to explain to the end.

"Because men have a kind of 'tool' between their legs and they put it inside the... the... you know... of women."

"What? My God, it's disgusting!" said Emily.

"Is this how children are made?" asked Catherine.

"Yes."

"So I'm pregnant?"

"It's not every time a woman gets pregnant. Are you sure he put the 'tool' inside you?"

"No, he definitely didn't."

"Then you need to tell your father about this. I knew... when I arrived in the room, although he had his belt open, he hadn't taken off his pants. He didn't have time to do anything."

"If I tell him this, my father will think that I have no more honour.

I don't know what happened to him."

The sisters cried hugging Eileen, who also couldn't understand what was happening in that house.

Before leaving, the Reverend went to the girls' room and found Catherine sleeping. Emily asked about their father.

"What happened to him, Reverend?"

"I don't know either, my dear. When I found him in the office, I thought he was going to have a heart attack. Then he cried with regret."

"Reverend, my sister didn't lose her honour. Fred tried but couldn't and he lied to Father."

"My dear, this man is very dangerous. I am very worried about how this story will unfold. Very worried. But how are you?"

"I'm fine. Eileen made me some brine water to put on my wounds; Father beat me with a whip. Worse than the physical pain is the emotional pain I'm feeling for my sister. She can't marry this monster, Reverend."

"My child, there is not much we can do about that."

"Reverend, are you going to tell Ian?"

"No, that would be like throwing fuel on a fire; it would only make the situation worse."

"Alright, I understand."

Catherine had a bad fever and was delirious all night. Eileen, who had stayed at the house that night to take care of her, thought it wasn't just because of her injuries, but because of the whole emotional issue involved. She was very sorry that the girl was going through all that. She had worked for a long time at the Crawford house and had seen how the girls' mother had raised them with love and affection.

Certainly, if she were still alive, things would be very different. The girls' mother always did everything her husband wanted, but her husband only wanted what, in a way, was also what she wanted. Eileen thought her mistress had a knack for getting things done, pretending it was her husband's will. He always had the last word, but the last word was always what his wife expected.

Emily couldn't sleep, so as soon as she heard a noise at the window she went there to see what it was.

"Are you mad?"

"Open the window, I need to see how she is."

"Did the Reverend tell you?"

"I realised something was wrong, he couldn't hide it. He's there waiting for me, he thought it would be safer to come with me. Open up, please."

Emily, then, opened the window.

"My love, how are you feeling?"

Catherine, who was burning with fever, took a while to wake up and probably thought she was just delirious.

"My love, what are you doing here? If my father catches you he will kill you!"

"I'd die for you. I would die if I couldn't see you."

"I love you," said the girl in a very weak voice, almost a whisper.

"I love you too, get better soon. Get better, my love, so we can go far away, to a place where no one will hurt you."

"Ian, please, I think you'd better go, I can hear footsteps."

"I will, but I'll always be around," said the young man, jumping out the window as the bedroom door opened.

"What was that? I seem to have heard voices."

"It's Catherine, delirious. I opened the window so she could breathe better."

"Well, close it. She'll be even worse with this cold air."

"I'm sure it would be less harmful than what you did to her," Emily replied.

"I know you two are very upset with me, but it's my responsibility to uphold this family's good name. And I'll do whatever it takes to make that happen."

"If our mother had been alive, this would never have happened."

"Do you think your mother would let you destroy our reputation? You're wrong."

"Father, Mother would at least listen to her daughters. Neither of us has ever given you a reason to doubt us. You were always our best companion, our friend, our hero. But suddenly, you no longer listen to anything other than what Fred says."

"We need Fred."

"We never needed him. Why would we need him now?"

"I need your sister to marry him. Your brother's been doing some business that didn't work out. We owe the Staffords a lot of money, my daughter. Your sister needs to marry him."

"Then it's even worse! You're selling your daughter!"

"I'm not selling her, your sister was happy to marry him before. I don't know what went on inside that girl's head to make her lose her way in life like that."

"She hasn't lost her way in life, Papa."

"You'd better go to sleep; I have too many problems on my mind right now."

After the third day, Catherine was showing the first signs that she was recovering. The Reverend entered her room to talk to her.

"My dear, how are you feeling?"

"I feel like I don't want to live if I must marry Fred."

"Don't talk such nonsense to me! I shouldn't get involved any further in this, but I will interfere, as I really think Fred is a dangerous man. Here, Ian sent you this letter."

"Thank you very much, Reverend."

"My dear, I know that advice when most needed is least heeded, but even so, I'll offer you some. I'm here to deal with the advance of your marriage. Just accept everything your father proposes, and don't argue with him. I also fear for his health, I think he could have a heart attack at any moment."

"Maybe then I'd be free."

"Catherine, the spoken word is like an arrow shot, it doesn't come back. I know you're only saying that because you're upset with your father. He's still that same man who walked for hours pulling your horse until you learned to ride, who used to go on picnics with you and your sister on the riverside so that you could remember these moments even after your mother died and who, until recently, was your best friend. He is still that man. You need to remember that."

"I know, Reverend, but he's also the man who's selling me to a monster."

"My daughter, he's not selling you; don't lash out at him. Well, I'll go now; I hope you're alright."

As soon as the Reverend left, she opened the letter sent by her lover.

"My love, I hope you are well. The Reverend took me out of the house. I'm staying near the port with a friend of his who is travelling. I miss you so much and I wish I could meet you and cover you with kisses.

I want to find you. Get your father out of the house tomorrow afternoon, and I'll come over there to work out the details of our escape. It will be soon. The Reverend is helping me.

We will be happy, my love. Your smile brightens my days."

She smiled again after reading his letter. And she barely had time to put it away before her father walked through the bedroom door and beckoned her to the office. She finally understood the Reverend's words: she could agree to anything, for the wedding would never happen.

Arriving there, she saw Fred, who was wearing a suit and was sitting cross-legged in an armchair.

"How have you been, my dear?"

"Very well, Fred. And you?"

"Looking forward to getting married soon."

"Well, let's not extend the conversation too long. I just called you here, my daughter, to tell you that you are getting married in fifteen days," said the father.

"I keep thinking that a wedding like this, in a hurry, will cause people to talk," said the Reverend.

"Well, I don't care about that. Whoever has the guts to say something, say it," said Fred, with an ironic smile on his lips.

"Fine," said Catherine.

"Fine? Where's your excitement, my dear? I don't see any joy in your eyes."

"May I be excused?" asked the girl.

"Reverend, could I speak privately with my fiancée?"

"I don't know if that should be the case, Eugene. She needs to recover," said the Reverend.

"Reverend, mind your own church business, I'll go talk to my fiancée now."

Eugene, cornered, just nodded. The two left the office and went to the living room.

"My dear, I won't save money, I want you to be the most beautiful bride Limerick has ever seen. Ten years from now, every girl will still dream of being you, getting married covered in wealth from head to toe."

"Aren't you ashamed of yourself? Look at the state I'm in because you lied to my father. I know nothing happened between us. Why are you doing this?"

"Because if you're not mine, you won't be anyone else's. Do you think I'm some fool, Catherine? I'm not!"

"No, I don't think you're a fool. I think you're a monster."

"Listen here..." he said holding Catherine by her arm.

"Is everything fine?" asked Emily who was watching from the living room door.

"Yes, my sister-in-law, are you still using brine water? Or do you need your father to renew your wounds?"

"You're such a fiend. Come on, Catherine. Come to the bedroom."

In the bedroom, Catherine revealed to her sister that she thought her fiancé actually knew that it was she who was involved with Ian, not her sister and that she feared he would do something against her great love. It was too risky for him to come to their house the next day. Emily needed to warn the Reverend, so he would warn Ian.

Emily went to the Cathedral to talk to the Reverend, but when she got there and told the story, he said it would be impossible to alert Ian. He, Eugene, and Fred were heading over to another friend's farm for a game night and wouldn't be back until the next day. There would be no way to warn the young man. So Emily offered to go, as neither her father nor Fred would be in town that night.

"But that's too dangerous. I think if Fred said that, he'd probably put someone on guard."

"Reverend, tell me the address. I'll find a way to get the message through to someone."

He agreed to inform the young man's whereabouts to the girl who, as soon as she found out, ran to tell her sister. Together they would come up with a plan and find a way to get the message to Ian.

"I'll go there and talk to him."

"No, have you lost your mind?"

"It's my only opportunity. I need to talk to him so we can agree on our plan. In fifteen days I'll be married, that is, I have exactly fifteen days to escape, my sister."

Emily stared at Catherine, but couldn't think of any way to help her until Eileen came into the room and the girl had an idea.

"Eileen, will your husband come to get you?"

"Yes, he should be arriving soon. Why?"

They revealed the entire plan to Eileen. As she lived near where Ian was hiding, Emily suggested that Catherine hide inside the carriage. Once there, she would talk to the young man and then go to Eileen's house. The next day, when she came to work, Catherine would come again hidden inside the carriage.

"But what if your father finds out?"

"He won't find out. They won't get here before we've returned."

"I know, Catherine, but I don't like the idea of leaving you at another man's house either."

"My father already thinks I've been dishonoured. What difference will it make?"

The woman thought for a moment and agreed. They would put her inside the carriage and cover her with the tarp. Eileen thought about the girls' mother. She was doing this for her too, as she would never have accepted the idea of her daughter marrying a man like Fred.

Then they began to put the plan into action. As they passed the gate, a man who was standing nearby waved. Surely he was there watching, at Fred's behest. He didn't suspect anything, as Eileen's husband used to take her to work and pick her up at the end of the day.

Upon reaching Ian's place, Eileen's husband went ahead to make sure it was the right place. The young man took a while to open the door, but when he heard that Miss Catherine had come to talk to him, he opened the door.

Eileen's husband took the girl, covered in a cloak, to the door and recommended that Ian take her back to her house afterwards, as it was not far from there.

When he closed the door...

"My love, what are you doing here?"

"I came to see you, as tomorrow will be very difficult. I think Fred put some guards to stop you from going to my house. I think he knows it wasn't Emily who was involved with you, but me."

"How did he find out?"

"I don't know, my love. Just kiss me, let's not talk about him now."

She lost track of time kissing him, and only after the urge to touch her lips again was sated, Ian told her that if she was willing, they could run away in four days. Everything was already arranged: they would leave in the middle of the night and would have to walk about 20km through the woods, but at dawn they would be at the farm of a friend of the Reverend who would take them under concealment to Dublin, to take a boat from there to Scotland. The girl agreed that she could arrange everything within four days.

Ian caressed her face, touching one of the bruises left by her father, while Catherine recounted what had happened: Fred's scheme and the beating she took from her father when she told him that she was the one having an affair with Ian.

"I wish I could kill Fred."

"But he didn't do anything to me, Eileen got there first."

"I would kill him if he had caused you this harm."

"I want to be yours."

"You will be mine. You will be mine forever."

"No, you don't understand. I want to be yours today, here."

"Are you sure?"

"I've never been so sure of anything in my life."

They kissed with even more passion.

He took her to the bed, gently releasing the hair that was tied in a bun. They were looking eye to eye and as her hair loosened, he lightly kissed her mouth. Their lips were both hot and moist. He kissed her neck while he opened his beloved's dress with his skilful hands. Her dress fell, and he covered her shoulders with fervent kisses. Seeing herself only in her petticoat, she blushed. She had never imagined herself like this in front of a man, but at the same time she was not ashamed before him, it was as if they had belonged this way for a long time.

He was looking at her breasts, visible through the thin fabric of her petticoat, and the sight made him excited and nervous. Then he took off his shirt, showing his muscles even more prominently with his bare chest. The strong, rapid breathing was the only noise that could be heard in the house. For a moment, trying to control himself, he stopped and asked:

"Are you sure? I don't mean to disrespect you."

"Yes, I want to be yours."

It was cold, but they were both sweating. He continued kissing the girl's entire body. Catherine stared into his eyes as she ran her hands through his red hair. Looking down, she understood what thing Eileen had been referring to and felt it coming in, a mixture of pain and pleasure. The pain she felt was immense at first, she was tense and afraid of what was to come, but little by little she started to feel more comfortable. He moved slowly, with delicacy, and she, not quite knowing what was happening, felt a wave of pleasure that she had never felt in her life, which made her moan, and grip his hair tightly. Her reaction had the same effect on him, making him moan too, falling on top of her, filling her with hot love.

They embraced and remained in bed for a long time while Ian stroked her hair.

"Was that making love?"

So, it was like feeling love enter your body and be completed by someone else. She wanted this for the rest of her life.

When they stood up, she saw the mark of her honour. The honour she had supposedly lost a week ago. She somehow felt avenged, she would have liked to take that sheet and rub it in Fred's face, and even in her father's face, but she knew she couldn't.

Ian took her to Eileen's house and said he would send a message to the Reverend to confirm the time and place to meet on the day they would run away.

Everything went well on the way home, and when her father came back, he didn't suspect a thing. Her sister still had a surprise.

"Here, it's yours," Emily said, handing back the ring Catherine had gotten from Ian.

"How did you manage to get it back?"

"The day Father hit me in the office, the ring fell to the floor and ended up behind the big bookshelf. I hadn't had a chance to go in there yet to try to get it until last night. I had to remove almost all the books, but I got it!"

"What would I do without you? I love you so much, my sister! Leaving you here is the only thing that makes me sad when I think about leaving."

"My sister, don't think like that, we'll meet again. Take this time to find me a good man, as I will never find one around here again after you leave."

The two laughed and hugged each other. They had a lot to organize for Catherine's departure.

It was agreed that Ian would wait for Catherine at the Reverend's house. It was the Reverend himself who communicated the plans to the girl when he visited her the day before the plan was put into practice. It would be the night they used to get together to play cards, so her father and fiancé would be out of the picture. The Reverend would say he needed to leave early and she would already be hiding inside the carriage. They would go home together, and by dawn, Catherine and Ian would be gone.

Catherine agreed to everything.

On the day of departure, as soon as the Reverend arrived, she and her sister began to carefully load some things into the carriage. The Reverend had said he would leave close to midnight, not before that, so when it was close to that time, Catherine would hide inside the carriage to be with her great love.

It was very difficult to say goodbye to her sister, her great companion in life. Catherine left Emily all the things she had ever wanted. The biggest present was the green dress that had belonged to their mother. Catherine had never even let Emily wear it. She couldn't think of a present that would mean so much to both of them and make them so happy. She also left behind the diamond ring, but asked her sister to give it to their father after some time so that it could be returned to Fred. She didn't want to start her new life with anything that came from a man as abominable as he was. Emily went with her sister to the carriage and, after making sure that no one would see them, amid tears and promises that as soon as possible they would meet again, the two said goodbye.

That day the game was strange. The Reverend felt a different mood in the air. Fred was more arrogant than usual and seemed to be dropping many hints. The Reverend pretended not to understand, but apparently Fred seemed to be suspicious that something was going on. This may have been heightened by his realisation that Ian was no longer living in the Reverend's house. How could the man disappear and the Reverend not comment? He should have been suspicious of something, but he hadn't asked, which could be another indication that he might be up to something. It was a night full of guesswork.

When the Reverend announced that he had an early appointment and that he needed to leave, he almost had a heart attack at the reaction of Catherine's fiancé:

"I will accompany you, Reverend."

"But my son, did you not come in your own carriage?"

"I did, but tomorrow I can send one of my employees to come and get it. I don't feel well either, I'd rather go with you."

"But how are you not feeling well, my son? You look so good."

"Reverend, what's this, are you denying me a lift?"

The Reverend just took a deep breath, but a million things were going through his head. How could he refuse to give him a lift? And how would he handle this situation? Certainly, Catherine was inside the carriage. He couldn't warn her sister, as she was supposed to be sleeping at that time. He didn't have time to think, as Fred was already waiting for him at the door. The only possible answer was:

"Of course, my son, let's go."

Catherine, from inside the carriage, watched as Fred and the Reverend came toward her. What was happening? Would Fred go along with the Reverend? Had Fred found out about their plan?

As they approached, the Reverend was trying to speak Fred's name out loud to alert Catherine that he was about to give her fiancé a lift. Catherine had gotten the message, but she could feel the sweat running down her back. Why would Fred be going along? Was he suspicious of something?

The Reverend was driving the cart, static, tense, and unable to act naturally. Fred started asking questions.

"What do you have to do tomorrow?"

"Oh, church matters, I have some documents to organise and send to Dublin."

"It must be something important to keep you from staying longer, is it?"

"It is, just as you must be feeling very sick to have left so early," said the Reverend, no longer playing along with Fred's game.

"Actually, Reverend, I asked to accompany you because I think we should talk. I don't know what you did to that Scottish friend of yours, but I want to warn you to keep him away from my fiancée. Otherwise, my men will finish what they started that other day. If I see him one more time, he will die."

"I can't believe you have the nerve to threaten him in front of me."

"That's not a threat, that's my word and that goes for you too. Stay out of this because no one wants to come between me and my goals."

"Fred, do you think the world revolves around you?"

"Reverend, if it doesn't, I'll set it straight. One thing you need to understand is that the world revolves around money and money is something I have."

"The world turns according to God's will, Fred."

"Then I tell you, it's good that not even God tries to mess with me, Reverend."

The Reverend just widened his eyes and continued driving his carriage home. He feared that something bad would happen to Catherine and Ian. The girl, terrified, heard everything from her hiding place. She needed to run away; she could never stay and marry this man who seemed capable of anything.

Ian watched as the carriage arrived and didn't understand when he saw the Reverend accompanied by Fred. He thought something had gone wrong and stayed hidden until Fred was gone. He felt more relieved when he saw Catherine getting out of the carriage. They had to be quick.

"My children, I don't know if it's a good idea for you to go today."

"Reverend, you, better than anyone, know that Fred is suspicious and if we don't go today, we may never be able to leave," said the girl running into the house."

"He has become a dangerous man, I don't recognize him," added the Reverend.

The Reverend conceded that the couple should run away that night, but advised they should wait at least a few hours before leaving, just to make sure it was safe. Ian then asked:

"Reverend, can I ask you one more thing?"

"Yes, sure you can, my son, anything."

"Can you marry us?"

"Marry? Now?"

"Yes, we'll do it anyway and we would love for it to be officiated by you."

"If that is your will, I can give the sacrament."

"Here, my love, this will be our ring," Catherine said, handing the Reverend the ring she'd received from Ian. The Reverend performed a beautiful and quick ceremony that moved the bride and groom. He spoke of the love of God, the love that breaks boundaries, that spreads and is capable of anything. Even the Reverend was moved. At the same time, he was worried because he knew that his friend Eugene would never forgive him for marrying his daughter without him knowing. But he did it out of love.

When they were about to leave, the Reverend gave Ian a big hug and put an envelope inside his bag.

"I know you won't want to accept it, but this is a small contribution to start your life. You are very important in my life. I've been friends with your family for decades and Catherine took her first steps inside my church. More than anyone else, I want and hope that you are very happy."

"Thank you so much, Reverend. You have been like a father to me. I don't know what I would do without you here nor how to thank you."

"Make this young lady happy. Her mother, like yours, was a very good friend of mine and her wish was always to see her daughter very happy."

They embraced and, without wasting more time, the couple began the journey.

The Shannon that day was at a very high water level, so the path they were thinking of taking, going along the riverbank for some distance, became unfeasible. They had to go behind the church and around the castle. The whole area of the medieval city was quite dark. On that particular day, a thick fog had taken over the city, and at that hour, it would be very difficult for anyone to see them.

They walked at a brisk pace to cross to the other side of the Thomond Bridge and catch the horses in order to reach the farm of the Reverend's friend more quickly.

When they were about halfway across the bridge, they saw someone coming towards them.

"Did you really think you could run away?" Fred said, and then fired, hitting Ian's chest on the right side.

Ian fell to the ground, not even having time to understand what had happened. As soon as he fell, he started bleeding and he felt an inexplicable weakness, but he knew he needed to get up.

Catherine threw herself to the ground to help her lover and Fred started to reload the gun.

"You are the biggest slut in the city of Limerick and I will cleanse my honour with your blood."

"Drop that gun and come fight like a man," Ian said, getting to his feet with Catherine's help and lunging at Fred.

"You barely have the strength to stand, you Scottish bastard."

The two began to fight, while Catherine screamed for help. Ian was much stronger than Fred, who looked as if he'd never even been involved in a fistfight. Her loved one would easily win, if he hadn't been shot and if his opponent was willing to fight using only his hands, and not using all the weapons he could.

As they fought, Fred pulled a knife from his pocket and stabbed Ian in the side, just below the ribs.

Ian felt the stab and cried out in pain. It was as if his life was leaving his body along with the knife.

"Die, you bastard!" Fred said as he used all his strength to spin the knife, still inside Ian's body.

Catherine rushed to help Ian, who was losing a lot of blood.

Fred took advantage of that moment to reach for the gun that had dropped during the fight against Ian. He wanted to take Catherine's life too. He stood up, and pointing the gun at Catherine, said:

"Now it's your turn!" But luckily for the girl, the gun jammed and Ian had time to gather his last strength and go for him. The man threw his body on top of his opponent, no longer able to do anything else. The important thing was to keep him away from the woman he loved. At that moment, Ian could only scream:

"Run, my love."

In the middle of the fight, Fred pushed Ian against the railing of the bridge, causing him to fall into the river.

"Nooooooooo! Nooooooooooooo!!!! Nooooooooo!" said Catherine, trying to jump after her lover, but she couldn't see him anymore. The river was almost overflowing that night and the fog made it impossible to see anything at that distance. Then she started to run, looking for the head of the bridge to try to get down to the river, swim, and find Ian, but she couldn't see him.

Fred ran after her with the gun, yelling that Catherine wouldn't get out of there alive, that if she wasn't his, she certainly wouldn't be anyone else's.

He shot once more, but luckily it didn't hit the young woman.

Catherine ran around the castle in desperation, lost her shoes, and felt her feet sink into the muddy banks of the Shannon. She couldn't see anything in the river and something inside her told her that she had already lost her great love forever. What reason would she have to live? Even so, her survival instinct made her run as fast as possible. Even without her brain's command, her legs seemed to know that she should run to the Reverend's house to try to escape the rage of the betrayed man.

If she was going to die, she wanted everyone to know that Fred was responsible for her death, so she started screaming desperately for help. She knew that her fiancé was powerful and that he would be able to cover up Ian's murder. However, killing her near the church would draw a lot of people's attention and it would be very difficult for Fred to silence all those voices.

"Help, heeeeelp. Help me!" Catherine screamed, when she finally managed to get back on the road, up the side of the Potato Market, just before the bridge. Fred was less than a body length away; she could hear his footsteps very close, but she wouldn't give up.

From inside the house, the Reverend began to hear strange noises. First, a noise that sounded like a gunshot. Hearing it, he felt his heart sink; he imagined that the plan had not worked. He picked up his hat and was already out on the street when he started to hear Catherine's screams for help.

He was reaching the church door when he spotted Catherine, who opened her arms as soon as she saw him. She didn't have time to reach him, as Fred's shot hit her in the back, causing her to fall to the ground.

The Reverend couldn't quite see who fired the shot, but his intuition said it was Fred. The man fled in the darkness, and no one who arrived at the scene, attracted by the cries for help, had managed to identify the shooter.

"Help me, help me!" said the Reverend to whoever arrived.

The bullet had passed through the girl's body, entered her back at the level of her lungs, and exited through her chest. The Reverend knew the bullet was no longer inside the girl, which he thought was a good sign, but they needed a doctor to examine her. One man offered to go get the doctor and another to go to the Crawford house to call the victim's family.

The Reverend, with the help of the people who arrived at the scene, took her inside and tried to stop the blood, until the doctor arrived.

Luckily, the doctor was at home and he managed to arrive at the scene even before the girl's family.

As soon as she entered the room, Emily hugged her sister and cried profusely. Their father didn't know what was going on. How had his daughter been shot in the dead of night? She had gone to sleep... how could this have happened? Despite being very worried, when he saw his daughter and realised she was wearing the damn ring given to her by the Scotsman, his behaviour changed. Was his daughter running away from home with that scoundrel? What had happened?

"Reverend, what happened to my daughter?"

"Eugene, you need to stay calm," said the Reverend, taking his friend by the arm and leading him into the other room.

"What was she doing on the street? Don't tell me she was running away with that shameless man."

"Eugene, don't talk like that. I'm afraid she's dead and your son-in--law did this to her."

"If he did, he did well to cleanse his honour. Emily, come home."

The Reverend, holding the man by the arm, asked him, "What are you doing, Eugene?"

"I don't have a daughter anymore."

"Father, have you gone mad?"

"Emily, come at once. I don't have a daughter anymore."

Emily stood up and shouted at her father, "So if you don't have a daughter, I don't have a father anymore. I won't leave my sister alone here."

"Stop it, if you want to resolve these issues, go outside because I need to try to save her life," said the doctor, who was still trying to stop the blood and then stitch her up.

Eugene turned his back and walked out of the Reverend's house, while Emily returned to the room to hold her sister's hand.

The next morning the murder attempt was the only thing that was talked about in the city, but no one understood what had happened. Along with the stories about Eugene's daughter, there were also theories on the origin of the blood found on top of the Thomond Bridge.

Only Catherine could tell the Reverend for sure, but somehow he knew that all that blood was Ian's.

Catherine kept fighting for her life, but she was paler than a sheet of paper. The doctor said that she had a chance to recover, but her sister should trust in God. From then on it was no longer a matter of medicine, but faith.

Someone knocked on the door and Emily gaped when she saw that it was Fred.

"Is my fiancée's body here?"

"You have no decency, what are you doing here?"

"My sister-in-law, I came here to see what happened to my fiancée. I was told that she was shot and that she is dead. Who was it?"

"What's going on?" asked the Reverend who had just arrived and couldn't believe the scene either.

"Reverend, what happened to my fiancée? Please, I can't bear to lose her like this."

"Your fiancée is recovering well, but she can't have visitors, Fred."

"Recovering?"

"Yes, the doctor managed to save her."

"Thank God!" said Fred, making anyone who didn't know him believe his words.

"You thought she was dead, didn't you? You thought you had killed her just like you killed..." The Reverend took Emily by the arm, preventing her from finishing her line so as not to arouse even more anger from Fred.

"Not at all! I'm relieved to hear that my beloved Catherine is alive."

"Well Fred, come back tomorrow to see her, maybe she'll be awake by then," said the Reverend.

"I'll be back, we have a lot to talk about," said the man, as cynical as ever.

When he left, Emily and the Reverend were staring at each other. Surely, he had gone there to avoid attention. Did he really hope she was dead and now he was afraid the whole truth would be revealed? Was her sister at risk at the Reverend's house? Would he come back to finish the job? Both the Reverend and Emily were very concerned and decided to try to reach Eugene for help. The Reverend did not believe that his friend would uphold the words he had said the night before. He was a good man; he couldn't abandon his daughter like that.

The Reverend went there, but he was very disappointed because Eugene repeated that he no longer had a daughter and that he would do nothing to help Catherine.

"But Eugene, would you rather see your daughter married to a man who was capable of trying to kill her?"

"I would do the same in his position. An honest girl wouldn't get involved with another man."

"You would never do the same, my friend. What's the matter with you?"

"Too many things! My life is falling apart. I've lost control of my daughters, and my fortune is slipping through my fingers. This marriage was the only solution, but look what she did!"

"Your daughters should be more important than your money. I don't recognise you."

"I don't recognise them either. How could they turn against me like that? How could they betray me like this?"

"Eugene, you can't abandon them. God, like a good father, never abandons us. You can't abandon your daughters."

"I don't want her inside this house. I don't want her here staining my home."

"Would you rather leave her there, at the risk of Fred trying to finish the job?"

Eugene reflected and then said, "Take one of my men; no one will enter your house. Leave him on guard there. I can give you some money too to pay for the necessary treatment."

"Very well, send one of your men to my house, but save your money. I think it's very important to you..." said the Reverend, turning his back on the friend he no longer recognised.

With the man serving as a guard, they felt safer, and little by little Catherine began to show small signs that she was recovering. She was still very weak, and Emily was afraid her sister wouldn't find the strength to keep fighting for her life. Four days later, Catherine opened her eyes and began to cry. Emily was at her bedside, happy to see her finally regaining consciousness.

"My sister, I'm so glad you're awake! Thank God you're alive!"

"I'd rather not be. He killed Ian, threw him into the river, and I couldn't save him. I couldn't jump after him."

"Stop, my sister," said Emily, hugging her. "There's nothing you could have done to save him. I went to the bridge and saw the bloodstains. He lost a lot of blood. Even if you had found him, he would have been dead, and both of you would never have been able to get out of the river anyway. It would have been impossible given the state of the river that night."

"But I would rather have died with him."

"Don't talk nonsense! Don't even think about it!"

"We were married before he died."

"How so?"

"Before we ran away, the Reverend married us. I remember every word; it was the happiest moment of my entire life," said Catherine, opening her arms to receive another hug from her sister.

As they were talking, Catherine confirmed what they already knew: Fred had spinelessly killed Ian and had tried to kill her. Emily said that the day after the crime, Fred had gone to the Reverend's house, hoping that Catherine was dead. After that day, he disappeared and was probably no longer in town.

Catherine asked about her father and why they were at the Reverend's house. Emily told her sister the truth. She knew their father would be very hurt, but she hadn't expected him to throw her sister out of the house either. This whole situation with their father made her very sad. He had been an amazing father, far better than any father she knew, friendly, playful, generous, and always present. When had they drifted away from each other?

The doctor examined Catherine and was satisfied to see her conscious and recovering from her wounds. He stated that it would take a long time to fully recover, as the left lung was very affected, but that with rest and care, she would get better. The Reverend believed that God's will, combined with the modern techniques used by a young doctor who had just arrived in the city, were the two factors that had helped save the girl.

As the doctor had warned, Catherine's recovery was quite slow. Gradually she felt stronger, despite having great difficulty breathing. As the days passed, she was able to stand up, take her first steps, and go back to feeding herself. She was almost two months into this recovery process when Catherine started feeling sick every morning. The Reverend thought it would be better to call the doctor to examine her.

The doctor started with the normal tests, checking if the symptoms could be consequences of the shot, but decided to move on to another line of investigation.

"When was the last time you had your period?"

"My... my period?"

"Yes, when was the last time?"

Her sister answered on behalf of her, "She hasn't had any since she was shot, doctor, but that must be because she's too weak."

"Well Emily, I think your sister is pregnant."

"No, there is no possibility."

Catherine began to cry. She knew there was a chance, and if that were really true she would be the happiest woman in the world. It would be the chance to have at least one more piece of her lover with her, but undoubtedly it would be another scandal.

The doctor ran some more tests and confirmed the pregnancy. The Reverend was intrigued and felt guilty, as he didn't think Catherine and Ian had really got to that point. What would she do now? If it was difficult for his friend to accept his daughter back before, imagine now that she was carrying a child as a widow.

"What are we going to do now?" Emily asked, visibly startled by the news.

"Now everything gets even more complicated. We need to talk to your father again," said the Reverend.

"No, he won't take me back, even less so now."

"But we need to find a solution. You can't stay here if you're pregnant. You know they're going to force you to give the child up for adoption and we can't allow that to happen."

"No, no one will touch my son. He is what makes me want to continue living. From the moment the doctor said I was pregnant, it was as if my life had found its meaning again."

"I know, my dear. I'm also happy to know that at least a little piece of our Ian still lives in you."

"Reverend, I've been wanting to ask you this for a long time and I don't want to seem nosy or anything like that, but what was your relationship to him?" asked Emily.

"I've always liked Ian very much. Since I first laid eyes on him, I viewed him as if he were my son."

"But where did so much love come from?" insisted the girl.

"Sometimes we choose paths in life that completely exclude other possibilities. When I chose to serve God, within my heart I decided not to have my own children. I chose only to guide God's children. It was my choice to serve God alone. But when a young man chooses that, he often doesn't know that life will give him many trials and one of them was Ian's mother.

It was an overwhelming passion that almost made me abandon my path to becoming a Reverend. I wanted to move to Scotland and do whatever she wanted to have her by my side. She was the most beautiful, sweetest woman I've ever seen in my entire life, perfect in every way. I fell in love, but she was already committed to Ian's father."

"But did she also fall in love with you?"

"No, she loved her betrothed, who, coincidentally, was here in Ireland at the time I met her. I didn't stand a chance with her. We became good friends and I managed to turn all the romantic love I felt into a great friendship. Then I became friends with Ian's father too, a great man. Whenever I went to Scotland, I visited them, so I was able to watch Ian grow up. We always got along very well, ever since he was very little. He always was a very good boy, hardworking and polite, he was certainly the closest thing I had to a son. If I could choose, I would have liked to have had a son like him. He also had hair and eyes like his mother's. I couldn't help but love him. But I feel guilty, I shouldn't have encouraged this madness. I ask God's forgiveness every day."

"Don't blame yourself that way, Reverend. If you ask for forgiveness every day, then I will thank you every day for believing in our love, for reaching out and helping us fulfil this feeling that we had so strongly for each other, which has now left a seed."

"Reverend, we will never be able to thank you for everything you are doing for us," said Emily, hugging him.

The next day they were surprised by two events. Firstly, by the visit of the girls' father, who arrived unannounced.

He knocked on the Reverend's door and asked to talk. The man looked fifteen years older than when they had last seen him: long hair and stubble, clothes rumpled, bags under his eyes that went halfway down his cheeks. Emily couldn't take it anymore and hugged him, still at the door.

"Father, what happened? Are you alright?"

"I'm not well, I was abandoned by my daughters and my friend," he said, referring to the Reverend.

"My friend, it was you who abandoned us."

"I'm sorry and I want you to come home. I will forgive everything you've done."

"Father, we're the ones who have to forgive you. It's we who have to think about whether we'll grant you our forgiveness," said Emily visibly upset.

"Please calm down. Let's talk and be reasonable," said the Reverend, while Catherine just cried in the corner of the room.

"I came here to take the two of you home. I don't want to live without you anymore; I need you to stay with me. I'm sure that in a while I'll be able to find another fiancé for Catherine..."

"No, Father, you don't need to find me another fiancé. Now I'm a widow."

"Widow? What do you mean widow?"

"Ian and I got married before Fred killed him."

"Married? Who performed the wedding?"

"I did, Eugene. I couldn't let them live in sin."

"If it was you and they were married just before the man died, that marriage can be annulled. I still have some leverage, we can claim it didn't have time for consummation, so it can be annulled."

"Father, we consummated the marriage before the Reverend's blessing happened. But what difference does it make? I was a virgin when Fred made up lies and you chose to believe him. I had never done anything wrong, not to my fiancé, not to anyone, and yet you called me a whore and hit me."

Eugene, visibly out of control, was crying inconsolably as he covered his face with both hands.

"You know, I won't hide this from anyone. I'm pregnant. I'm expecting Ian's baby."

A deafening silence took over the room. Only the tense breathing of the four people in the room could be heard. The moment was interrupted by Eugene who, having come out of practically a trance, shouted:

"That can't be true! You really want to kill me!"

The man turned red, couldn't seem to breathe, and started to rip his shirt off. The Reverend went to him to help.

"What are you feeling, my friend?"

"My heart... my heart..."

"Emily, call the doctor! I think your father is having a heart attack!"

Eugene was indeed having a heart attack, but thanks to the speed of care and some pills, the doctor gave him, his heart seemed to have stabilised.

"You have to take care of yourself. I will prescribe some pills that will help you, but we need to do some more concrete tests to find out what is wrong," said the doctor before leaving the room.

Eugene got up and announced that he was also leaving.

"Slow down, my friend, we have to talk."

"I don't think we have anything else to talk about." He said this and left the house.

But that wouldn't be the only important event of the day. Earlier in the evening, they received another visitor, but this time it was someone looking to speak to the Reverend. This was not just any visit, it was the Bishop of Dublin who had come to bring bad news: they were transferring the Reverend to another city.

"What do you mean? I've been here for over 25 years and I have had no complaints."

"Yes, you are an excellent Reverend, loved by all, but we need you elsewhere."

"But my whole life is here, everything I've built is in this diocese."

"When we choose to serve God, we know that we have become his instrument and that we have to go wherever he sends us."

"But Bishop, would there be the possibility..."

"There is no possibility."

"I don't even know what to say..."

"You don't have to say anything, just pack your bags. In a week you will be introduced to the new church. You will have time to organise your things and say goodbye to your congregation."

It broke the Reverend's heart into more pieces than he thought would be possible. His whole life was in Limerick, all his history, all the people he could call family. He tried to argue, but the bishop was unyielding and he had to leave in just a week. He had nothing else to do, although he couldn't think of what his life would be like far away from there.

"You're staying for dinner, aren't you? I'll put another plate on the table," asked the Reverend, out of politeness.

"Not this time my friend. I'm having dinner at the Stafford's."

Hearing that, everything started to make sense: Fred was responsible for this decision; his power really knew no bounds. He had probably used his influence and money to force the bishop to make this change. The Reverend felt tiny in the face of it, weak. His hands were tied.

This change had yet another consequence: he could not take the girls with him. He could not arrive in another city with two young women, one of whom was carrying a child conceived in sin. They were at a dead end. He told the sisters about the situation and said he had no choice but to go to Eugene's house to find a solution.

Catherine felt very bad because the person who helped her the most would suffer this severe consequence. She knew how devoted the Reverend was, how beloved by his community he was and how unfair it was for him to be thrown out in this way.

To his surprise, when the Reverend reached Eugene's house, Fred was already there. The despicable man was on his way out, but he still had time to say:

"Well, well Reverend, I thought you'd be packing by now. Aren't you leaving?" the man said as he mounted his horse and galloped off, making the Reverend very upset.

The Reverend, more than anyone, knew that it was a great sin, but he had never wanted anyone dead as much as he wanted this man to die.

Once inside the house, he was shocked to hear Eugene's solution. Eugene had told Fred that his daughter was pregnant and, to his surprise, the man had said that he would marry her and take responsibility for the child.

When asked by the girl's father about the reasons for such a decision, Fred said:

"I always get what I want. I've dreamed of marrying your daughter for years. I won't die before I achieve it."

The truth is that everything had been hushed up and a story about a kidnapping was fabricated. Nobody knew that Catherine had been found running away with another man, so Fred's honour wouldn't be tarnished.

"Do you really want to see your daughter married to the man who tried to kill her?"

"If my daughter agrees to marry him, he will forgive my debts. What other solution do I have? Besides, I won't take her back with a bastard child, although, I would have taken her back without the child. This will be the perfect solution."

"Perfect solution?"

"Yes, if she marries Fred, I have my debts forgiven. We erase this scandal, name the child and Emily still has a chance of finding a good husband. Everything will go back to normal."

"I can't believe you want your daughter to marry this man!"

"I don't see any other solution."

The Reverend got up and, without saying anything else, just went to his house. He told the story to the girls. Emily looked like she wanted to foam at the mouth, she was so angry at the thought that her father might actually be thinking about such an absurd idea.

"I'll accept."

"What? Take it easy, calm down, I think she's sick, maybe insane, Reverend! What are you talking about, Catherine?"

"I will accept the proposal, but on one condition."

"No, you won't," said the Reverend.

"I'll talk to Fred, and if he can reverse the decision to take you out of Limerick, Reverend, I will accept the proposal."

"I agree with Emily, you've lost your senses. I won't let you do that."

"It's the only way. I can't destroy your lives. I'm afraid that even if we resist, my father will put the baby up for adoption. I can't even think about the possibility of never seeing my child grow up."

"We can run away, cross the sea, and live in America."

"Emily, you know the reality is very different. What power do we have? Two women, one pregnant!"

"We..."

"No, I'm tired of all this. I'll marry him, keep my son close to me, the Reverend stays here, and you get a good husband."

"I don't want a good husband, I want you to stay safe and away from that monster."

"I'll talk to him. That's the only way."

The two still tried to argue, but Catherine was unyielding. They couldn't get that idea out of her head. As if anticipating their attempts to dissuade her, she woke up very early the next day and went to Fred's house.

It wasn't an easy conversation. Catherine couldn't look at Fred without thinking that he had killed her great love. But it had to be done, not for herself, but for everyone she loved. That was the only solution. When he agreed to keep the Reverend at St Mary's Cathedral, she made the deal. It was decided that they would be married in a week.

Catherine and Emily returned to their father's house, but Catherine would only stay there for a short time since in a few days she would live with her future husband.

Only the families of the bride and groom attended the wedding, but even so, it was a very ostentatious ceremony. Fred was cunning and maintained the appearance that everything was fine and that he was happily awaiting his son. He even bragged to his friends, telling a made-up story about how he got his bride pregnant before the wedding without her father knowing.

The debt of the father had indeed been forgiven and the Reverend got to stay in town. Catherine was also happy, as she had seen her sister's eyes on Geoffrey, the doctor who had been treating Catherine and her father. He was a good man and she was glad to realise that Emily could potentially be happy with him.

On her wedding night, she got the gist of what her life would be like with that man. Even though she was pregnant, she had only been with a man once and it was nothing like the experience she had that night. Fred hit her face until her nose bled, then forced himself on her in every possible way. She felt no pleasure whatsoever. She was very disgusted by him as the man moaned in pleasure over her body.

And it would be like that pretty much every night. Fred behaved like an animal, and Catherine had no choice but to endure his brutality. As the pregnancy progressed, he became increasingly violent and she was beaten even more. At home, he was always drunk, but in public he played the good husband, introducing his wife to everyone and saying he was looking forward to the birth of his heir.

The romance between Emily and Geoffrey went from strength to strength. Shortly after Catherine's wedding, the doctor found the courage to ask her father for permission to court his youngest daughter. Ignoring the reality experienced by Catherine, the patriarch thought that everything was finally back on track.

One night, Fred said to Catherine:

"I can't wait to have our own son, because this one won't survive."

"What do you mean it won't survive?"

"Children are fragile; they die easily."

She had understood the warning. It was clear that he would not raise another man's child. This child was in serious danger. So, Catherine went to talk to her sister about her concerns. She found her at the Reverend's house, where she was accompanied by Geoffrey.

Catherine told him what Fred had said and that she knew her son was in danger. The Reverend wondered if Fred would really harm a baby, but he knew that man was capable of anything. Everyone fell silent when Geoffrey spoke:

"I have an idea."

"What idea?" asked Emily.

"It might sound a little crazy, but it might work."

"Tell us, we need a solution."

"Emily and I could raise the child."

"How so?" asked Catherine.

"I would be happy to raise this baby as my own so I don't leave him in this man's hands. I've seen what he's done to you and Ian and what he does to you every day. I can't let him do the same with the baby. Especially a baby born from a pure and beautiful love such as you had with Ian. I'll deliver the baby and I'll say the child died. He won't care to see the body, because he has no appreciation for the child. I can say that the child was born with some deformity. Emily and I would run away to another city and raise the child. The child will always be yours. However, we will only return when the child is old enough that it won't raise suspicions."

"Running away? My father is going to die..."

"No, my love... we're going to bring our wedding forward. Then we move and take the child with us."

"But Geoffrey, are you willing to do all that to help me?"

"Yes, we'll just be bringing things forward a little. I swear to you we'll raise this child with all the love in the world."

Catherine didn't want to give up on her son, but it would also be an act of love. She could bear all her husband's abuse, but she couldn't bear to see him do anything to the child. It would be a difficult decision to separate from her son, but she would find strength, for the child's own safety.

The wedding was brought forward and Emily could not hide the happiness of having found a bridegroom that she loved so much. The diamond in her engagement ring wasn't even half the size of her sister's old ring, but she had lived long enough to know that that was of little importance. What mattered was the love they nourished for each other and that they had in abundance.

On the day that marked eight months since Ian's death, Catherine paid him a tribute by publishing a note in the newspaper:

"My beloved Ian Alexander McLeod
Eight months of missing the one who will always be my great love.
C.C.M."

She signed C.C.M., the initials she would have used if she had been able to live her life alongside Ian: Catherine Crawford McLeod. As she didn't have a grave to light candles and place flowers on, she spoke to the Reverend about burying her ring in the cemetery and placing a small headstone with her lover's initials. That way, at least she would have a place to pray and pay her respects. The Reverend said the cemetery was a sacred place and he couldn't allow it, but if he didn't see it... he couldn't do anything. He didn't want to commit, but he hinted his support for her idea.

Catherine asked Geoffrey to order a small stone with the initials I.A.M. As soon as her brother-in-law brought it to her, she put Ian's ring and a note in a bag and buried them in a corner of the cemetery, declaring all her love for Ian. There she could light candles and leave flowers for her lover. Unfortunately, she didn't have much time to visit.

That same night, when she got home, she found Fred holding the newspaper in his hand, completely possessed.

"Once a slut, always a slut. Don't you miss any chance to humiliate me?"

"What are you talking about?"

"You think I don't know it was you who wrote that message to your lover?"

He didn't wait for an answer and started beating her. Catherine fell to the ground and Fred started kicking her in the belly and within minutes she started spitting blood out of her mouth. The servants always saw how he treated her inside the house and they didn't usually intervene, but that day, seeing the level of violence, they were forced to take action. Catherine was almost dead.

The man seemed possessed. It seemed that he really wanted to take his wife's life and even though he was completely drunk, it took two servants to stop him from killing her. He stumbled into the living room and sat on the couch, holding a bottle of whiskey that he drank like water. He tapped his shoes on the floor rhythmically, as if playing a happy song.

The employees, frightened by the man's attitude and showing affection for Catherine, went to Geoffrey's house to ask for help. When they found Emily, they said that it would be good for her to go along, as they didn't know if Catherine would survive.

When they arrived at the Stafford's house, they found Fred still drinking in the living room and Catherine in labour, but the child was not in the right position. The employees called the Reverend, in case she needed last rites.

Geoffrey asked all the employees to leave the room, as they would have to do everything they could to get the baby out of there.

Just seeing her sister-in-law's condition was enough to make him realise that things were more complicated than he could have imagined. Catherine was losing a lot of blood and appeared to have some internal bleeding.

Emily was holding her sister's hand when Geoffrey looked at the Reverend and shook his head to indicate that the baby was not alive.

Catherine was still struggling, hoping for her little baby to be born strong and healthy. Realising that the baby didn't cry, she despaired and tried to scream, even though she was too weak:

"Let me see my baby! Let me see my baby!"

Geoffrey held the tiny baby, a boy with red hair just like his father, and very carefully and through tears, handed him to his sister-in-law who, crying, took one last breath.

The bleeding stopped and Geoffrey knew what that meant. His sister-in-law's heart had stopped beating. He tried in every way to revive her, but he couldn't.

Catherine was dead.

Silence took over the room. Emily, as if in shock, didn't speak or cry. The Reverend prayed silently beside the bed and Geoffrey sat beside the pool of blood, the blood that had soaked through the bed and was now pooling on the floor.

That was the scenario Fred encountered when he opened the door, cigar in hand, drunk as a skunk, and said:

"My bastard was born."

Geoffrey lunged and punched him in the face, and he fell unconscious.

As Geoffrey was getting up off the man, Emily, with her husband's scalpel in her hand, cut a deep gash in her brother-in-law's neck, splitting it from side to side.

The Reverend got up and closed the door, saying:

"Lord, have mercy! We are lost!"

They had committed a murder.

Emily, starting to cry, hugged her sister and said:

"We should have done this a long time ago!"

The Reverend was perplexed by the scene.

Geoffrey thought of a solution. He was quick-thinking and, perhaps from his practice as a doctor, was able to act quickly when under pressure. He turned to the others and said:

"We have to do something. Reverend, go outside and ask the employees to look for Fred, because he ran out the window and you're afraid he'll do something crazy. Make sure the employees leave and come back to help. We'll wrap the body in some sheets, put it on your carriage and throw him in the river."

"My son, we cannot do this."

"Then I will turn myself in to the police, saying I killed him. I won't let my wife be arrested for killing that bastard.

"No, Geoffrey , I won't let you disgrace your life, your career. I have no regrets, I would do it all over again. The only regret I have is that I didn't do this sooner to prevent this tragedy." She said looking at her sister who died hugging her nephew's body.

Another tragedy was being announced.

The Reverend could not allow another person's life to be destroyed because of Fred. He decided to accept the plan and do what was agreed.

When the servants left the house, the two carried the body to the Reverend's carriage. They proceeded to a stretch of river where they knew the plan would work. The strong current would carry the body far away by daybreak.

The Reverend said one last prayer, and together they threw the man's body into the Shannon. The same river that had already witnessed the end of Catherine and Ian's love was now witnessing the end of this story.

New times

Beep, beep, beep.

Beeeeeeeeeeeeeeeeeeeeeeeep

"We're losing her!"

"Bring the defibrillator," said one of the doctors.

"Charge 200!"

"I don't know if she will respond, doctor."

"Clear!"

The doctor applied the defibrillator to Olivia's chest, but there was no response.

"Damn it, come on, come on. One more time."

"Clear!"

The doctor once again applied the defibrillator to the girl's chest.

Beep, beep, beep.

"She's reacting! Come on, girl! Come on!"

Olivia woke up disoriented and with a dry mouth. Her eyes were sensitive to the light. She heard voices but couldn't understand what the people around her were saying. They came closer and began to examine her. She was still very confused. Where was she?

"I'm glad you're awake! I never lost hope!" said a nurse, in English, but Olivia couldn't reply as her vocal cords were weak. She tried to speak, but the same nurse warned her:

"Take it easy, don't try to talk now, little by little your voice will return."

Return from where exactly? What was she doing there? Olivia was utterly confused about what was going on.

Her whole body ached. The pain in her ribs was so bad it felt like she'd been run over. Had she been run over?

Gradually all these unanswered questions made her very agitated. She wanted to get up, but she didn't have the strength to do so. The nurse approached and said:

"Calm down, Olivia, calm down. Try to rest, you've just been extubated."

The nurse must have administered a sedative through one of the IVs attached to Olivia's body because she calmed down and fell asleep immediately.

When Olivia woke up again, two doctors and two nurses were looking at her.

"Welcome back, Olivia."

Her voice was still very weak, she tried unsuccessfully to make sounds through her vocal cords. Finally, after coughing a few times, in a very weak and low voice, she said:

"What's going on? Where am I?"

"You are at University Hospital Limerick. You arrived here with Covid-19 in March and needed to be intubated as soon as you were admitted because your lungs were severely damaged. Your heart became overloaded, there were complications and you had a cardiac arrest followed by a coma."

"What do you mean, I was in a coma?"

"Yes, we had little hope of you coming back to life without severe side effects."

"How many days was I in a coma?"

"How many days? Well, 124 days to be exact."

"What!?"

"Yes, you were in a coma for four months."

"It can't be true!"

Suddenly, Olivia began to cry uncontrollably. She felt confused but remembered that her baby was stillborn. The baby she'd waited so long for and loved so much. Why was all this happening?

"Please, calm down. Everything is fine now. Your exams are all normal, which is amazing. We are delighted with your recovery."

"Where's my family? My phone? I need someone to come here."

"Take it easy. We can call your family. But first, we need to know your name."

"My name is..." She was going to say 'Catherine'. She remembered everything she had experienced. Had that been a dream? How could it be? It was too real to be a dream. What had happened? Catherine, Ian, the little baby… all dead. Fred, that monster, and his sister killing him... She had a lot inside her head. She felt her body soften and a cold sweat ran down her back.

Olivia had a sudden drop in blood pressure and was quickly treated by doctors. It was normal; she had been in a coma for a long time, in a hospital bed, and her body was still readjusting. Gradually she regained consciousness and the doctors asked her to go slowly. It was okay if she couldn't remember things as soon as she woke up. That was absolutely normal.

Who was she? The only name that came to mind was Catherine Crawford, but she knew that wasn't her name. Olivia paused for a long time and stared at the doctor. What was her name? She didn't remember, so she started crying again. The doctor approached her and calmed her down.

"Have a little patience. It's normal for you to be disoriented. Matt, get her some fresh water."

"Matt? Matt!"

When she heard that name, her memories came back and she knew exactly who she was.

"My name is Olivia. Olivia Walter Kalckmann. I'm Brazilian, from Alfredo Wagner, and I study at Mary Immaculate College."

The doctor looked at her and was very intrigued. He remembered months ago talking to the Director of the International Office at that college to give her some very sad news: one of her Brazilian students had died of Covid-19. He remembered that the burial had to take place on the same day and that no one from the deceased's family could attend.

"Are you sure?"

"Yes, now I can remember, my name is Olivia."

"Who can we contact?"

"Where are my belongings?"

"No, no, you arrived here with nothing. That's why we didn't know your name."

"Could you call the college and ask to speak with Seoidín, the Director of the International Office? I used to live in the student accommodation at Mary I, but I don't know the number there."

"Alright, I'll check it out. I'll be back soon and in the meantime, we'll do some more exams. Don't worry, everything is going to be okay."

The doctor reported the case to the hospital administration. It didn't take long for them to find the obituary details and to understand that a terrible mistake had been made: they had reported the death of the wrong person. Olivia was actually alive.

The hospital administration was concerned about this terrible misunderstanding. How could such a mistake have happened? They contacted the lawyers in the first instance, as only they would know how to proceed in this situation. A person presumed dead remains in a coma for four months, while everyone who knew her, most of them in another country, believed she was dead! This didn't look good for the hospital.

Later, the doctor returned saying he had spoken to the Director of the International Office and that she was coming to the hospital.

Olivia felt deeply weak and her body was very sore, as a result of having been lying down for the last four months. She didn't know how to define what she was feeling, didn't know how to behave. It all seemed so far from reality, it seemed to be part of a dream.

Olivia lost track of time. She couldn't tell how many hours or minutes passed before the director arrived at the hospital.

She heard her friend's voice from down the hall. Finally, something familiar.

The director came in and her inevitable reaction was to start crying. Olivia looked scared, somehow the presence of the director there, crying like that, brought meaning to the doctor's explanation.

"Olivia, my God, it's a dream to see you alive again."

"I didn't even know I had died."

"How are you feeling?"

"I'm so confused. Was I really here for four months? I can't believe it! What about my family? My boyfriend? Where are they?"

"This seems very surreal. I don't even know where to start."

"I just remember that an ambulance collected me at home, we had an accident on the way or we stopped to help someone, and then I remember some flashes here in the hospital, some confused dreams and nothing else."

"Olivia, there was a big mistake. They said you had died."

"How so?"

"That's it. It looks like there was a mix-up on your arrival because of that accident. They registered another person under your name and you were registered as 'Unknown Person' because they couldn't find your documents."

"But how?"

"I don't know, I don't know how this could have happened. This place was in chaos because of the Covid cases."

"What do you mean? My family thinks I'm dead?"

"Yes."

"My God, my grandmother!? Is she okay? She must have been really worried! We have to call her now!" Olivia said this as she tried to get up but soon got dizzy.

"Take it easy Olivia, take it easy. We'll clear everything up. I needed to come here first and confirm that you were alive."

"Where's my phone?"

"I have it."

"I need to talk to my mom, to Matt... does he think I'm dead too?"

"Yes, everyone. It was horrible, everyone suffered a lot."

Olivia cried as she listened to the story. She couldn't imagine how all of them had suffered because of her death."

"My family, Matt... no one came to see me?"

"No, because you supposedly died the first day you were hospitalised."

"No one saw that it wasn't me inside the coffin?"

"No, we couldn't even get close. The coffin was sealed and buried almost immediately. The girls and I followed it from afar."

"And the girls, are they okay?"

"Yes, they are all fine, they have all returned to Brazil."

"Please help me, I need to talk to my family."

"Yes, you can use my phone."

Olivia took her cell phone in her hand and stared at it.

"What?" asked Seoidin.

"Am I going to give my mother a heart attack? She thinks I'm dead."

"Yeah, I think we'd better calm down and think about how we're going to do this. How are you feeling?"

"I feel weak and dirty and lost."

"It's ok, everything will be fine. Let's call the nurse and see if you can take a shower. Do you want something different to eat? I can get you whatever you want."

"I just want to talk to the people I love, but without giving them a heart attack."

The director hugged Olivia who looked more scared than ever. After that, she called the nurse and together they did everything they could to make the patient more comfortable. She still couldn't stand up, it felt like all her muscles had tightened and she felt immense pain whenever she moved. According to the nurse, this was absolutely normal and with the help of a physical therapist, she would soon recover. The girl took a shower, sat in a wheelchair and had her hair brushed. She was sitting on the bed when she said to the director:

"I think I better call Bella first."

"Who is Bella?"

"Bella is my best friend. I think she'll react better than my mom and maybe she can help me tell my family without causing too much fuss. My family is pretty dramatic, I imagine it'll be crazy when they know I'm alive."

"Sure, great idea. Do you know her number?"

"Yes, I know it."

"Do you want to call her now?"

Olivia took a deep breath and nodded. Seoidín gave her the phone and she entered her friend's phone number. It was the same number that she had already called so many times and that would now allow her to contact her friend to give her news that she never imagined she would. The news of her "non-death", the news that she was alive.

Riiiiing... Riiiiing... Riiiiing...

On the third ring, Bella picked up. Olivia was already getting upset because her friend didn't always answer calls, but the strange number from Ireland had probably caught her attention.

"Hello."

"Hello, Bella?"

"Who's talking?"

"It's me, Ol..."

"What kind of bad joke is this?"

"It's not a joke, it's me."

"It can't be, please, what is going on?"

"Bella, listen, I'm alive. I was in a coma this whole time."

"Olivia, Olivia, is that really you?"

"Yes, it's me!"

The two friends burst into tears as Olivia explained to Bella what had happened, all the mess with the name change at the hospital, the fact that she had just come out of her coma, and didn't know how to tell her mother without killing her.

"I thought it was a prank call, Olivia."

"Yes, I noticed."

"Your mother is going to be very scared, but undoubtedly this is the best news any of us could get right now. I still can't believe this is true!"

"How is my grandma doing?"

"Your grandma is strong. She was visibly shaken, like everyone else, but she said you would always be with her and wouldn't want her to give up on life."

"But is she okay?"

"She is. I saw her last week."

"And my mother?"

"I can't even explain to you how your mother reacted. I've visited your house a few times to talk to her."

"How do I tell her?"

"I think I should go there and tell her in person before you call. I think it would be better, at least to have someone with her when she gets the news."

"Yes, that would be fantastic. Can you go over there now?"

"Yes, in a few minutes. In fact, I can't wait to tell everyone you're alive. You know when you wonder what would happen if you died?"

"Yes, we used to talk about that."

"I can tell you exactly what happened when you were presumed dead. Who cried the most, who went to your funeral. Yes, you had a symbolic burial here, even though there was no body. And you can check your Facebook. There are hundreds of messages there."

"I still haven't picked up my phone and haven't even talked to Matt. I'm scared."

"Why?"

"I'm afraid he's forgotten me."

"Never! He'll never forget you. That's what he wrote on your Facebook a few weeks after you were presumed dead."

"I need to see this."

"You'll have plenty of time to do that. I'm going to your house now. Get ready, I'll call you in a bit."

Bella hung up and headed for Olivia's family home. It was only a few minutes by car and Bella felt so happy to bring this news. Not even in her wildest dreams did she imagine that it would be possible, in this life, to see her great friend again.

When Bella had received the news of Olivia's death, she couldn't believe it. She wanted to go to Ireland, she wanted to fight everyone. How could they have let her die? They should have done more, fought harder. After that, she was never the same; she always seemed angry at everything and everyone, knowing it was a result of this whole situation. Covid-19 had affected everyone's lives in a variety of ways, and in her case, it had taken her best friend. Olivia and Bella were like sisters. There were no secrets between them; they could say anything to each other. They could argue and have different opinions on different subjects, but at the end of each discussion everything was fine and the commonalities always stood out. Even after Olivia's death, Bella still picked up the phone to call her friend whenever something new, a problem, or even a silly everyday thing happened. She thought she would never break that habit. Bella had always been an introverted person, who didn't like to expose herself, didn't like to show her weaknesses, her limitations, but she felt comfortable talking about anything with Olivia. She still hadn't gotten used to what it would be like to live without her friend, but now that wasn't an issue anymore. She wanted to tell everyone that Olivia was alive, but first, she needed to inform Olivia's mother, who until then believed her daughter was deceased.

It was undeniably exciting!

"Hi, how are you, Mrs. Kalckmann?"

"Hi, Bella! What a surprise! I'm all dishevelled, I was writing..."

"Are you writing now?"

"Yes, Olivia always said that I should be more organised with the things I write. I decided to put all my poetry in this notebook, I think she would like it."

"What if I told you that you could show her this notebook?"

"Yes, I believe that one day we'll meet again... I even think she can see everything."

"That's not what I mean. I have something very important to tell you regarding Olivia."

"What? What happened?"

"I think you'd better sit down."

"Tell me at once Bella, what happened?"

"I just got a call from Ireland and I just spoke to Olivia."

"What!?"

One of Olivia's brothers who was at home at that moment overheard the conversation and asked:

"Is Olivia alive?!"

"Yes. She's alive! She's been in a coma all these months! There was a mix-up at the hospital and they registered someone else with her name."

"No, Bella, you're kidding me. Don't do that."

"She's really alive!" confirmed Bella, already crying. Olivia's brother, hugging his mother, also began to cry.

"She's really alive, Mom! She's alive!"

Olivia's mother was in shock, but this time it was from joy. How many times had she prayed and asked to kiss and hug her daughter at least one more time? God was being very generous, allowing this to come true. More than that, He was giving her back her daughter.

She wanted to take the first plane to Ireland, bring her daughter home, and never let her go again. She wanted to keep her forever within her embrace.

"And how is she? Who's there with her?"

"She came out of her coma yesterday, as far as I know. She's still very weak, she can't even stand up. But Seoidín, the college's international director, is there. No need to worry, Olivia is in good hands."

"I'm going to go get my daughter! She won't be far from me any longer!"

"Unfortunately, we'll have to wait, Mrs. Kalckmann. No one from Brazil can enter Europe due to the pandemic restrictions."

"But there must be something we can do, right?"

"Yes, there must be and we'll find a solution. Soon we'll have Olivia here with us again. I can't believe this is true!" said Bella with tears in her eyes.

"I can't wait to hug my daughter again."

"Well, you can't hug her right now, but how about a video call?"

"Do you think so? My God, I don't know if I'm ready..."

Mother and daughter spent hours on the video call. Olivia was pale and several pounds lighter, had deep circles under her eyes but a genuine smile on her lips as she spoke to her family. As a neighbour had arrived at her house in Brazil while the two were on the phone, and it wouldn't be long before the whole town knew she was alive.

When they ended the call, Seoidín said that she would go home to get some things to spend the night at the hospital and that she would bring some of Olivia's belongings that she still had, such as her phone, computer, and some clothes.

Olivia couldn't wait to talk to Matt. She wanted to know how he was and if they could meet again. She wanted to tell him about the dream she'd had involving his ancestor, a dream that felt so real. Whenever she closed her eyes it was his face that she saw. Matt was the love of her life and she strongly believed that he had been her love for many lifetimes.

She fell asleep, as she still felt very weak. She woke up a few hours later when the director had already returned with her belongings. Olivia saw Seoidín sleeping on the couch. Seoidín also woke up when she realized that Olivia had awakened.

"That couch doesn't look very comfortable."

"Don't worry, it's comfortable enough."

"Thank you so much for doing all this for me."

"No problem, I'm so glad you're alive. It was horrible for all of us to lose you. The entire college was inconsolable. The president is coming to see you tomorrow."

"Is everyone doing okay?"

"Yes, it looks like we are overcoming the Coronavirus. Little by little places are reopening and most pubs are already working again. Things might get worse again in winter, but until then, we are relearning how to live. We are adapting to the 'new normal.'"

"So, has everything reopened?"

"Yes, most places are reopening, but with a lot of restrictions."

"What about Nancy's?" Olivia asked jokingly, knowing she couldn't go anywhere anytime soon.

"Soon it will be open again and soon you'll be well enough to go there too. Guinness on me!"

"Oh, I wish I could have a Guinness! In fact, I'd give my life for a very cold Coke right now. You know when you take the first sip and it's so refreshing that you tear up?"

"Let's fix that, I'll get you a Coke."

"No, there's no need."

"Olivia, you just said you'd give your life for a Coke. I'm not willing to see you lose your life again while you're here in Ireland. I'll bring you the Coke at a much lower cost. Here, I charged your phone. I know you're anxious to talk to Matt."

"Yes, I am. I can't wait."

"Then enjoy this moment. I'll be back in a few minutes."

The director handed Olivia the cell phone and left the room. Olivia thought her phone would crash when she finally connected it to the internet due to the number of notifications she received. Would she have received all these messages in the afterlife? She didn't think so, but she was flattered to see that a lot of people had texted her to express their longing feelings.

She saw dozens of messages from her mother, many from her brothers, and long audios from Bella, probably cursing her for abandoning her. Friends from Brazil, Ireland, and even Cristiano. But she didn't want to read or hear anything else, she just wanted to talk to Matt.

He had also sent messages saying that everything must be a nightmare and that it couldn't be true he had lost the love of his life. In another message, he said that nothing else made sense and that he was the most unhappy of human beings. Matt confessed that he no longer had a reason to live knowing that he would never be able to share his life with her again.

His last online activity was over three months ago. Olivia thought it was very strange, but she decided to try anyway. She just sent a "Hello" to see if he would see it, but the message was not even delivered. She needed to talk to Matt as soon as possible, her heart was overflowing with longing. She tried calling, but he didn't answer. She called until the connection was dropped and nothing happened.

The girl went to look for him on Facebook, Instagram and other social media platforms, but she couldn't find his profile on any of them, which made her worried.

The director came back and Olivia commented that she was finding it all very strange.

"Do you think something happened to him?"

"No, I don't think anything happened. He probably deleted his accounts."

"Yeah, maybe. He was never too interested in social media, he must have deleted it."

"I brought Cokes for both of us. Let's toast to your life. Seriously, Olivia, I'm really glad you're well and recovering."

Seoidín was a fantastic person. A powerful and respected woman who treated everyone with kindness and as an equal. It didn't matter that she held a prestigious position within the college. She had become a great friend to all the Brazilian students who had spent that year in Ireland. Everyone knew they could count on her for anything. Olivia could imagine how much her supposed death must have affected Seoidín. She knew that Seoidín felt responsible for all the international students, and losing one of them, even if not true, had certainly been very difficult. Olivia felt a little guilty that she had caused so much trouble for everyone.

"Again, thank you so much for everything and I'm sorry."

"You don't have to apologise Olivia. It wasn't your fault."

"But look at the suffering I've caused everyone. To you, to my family, to my friends."

"No, it was the hospital that caused that suffering when it made this big mistake."

"Yes, but I also understand. The hospital was in chaos, I remember how crowded it was when I arrived."

"Okay, but they should have made sure what happened before confirming. They shouldn't have assumed that you had died, knowing that there was an unidentified person who had arrived that same day, at the same time. It was an accident, but it was above all irresponsible."

Seoidín was right, but Olivia didn't want to think about it at that moment. She just wanted to talk to Matt, but it was already too late and maybe it was better to leave it for the next day.

Early the next day, a medical team came to Olivia's room and ran some tests. They wanted Olivia to start physical therapy, including getting up and walking around the hospital. They thought she would need to stay at least another week there so they could follow her recovery. It wasn't easy to get up, she couldn't stand up without help and she almost cried when she saw herself in the mirror. She felt like a shadow of her former self.

It would be a long recovery, with intense physical therapy and, above all, with a lot of patience because it could take a while for her to fully recover. However, the doctors were optimistic, as she didn't appear to have serious side effects, just difficulty in movement, which is normal in such cases.

Olivia could hardly believe she'd spent four months in a coma. Everything was scrambled in her head; it felt like she had just woken up from a long dream. A confusing dream that mixed reality with fiction. But she felt all the emotions from the dream very strongly. She spent hours lost in thought, trying to remember and piece together each part of the story.

Gradually, the news of her survival was spreading. Lots of people were calling and texting. Even Brazilian television was interested in covering the story that had gone viral on social media. But Olivia didn't want to talk to anyone. In fact, the only person she wanted to talk to was Matt. She had sent an email, but got no reply. She no longer knew what she could do.

Fabiana, her friend who was living in Ireland when Olivia went to the hospital, had now returned to Brazil. She was the one who had told Matt about Olivia's supposed death. In a phone call, the friend said:

"Olivia, he was devastated. We chatted a few times, but he seemed to have lost his will to live."

"What do you mean? What exactly did he say?"

"He said exactly that, that without you, life had no more meaning. Everyone was very shaken by your supposed death, but he was absolutely inconsolable."

"I can't talk to him. Do you think something bad might have happened?"

"I don't know. Don't you have his parents' number or his friend's?"

"No, I don't. I never needed to."

"What if I contact the college where he was studying? Usually, they require the 'next of kin' contact in the application form."

"That's a good idea. I'll try to get in touch or ask Seoidín to do it. I feel completely helpless."

"It doesn't feel like we live in a globalised world where everyone connects easily anymore."

"Yes, it's surreal! That's why I'm worried; something might have happened or maybe he doesn't want to talk to me anymore."

"Olivia, please don't be silly. First of all, to him, you're still presumed dead. I was the one who told him, remember? I saw how shaken he was, I just told you. If there was any chance he could talk to you again, I'm sure he wouldn't miss it. There must be another explanation."

"But his disappearance is very strange."

"Yes, but call the college. They should have additional contact details."

"Thank you for the tip, Fabiana. I'll do that later today."

After hanging up, she immediately tried to contact Matt's college. However, she couldn't reach them by phone, as the international office was probably not open yet. She then sent an email explaining the situation and asking for some information.

She hated waiting. Olivia always liked having all the answers right away. That was her personality. If she created something, she wanted to see the result immediately, she wanted to see things happen without having to wait for anything or anyone. In her current situation, she was forced to learn to wait, as she had no other choice.

She was waiting to recover, waiting to get in touch with her love, waiting to see her family again. She had already understood that there was no point in swimming against the tide; it would only cause unnecessary suffering. The only thing she could do was wait and follow the doctors' instructions to recover as quickly as possible.

Olivia had found out through the news that the pandemic in Brazil was out of control. The country had one of the highest numbers of infected people on the planet. The virus was spreading fast, and most of the population didn't seem to believe in the pandemic's catastrophic proportions. The president himself had called it just a "little flu."

Every day, an exorbitant number of Brazilians lost their lives, and even more contracted the disease. This was just what the data showed, as cases were underreported due to a lack of tests. At one stage of the pandemic, Brazil had half as many cases as the United States but had conducted 20 times fewer tests. The country seemed to be the worst place to be during the pandemic, closing the world's doors to Brazilians and making it difficult for Olivia's family to come to Ireland.

While European countries began to reopen borders and economic activities, Brazil was experiencing a health crisis due to Covid-19. When Olivia awoke from her coma, Brazil had been without a health minister for almost two months. Brazil seemed to be adrift, and Europe didn't want to risk a new wave by receiving visitors from Brazil, so the border was closed to Brazilians.

This decision directly prevented any member of Olivia's family from entering Ireland. Bella, however, had dual citizenship and could secure her entry via Luxembourg, where her ancestors had emigrated from over a century ago.

It was decided: Bella would come to Ireland to "rescue" her best friend. She only needed a few days to find a flight and make arrangements to stay in the country as long as necessary. Mary Immaculate College offered one of its student accommodations, but Seoidín insisted that Olivia and her friend stay with her. Seoidín's house was close to where Olivia would have physical therapy, in addition to being a more familiar and much cosier place. The director was happy to finally meet Bella and to be able to welcome them both.

A few more days passed, and Olivia was still unable to contact Matt. She had already done everything in her power to try to reach him. She had even looked up his name among the pandemic victims in her desperation for answers.

While Bella hadn't arrived yet, the director was by her side, trying to ease her anguish.

"Do you think something might have happened to Matt?"

"No, Olivia, don't worry, we'll find a solution. I'll call the international director at his college and explain the situation."

"Can you call now?"

"Yes, let's see if she has any information. Just a moment."

The director left for a moment to make the call. She returned a few moments later with some phone numbers and emails. College staff were also trying to contact him but had received no response. They had passed on his parents' email. Maybe she could email them instead. That seemed promising. Surely they could tell her where Matt was.

Olivia had never met her in-laws personally. The meeting had been planned, but everything had gotten out of hand. She was embarrassed to send the email, especially to explain the crazy story about her "mistaken death." She spent hours choosing the right words and felt her heart race when she finally hit send. She hoped they would respond soon and end her agony.

Olivia was packing to leave the hospital when she received a notification on her phone. She had received a new email.

Olivia,

I can't believe you're alive, but I can't say the same about my son. Matt is dead. Since he received the news of your death, he gave up on life. He started drinking and lost his life in a car accident.

Knowing that you are alive does not lessen our pain; it only increases it. You took our son's life. Please stay away from our family. I don't know what I'm capable of if one day I find you in front of me.

Please do not contact us again, please leave our family alone.

As she finished reading the email, Olivia collapsed onto the bed, sinking her head into the pillow. She froze, lost for words, not knowing whether to cry, scream, or remain still, waiting to wake up from this nightmare. This couldn't be true! Was Matt dead? How so? Were his parents mad at her? What kind of email was that?

Seeing Olivia's state, Seoidín asked what had happened.

"What's going on, Olivia? You're so pale, are you okay?"

Olivia was still trying to process those words and handed over her phone so Seoidín could read the email.

The director couldn't believe what she had just read either.

"Calm down, Olivia! My God, I don't know what to say!"

"He's dead. Matt is dead, Seoidín!" Olivia cried profusely.

"My God, what a tragedy! Calm down, please!"

Seoidín hugged her in an attempt to support her during this difficult time. But the truth was, she couldn't find words to comfort her friend. She couldn't believe it; she knew how much they loved each other. And worse, how could his parents write such an email, blaming their son's death on Olivia? It was incredibly cruel! She knew Olivia well enough to know it would take her a while to recover from this -from Matt's absence and the guilt over his death. Even though she wasn't at fault, she knew Olivia would be willing to take the blame for what happened.

How could Olivia give up all her dreams? How could she abandon the future she'd dreamed of experiencing alongside him? The marriage, the children... How could she live without hearing him tell stories? Without seeing him smile again, without feeling his soft and, at the same time, breath-taking kiss? She wouldn't be able to live in a world without him. Amid this suffering, she remembered, as if it were a recent memory, that she had been through this before. She knew exactly what she was feeling because she had felt the same when Ian died. Her feelings mirrored Catherine's when she received the news of Ian's death. Olivia felt a brutal, physical pain as if someone were ripping her heart out. She couldn't stop crying and felt like she didn't want to live anymore. Seeing her condition, the nurses gave her a powerful sedative, and she fell asleep.

"Olivia, Olivia, wake up! Today we're going home and Bella will be with us soon. Let's go!"

"I don't want to go anywhere."

"But you will. You need to calm down. I don't know what to say, but I won't let you give in to this pain. You are a brilliant woman, and many people love you. I won't let you forget that and lose the will to live. Come with me."

Olivia was too weak to argue. She wouldn't insist on staying or doing anything that would cause Seoidín more problems. She agreed to leave, but what she really wanted was to lie in a dark and empty room.

From the car, she could finally see Limerick again. Her heart was falling apart inside her chest; every corner brought back memories. The restaurant where they had their first date, the corner where they had one of their first kisses, the bus stop that took her to Matt's house, the sushi place they liked to go to, the place where they had heard the best traditional music, the best food...

The entire city was the backdrop of the great love Olivia had experienced, and now she still had memories of the dream she had had during her coma. The bridge where Ian had been killed, the place where Fred had chased Catherine, the house where she'd spent the first night with the Scotsman. The street that led to the house where the Crawford family had lived.

A lot was happening at once. She still needed more time to organise her thoughts and reflect on everything she'd dreamed about. One thing seemed clear: if her dream was related to another life, then her love with Matt was doomed to failure. In this life, as in the next, she had lost her great love. Her soul was destined to suffer—that was certain.

Upon arriving at Seoidín's house, she went straight to bed. Her only wish was to sleep and never have to wake up again as her life had become a nightmare. Sleeping was easy because they had given her some medicine at the hospital to help her feel more relaxed and calmer. Unfortunately, when she woke up, she would still have to deal with this terrible pain.

She slept the rest of that day and spent the next day in bed, lost in her thoughts, sometimes crying, sometimes sleeping, but constantly grieving Matt's death.

On the third day, she was awakened by someone speaking Portuguese. She opened the bedroom windows and let the sunlight, which finally reappeared in Limerick that day, into the room.

"What a great friend I have, huh?! First, she dies and leaves me alone in the world. Then she leaves me lost among people who don't speak Portuguese, knowing I only have the English we learned in our classes in Silva Jardim. What a great friend this Olivia is!"

"Must be what you deserve," Olivia teased, opening her eyes and smiling at Bella. Her face soon filled with tears.

Bella had arrived the night before, but since Olivia was sleeping, she thought it would be better to talk to her friend the next day. Seoidín was very worried about Olivia, who, since she had come back from the hospital, had been locked in her room, crying practically all the time. Bella knew how much her friend must be suffering, as she had never seen her love someone like that.

"Shh, I'm here. It's going to be okay."

"Nothing is going to be okay. He died, Bella. He died."

"He died, but you didn't. You have lived many years without him. You have a life, Olivia. Everyone in Brazil is waiting for you with open arms. Your life is not over."

"But how will I live without him?"

"As you always have."

"It's not that simple, Bella."

"I know, I know it's not. I can't even imagine what you're feeling. Seriously, I can't put myself in your shoes. I just want to tell you that one day this will pass, and you'll still have a lot of good things in your life."

"If only I had a child with him…"

"Olivia, have you forgotten that you spent four months in a coma? If you were pregnant, neither you nor the baby might have survived."

"Maybe that would be better."

"Wow, you're being really selfish."

"No, I'm not."

"Of course you are! I saw the suffering of your family and friends when you supposedly died. I wish you could have seen how your mother and grandmother took the news. I'm sure you would never say such a thing again. That's very selfish of you. Who has a chance like you did, Olivia? I was sure I'd never see you again, that I'd have to live the rest of my life without you. But maybe that reality would be better than hearing you say that."

"But how will I live now, Bella?"

"You'll be fine. Time will make you forget."

"Not even a lifetime would make me forget him."

"But time will make the memories less painful."

"Why did this damn virus come just when I found the love of my life?"

"My God, you came back from death more self-centred than when you left. Do you really think the pandemic happened because of you?"

"You're insufferable! But I know everything would be even more difficult without your company. Thank you for coming here for me."

"Not just for you, my friend. I also wanted to see the city that stole you from Brazil. What is so important about this place? I wanted to see it with my own eyes."

"Bella, I need you to be mature enough to hear what I have to say. But I know you so well that it feels like I'm already hearing you mock it."

"Oh, if you already know I'm going to mock you, then get ready, because I probably will."

"Seriously. I really believe what I'm about to tell you."

"Okay, Olivia. Tell me."

Seoidín peeked from the door and was happy to see Olivia talking to her friend. She'd been worried about Olivia, who hadn't spoken much since receiving the news of Matt's death. She knew that with her friend's arrival, things would change. She appeared at the door and, in Portuguese, offered tea. She had been studying the language for a while.

"Yes, please. Olivia wants to tell a story."

"That's good, Olivia. It would be good for you to eat something," said Seoidín.

"It's fine. You also need to promise me that you won't laugh at the story I'm about to tell, as I truly believe it."

"You have my word. I'll get the tea, and then you can start."

When Seoidín returned from the kitchen with tea and toast, they sat on the bed to listen to Olivia's story.

"Well, I'll start. First, I wanted to tell Seoidín that since I first set foot in Limerick, I knew I had to come back because I felt a strong connection with the city and that, in a way, part of my history had to be written here."

"Yes, you wrote that in a blog post, right?"

"Yes, I did."

"Yes, she did. It almost drove me crazy trying to figure out what that connection was," Bella added.

"Have you finally figured it out?" asked Seoidín.

"And what is it? Enough with the mystery, Olivia, please," Bella said.

"Calm down, I'll tell you."

"Go ahead."

"I think I lived here in another life. I think I was Catherine Crawford."

When Olivia said that, her two friends stared at her, waiting for more information to make sense of her statement.

"Really? Is this what you want to tell us after all that drama? For God's sake, Olivia!" said Bella, getting up from the bed.

"I asked you to listen before doubting me. Please, Bella, sit down and listen."

"Okay, okay. But don't give me one of those soap opera stories. You're not Elizabeth Jhin or Ivani Ribeiro..."

"As far as I can remember, before I 'died,' you used to like soap operas too," Olivia said, looking at Bella. Then, turning to Seoidín, she explained that Elizabeth Jhin and Ivani Ribeiro are Brazilian soap opera writers.

"Do you remember when I told you how popular soap operas are in Brazil? The two are famous for their narratives about past lives. Although Bella is making fun of me, she also watched these soap operas and liked them."

"Okay, keep going, Olivia. I won't interrupt anymore."

"Well, it all started during my first visit to Limerick in 2018. I felt something when we visited the Cathedral and saw the graveyard. I took a picture, not knowing why, but I felt the need to. That place caught my attention. Later, when I was living here, I felt something whenever I passed by, and I always took a picture."

"Always from the same place?" asked Seoidín.

"Yes, always from the same place, but I only realised it when I checked the photos on my computer. The photos were identical, all taken from the same spot."

"Yes, I remember when you told me that. It gave me goosebumps," said Bella.

"What did you do?"

"Well, I went to the graveyard the next day and walked around to see if I would feel something supernatural. One grave caught my attention; it belonged to someone named Catherine Crawford. Her family was buried there. I did some research, but it was impossible to find anything about her. With Bella's help, I convinced myself it was just a coincidence."

"Didn't you go to the library?"

"No, not at first, because we were busy with college assignments. I didn't have time to look, and to be honest, I ended up forgetting about it for a while. For me, the matter was closed; I had convinced myself it wasn't a big deal."

"Until the Crawfords crossed her path again," said Bella.

"That's right. One weekend, I went out to take pictures of places that were important to The Cranberries and passed by a house where I felt that connection again. A man walking down the street told me it belonged to the Crawfords."

"Is it a house located in the medieval area of the city?" asked Seoidín.

"Yes, that house."

"Are you serious?"

"I am! But what happened there?"

"I was shocked when I found out the house belonged to this family, as I had memories of what it looked like inside. I even felt lightheaded and had to sit down and drink water."

"Yeah, you had a friend with you when that happened, right? I remember you telling me," said Bella.

"Yes, Marcos was with me. Unfortunately, I didn't get to talk to the man who gave us the information about the house for long. I wish I had more time to talk to him. But as we approached the winter holidays, I was able to go to the library to research Catherine. I found some information about the family. I discovered she was engaged to a Fred Stafford and was supposedly pregnant with his child. He was a very rich and influential man in the city. But that's all I found out."

"Supposedly pregnant with his child? What do you mean? Wasn't he the father? Hmm, maybe this is a Mexican soap opera."

"Stop, Bella. Let her continue," Seoidín said, surprising even Olivia.

"Thank you, Seoidín. Bella is a good person, I swear, even though she always finds a way to go against me," Olivia said, winking at Bella, who smiled back.

"I believe you because only a good person would leave their whole life in Brazil, cross the ocean, and be here with you at such a time."

"Yeah, I'm a great person, but we'll still have to talk about the flight ticket because now I'm broke," Bella said, throwing a pillow at Olivia.

"Continue, Olivia," Seoidín said.

"Yes, yes, I will. In fact, I was relieved that I didn't discover anything impressive. It was around this time that I met Matt," Olivia recalled, pausing as her eyes filled with tears.

Bella hugged her and urged her to continue.

"When I met him, it was like I'd been waiting for him my whole life. Like I already knew the taste of his kiss and my body was his before he even touched me." She sighed deeply, missing him infinitely, but looked at her friends and said:

"Okay, I'll summarise. This story was erased from my mind until we went to Scotland. There, on a visit to the Isle of Skye, where Matt's ancestors came from, we found the name of a certain Ian McLeod, who had lived in Limerick."

"Here in Limerick?" asked Seoidín.

"Yes, here in Limerick. We knew little about him because there weren't many records. But according to an old book, he died mysteriously in the River Shannon."

"What do you mean?"

"It's not known. It seems the family didn't find out until a while later when a Reverend named John told them he had been stabbed and shot."

"But was that his only connection to Limerick?"

"No. The most impressive thing is that we found an old newspaper note that read:"

"My beloved Ian Alexander McLeod

Eight months of missing the one who will always be my great love.

C.C.M."

"C.C.M? What does that mean?" asked Bella, feigning doubt, even though she already knew the story.

"My God! Catherine Crawford McLeod?" concluded Seoidín.

"Exactly!"

"My goodness, now I'm the one who's got goosebumps! Once again this woman's name crosses your path, Olivia," said Seoidín.

"Yes, she seemed to be chasing me."

"But what about Reverend John? You didn't mention his name before. Did you find anything else? Did you have time to research?" asked Bella.

"That's where the story gets even more unbelievable."

"Even more? As if what you've already told us wasn't enough," snapped Bella.

"Oh God, you're just like Emily."

"Who's that?"

"Catherine's sister."

"How do you know?"

"I'll tell you everything. When I was in a coma, I started having these weird dreams where Matt was Matt, but not exactly. You, Bella, were you, but also someone else. At first, things were strange and confusing, but then everything started to make sense. I was Catherine, engaged to Fred, who was Jean, that crazy French guy I met. You, Bella, were Emily, my sister. Even you, Seoidín, were in the dream. You worked in our house; we knew each other since we were little. You were one of my best friends and always helped and defended me."

"Keep going," said Seoidín, while Bella listened in silence.

"Well... Catherine was engaged to Fred Stafford, a very powerful man in the city. She didn't love him, but he was undoubtedly a great catch. She didn't love him because she didn't know what it was to love someone. But one day, in the cathedral, she met Ian McLeod, a Scotsman who had just arrived in the city. It was love at first sight, just like with Matt and me."

"But her fiancé was very powerful, right?" asked Bella, engrossed in the story.

"Yes, he was powerful and unscrupulous."

"So this story ended up badly," concluded Seoidín.

"Yes, Fred killed Ian, and his body fell into the river but was never found."

"What do you mean? Why did he kill the Scotsman?"

"Catherine and Ian were more and more in love; it was an uncontrollable love. I experienced it all in the dream, and it felt very real. I truly feel that I was Catherine and lived her life in the past. I experienced her first kiss, her first night with Ian..."

"This all happened while you were in a coma? Not bad, huh, Olivia?" joked Bella, trying to break the tension.

"Yes, but I also felt the pain when her father hit her and every time Fred beat her. I felt her pain when her lover died and when she found out her son had died. I died with her when she lost her life after losing so much blood that day."

"Please, I'm bursting with curiosity. Tell me how it all happened," begged Seoidín.

"Okay, moving on. They fell in love and lived that love with the support of Emily and Reverend John, who believed in their love. John was Joseph, who works at Courtbrack, Seoidín. Bella, you don't know him, but just for context. Catherine and Ian were very happy and sharing a great love, but of course, Fred found out. At first, he suspected the Scotsman's involvement was with Emily, the sister-in-law, and then he was sure it was with Catherine, his fiancée. After he figured it out, he tried to end the romance. He paid some men to beat Ian up and they almost killed him. But he couldn't kill him or end their love. On the contrary, it strengthened their love and made them decide to run away together."

"What about her father?"

"Her father was practically broke and owed Fred's family a lot of money. He was a good man, but because of this debt, he was acting oddly."

"And her mother, did she have her support?" asked Seoidín.

"Her mother died when she was little, but her father had been very good since then."

"So, she couldn't tell her father she was in love with Ian?" asked Bella.

"It was another time... I believe the occurrences of this dream took place around 1867. Society and values were different. Calling off an engagement was frowned upon, especially with a man as powerful as Fred. You, I mean Emily, would never have found a good husband. The entire family name would have been ruined, especially because she would be turning him down for a Scotsman who apparently didn't have a penny."

"Yes, Limerick society at that time was very conservative and had its values were closely linked to religion," added Seoidín.

"Exactly. So, the only way out was to run away and live out their love somewhere else. But somehow Fred found out about the plan. When they were crossing Thomond Bridge, he was there, armed, waiting for them. Fred shot Ian, and they started fighting on the bridge, but Fred stabbed him. Ian fell into the river. I tried..."

"Catherine tried. Don't confuse things, Olivia," said Bella.

"Yes, Catherine tried to save him, but the Shannon was too full, and Fred was chasing her. He shot her in the back, and she fell in front of the Reverend. The place is the same spot where I used to take all those pictures."

"Did the shot leave a scar like this?" Bella asked, placing her finger where she knew Olivia had a scar.

"Yeah, like this one. That's exactly where the shot went, but I wasn't born with that scar, you know. This scar is from surgery, so unfortunately it's not evidence," Olivia said to Bella, who laughed at the joke.

"Keep going, please. If you write a soap opera about this, I'll definitely want to watch it."

Olivia smiled at Seoidín and continued:

"The bullet entered Catherine's back and exited through her chest. She was between life and death for several days. Her father disowned her and her sister."

"He was really a good man," scoffed Bella.

"And Fred showed up to visit her, even though the Reverend and sister were sure he was responsible for the shooting."

"He was trying to lessen the suspicions that might fall on him. He was certainly a cold-blooded man," said Seoidín.

"Exactly. I believe he thought his fiancée was dead, and that's why he went there. But when he saw she was alive, he vanished for a long time, knowing Catherine was a witness to his crimes."

"And he didn't come back or send someone to finish the job?" Bella asked.

"The Reverend was afraid this might happen and asked the girls' father for help. Although he no longer wanted his daughters in his house, he sent a man to the Reverend's house to protect them. When Catherine finally recovered, she found out she was pregnant."

"What do you mean? Pregnant? Did they have time to do that before Ian was killed?" Bella asked again.

"Actually, they had spent a night together a few days before. It was in a house near the port, where Dolans is today, Seoidín. Do you know it?"

"Yes, of course. I'm completely fascinated by your story, Olivia. Go on."

So, they had a night of love there, and Catherine got pregnant. She was about two months along when she found out.

"Pregnant and single in an extremely religious society. It looks like things are going to get even worse for you—I mean, for Catherine," scoffed

Bella.

"Yes. But she wasn't single; the Reverend had married them before they ran away that night. It was a beautiful ceremony, even the Reverend was moved."

"But anyway, I presume her father didn't take it well," said Seoidín.

"No. It was undoubtedly another big problem. Her father had almost accepted her back, but when he found out about the pregnancy, he made it clear he would never accept his pregnant daughter. The Reverend was also suffering the consequences of supporting Catherine and Ian's romance. Fred, with all his power, convinced or promised the Bishop something to get him to remove John from town. The girls could no longer stay with the Reverend, and Catherine feared she would be separated from her baby."

"My God! And what did they do?" asked Seoidín.

"Oddly enough, their father came up with a solution. Fred agreed to marry her even though she was pregnant with someone else's child."

"Crazy, this man was a maniac!" said Bella.

"Absolutely! A sadist, a bastard…" agreed Olivia.

"But Catherine didn't accept this solution, right? He was the one who killed Ian and tried to kill her. There's no way she would have accepted…" Seoidín said.

"She accepted! My God, I remember the engagement picture you found when you were researching her. Oh no, don't tell me she accepted!"

"Unfortunately, she accepted, Bella."

"No!"

"How so?"

"Catherine didn't want to be separated from her child and Fred promised he would raise the baby as his own. Besides, she wanted to repay the Reverend for everything he had done, so she set one more condition for the marriage to take place: the Reverend should remain with his congregation. Fred agreed to everything, and within a few days, they were married."

"I can't believe she did that. Did he keep his word?" asked Seoidín.

"In a way, yes. But he was extremely cruel and abusive. He felt like he owned her body. He beat her every night, even as the pregnancy progressed. She suffered a lot. Fred was a scoundrel; he treated her very badly at home but wanted to show they were a perfect couple in public."

"Wow, but it's not much different from what we see nowadays. Sometimes people are living in hell at home but show society they are living in paradise," said Bella.

"Exactly. If they were living in the present time, he'd probably be that guy who posts photos declaring his love for his wife on Instagram and then beats her to death."

"So, he beat her even though she was pregnant?" asked Seoidín.

"Yes. And Catherine began to suspect that Fred would do the same to the baby. So, with the help of Emily and her brother-in-law..."

"Hold on, hold on. Does Emily have a husband? Who is he? Please tell me he's someone I know and he's handsome," said Bella, making Olivia and Seoidín laugh.

"He was beautiful. He was the doctor who treated Catherine. Emily and he started dating, and it was his idea that as soon as the baby was born, they would fake the newborn's death and get him out of Limerick, raising him in another location."

"But who was he? Do we know him?"

"No. But at least he was handsome and a good man, I can assure you," joked Olivia.

"Go on, please. Did they manage to get the baby out of town? What happened?" questioned Seoidín, eager to know the end of the story.

"I'll tell you, but first... Do you remember the piece of newspaper Matt and I found in Scotland that had been written by Catherine?"

"Yes, with her initials," they said at the same time.

"That's right. It all happened because of that message. Catherine wanted to have a place to mourn Ian's death, so eight months after her lover's death, she decided to bury a ring he had given her."

"What ring was that?"

"A Claddagh ring."

"Oh, let me get this straight. A ring exactly like the one you gave Matt when he left?"

"Yes, Bella, that ring. As you may remember, I was very touched when I saw this ring for the first time. I felt it meant a lot to me, but I didn't understand why."

"That ring is very common around here."

"Yes, Seoidín, it's quite common. But I can't describe what I felt when I saw the Claddagh ring for the first time. It was as if it already had some meaning for me."

"Alright, Olivia, continue. I'll make my observations later."

"I can imagine what kind of observations, Bella, but it's fine. She buried the Claddagh ring and a letter to him, reaffirming all her love. She placed a stone with his initials on it on the ground above them and published that note in the newspaper. It turned out Fred was very smart. He saw the note and noticed that the initials were his wife's. When he got home, he asked her was about it. I don't know if she would have denied it, but she didn't even have time for that. He started hitting her in a way never seen before. The employees had to interfere so he wouldn't kill her and she ended up going into labour."

"That man was a monster," Bella said.

"He was. He was a horrible person and he definitely had a lot of psychological problems, probably a psychopath."

"Exactly like your Frenchman."

"Yeah, quite similar. He was sneaky, two-faced, deranged, and very violent. Maybe if Jean had as much money as Fred had, he would have turned out to be even worse."

"But what happened? Did she have the child?"

"Emily and Geoffrey arrived just in time to help. The Reverend was also called and the three of them were in the room when the baby was finally born. But unfortunately, he was stillborn. He was a beautiful baby, red-haired like his father," said Olivia, crying.

"How sad! And what did Catherine do?"

"She was very weak, Seoidín, but it was certainly the biggest pain in her life. I think the pain of losing a child is the worst pain a person can feel. Nothing compares," lamented Olivia, getting lost in her thoughts.

"But that's not your perspective, right? After all, you've never had a child," Bella said to reinforce the idea that she wasn't Catherine.

"I may not have had a child in this life, but I felt what Catherine felt."

"Calm down. Finish the story. We'll discuss this later."

"It's okay, Seoidín. Catherine died minutes after her son was stillborn. I think she had a haemorrhage. She lost a lot of blood and it was impossible to keep her alive."

"What about that unscrupulous man?"

"You killed him. I mean, Emily did."

"What do you mean? How did she kill him?" asked Seoidín.

"When Catherine died, they were all in the room. Fred came in mockingly, asking for the 'bastard baby.' Emily knew that Fred was the reason why her sister had gone into labour and died. She didn't think twice: she took her husband's scalpel and cut Fred's jugular."

"My God, what do you mean?" Seoidín asked in disbelief.

"She acted on impulse and when she realised it, she was sitting in the pool of blood spilling from her brother-in-law's neck."

"And what did they do? Were they arrested?"

"No. With the Reverend's help, they were able to get the servants out of the house, remove Fred's body, and throw him into the Shannon."

"My God! That's crazy!" "Did the Reverend help?"

"Well, he was already involved up to his neck in this story. If he didn't help, Emily would have been arrested for the murder of her brother-in-law."

"And they never found out about what happened?" asked Seoidin.

"I don't know. I woke up from the coma at that point."

"I've never heard anything about it. But we can certainly look it up. If he was that powerful, there must be some record of his death."

"Yes, there must be, but I didn't find anything when I did my research in the library. Maybe I didn't dig deep enough."

"Or maybe because it never happened," Bella said.

"It never happened? Of course, it did happen."

"No, Olivia. It was just a dream."

"I know it wasn't a dream. It was too real to have only been a dream."

"Can't you see all the evidence that it was just a dream? I was your sister, Fred had all the characteristics of that lunatic, Seoidín was your childhood friend, and the man who worked where you lived was the Reverend. Even the ring is the one that meant so much to you and to Matt."

"No. All of this I see as evidence that yes, I had experienced all that in another life."

"It's fantasy, Olivia. You didn't experience it. You know you dreamed it."

"I lived it, Bella. I lived it."

"What do you think, Seoidín?"

"Well, it's definitely an impressive story and you can tell it with immense detail. And there's some irrefutable evidence, like the photos, the tombs, the house, the newspaper itself. All this actually happened and proves that Catherine Crawford really existed."

"Yes, I'm not saying she didn't exist. This is all very impressive, but I'm just saying that Olivia, even in a coma, didn't give her writer's brain a rest and merged these elements of real life with fantasy. It was a dream, folks. It's obvious."

"Could she create such a story, in such rich detail, in a coma?" asked Seoidín.

"We're talking about the person who creates complex stories to distract herself before going to sleep and calls it 'a parallel life.' Isn't that right, Olivia?"

"One thing has nothing to do with the other. Yes, I could have created this whole story inside my head. But I know what I felt, I know what I experienced."

"But where are you going with this?"

"I don't want to get anywhere. I just wanted to share this with you and say that now I understand my connection with this city. Catherine was extremely passionate about Limerick. She knew a lot about the history here, she was a researcher, and she had loads of notebooks with records. Records about the Celts, records about the Vikings, about the entire history of the city."

"Exactly like you do in Alfredo Wagner?"

"Yeah, that's right Bella. Just like me."

"More proof that it's fantasy."

"More proof that my soul remains the same."

"Olivia, you're very stubborn, you've got it in your head and I know it's going to be hard for me to change your mind. But you have to be rational, this was just a dream."

"I don't know much about it, about past lives. But I don't think Olivia could be so wrong. What if she really had a paranormal experience through this dream?" asked Seoidin.

"I believe I had to come to Limerick and find Matt here. What are the chances, girls? I was living in a town in the middle of nowhere in Brazil, just like Matt in Canada, and we met in Limerick, another small city, not Dublin, the capital. Our souls had to meet. That meeting was predestined and it was destined to be here."

"My God. Now you're like Dinah and Otávio from the soap opera 'A Viagem'? What's the soundtrack? 'Linger'? By the way, was Dolores in your dream too? Who was she?"

"Actually she was, she was Margaret, another sister of Catherine."

"See, another piece of evidence," Bella said, mocking her friend.

"Yeah, another piece of evidence. I was, I don't know, seven years old and I heard her voice on TV and I was completely fascinated because it was so familiar. That was the first time I heard about Limerick. It was my first connection with the city."

"Oh, you sound like you're the only one who liked her voice. She had millions of fans around the world. It wasn't just you who liked her."

"Bella, Bella… And I'm the stubborn one."

"I'm trying to be rational. I know you. I don't want you to suffer because of your life and all the misfortunes that happened in Catherine's life. You can't do this to yourself."

"As if I needed even more tragedy in my life. I lost the man I loved. Twice."

"But you're still alive. You can't give up on your life. And I don't think you created all this inside your head. I'm going to look into Fred and Catherine and maybe we'll find some more evidence. I really believe in your story."

"Okay, Seoidín. But what if that's true, what changes? Olivia had a past life; so what? It doesn't change anything."

"It may not change anything, but I know that the love I felt and still feel for Matt was stronger than only one life can bear. Maybe our souls will meet again in another life…" Olivia said this and started crying again.

"Well, Olivia, if believing this is going to make you feel any better, you know I'll support you. I'll support you today and always. But I guess that's just a fantasy."

"Fantasy or not, Bella, I think it was good for Olivia to tell us this story. It was great to see her talking. It was like having the Olivia from before her coma again. I was happy to have this reunion. As I told you, I'll research more about all these characters."

"Speaking of 'characters,' why don't you write this story, Olivia? Put everything you experienced in the dream on paper."

"I don't think I can write. In fact, it feels like I'll never feel like writing again, Bella."

"No, that's impossible, there is no Olivia without writing."

"Yeah, maybe Olivia doesn't exist anymore."

"Stop it! I don't want to hear this conversation anymore. By the way, I think you should get up, take a shower, and get ready so we can go for a walk with Bella around town. She has to take the opportunity to get to know your Limerick, our Limerick."

"I don't know if it's a good idea. I still feel very weak."

"Well, it will be. Even if it's only for a few minutes. Do you think I came here just to pick you up? I came to sightsee too. I need a holiday, I need a little peace in a place where the virus is more controlled than in Brazil. You can get up. I don't want to hear any excuses," said Bella, pulling the covers off her friend.

Because of everything Olivia had told her about the story between Matt and her, it was impossible for Bella not to be annoyed as well. It all seemed so unfair! But she would not accept seeing her friend give in to suffering and would do everything to prevent that from happening. Because of this, she was adamantly against the theory that the dream could have really been another life.

She knew Olivia and knew that her friend would suffer for this and for all the past lives she had supposedly lived. This was Olivia, the person who felt everything so intensely. She gave of herself to others and was great company not only to share the joys of life but also the sorrows. Olivia wouldn't have the strength now to grieve for Catherine's losses as well as her own.

Leaving the room, Bella spoke to Seoidín.

"You must think I'm the worst friend in the world, right?"

"Not at all. You're here for your friend; few friends would do that, and I understand your point too."

"The dream is certainly very impressive, but I don't believe in past lives."

"I also don't know if I believe in this whole theory, but I can't deny that I was very impressed with Olivia's story. I want to research Catherine, who knows, maybe I can find out something."

"Yes, I think it's worth a try. Maybe you don't know Olivia that well. She's one of the most creative people I know, it wouldn't surprise me at all if she created this whole story, full of details, while she was sleeping."

"Let's see. But go get dressed; I want to take you to some places. I think you're going to love Limerick."

The three went for a walk. Nothing too exhausting, as Olivia was not yet ready for physical exertion and was still using a wheelchair because she got tired very easily. Despite all the sadness she felt, she was happy to have her best friend in this city. As they drove through Limerick, they passed Mary Immaculate College and headed to Courtbrack, where Olivia had lived for nearly a year. When they spotted Joseph, the manager, he looked happy to see Olivia recovered.

They talked a lot, and it seemed Olivia liked him even more now, as he reminded her of Reverend John, the man who had been so good to Catherine and Ian. Afterwards, Seoidín and Joseph started talking about some college issues, and the two friends took the opportunity to walk around the garden, with Olivia showing her friend the window of the room where she had lived.

Leaving the garden, Bella asked:

"Remember when you said that living here with a bunch of people you didn't know was like being in an edition of Big Brother Brazil? Well, if that was Big Brother, it seems you're the champion because you're still here."

"If I'm the champion, I want my one and a half million!"

"Maybe the prize is on its way."

"Oh yes?"

"You know you're going to get compensation from the hospital for all this mess they've caused in your life, right?"

"I'm not thinking about it, it won't make a difference."

"Oh, I'm sure you'll see it makes a difference when you see how much they're charging you. Or do you think being in a coma for four months is cheap?"

"How so?"

"You don't have to worry about that; you already have a lawyer taking care of everything. But the hospital is charging you an absurd amount, and you're suing for various damages. If Matt's parents are right and your death indirectly caused his death, it is the hospital's fault."

"That is so unfair. They took such good care of me."

"They did what they had to do. I agree they were very nice, but what about all the suffering they caused because of this mistake?"

Olivia stared at the horizon. She knew that Bella was right, but it was very strange to think about how a mistake, an isolated event, could have changed her life and so many other people's lives so much. It was only fair that they should face the consequences, but she wasn't happy about it either, as no amount of money would change the fact that her supposed death had contributed to Matt's death.

It started to rain, and the two went to the car. It didn't take long, and Seoidín met them there.

"Welcome to Limerick!" Seoidín said, referring to the rain.

"Welcome Bella, as I already told you, the only certainty we have here is that it will rain."

"You'd be surprised; during the time you were dead—I mean, in a coma—we had three months of sunshine. Real sun, blue skies, heat. Beautiful days."

"That's not true. I'll never believe it."

"It's true, three months with almost no rain."

"Oh, so this must be personal. All this rain must be my fault."

Bella, who was sitting in the back seat, put her hands on Olivia's head and started messing her hair, saying:

"Wow, this girl is very important. There was a pandemic because of her and the rain in Ireland is also because of her. Is she or isn't she a supreme being?"

Seoidín laughed and said:

"Then let's take this supreme being downtown for coffee. Are you hungry, Bella?"

"Yes, let's go."

They headed downtown. At the café, they talked about the places they would have to take Bella, and Olivia shared her travel experiences. She told them about when she was at the Cliffs of Moher with some friends, and they were almost blown away by the wind. She showed some videos, and Bella said that after watching them she was almost losing the desire to visit the place. But the two friends also showed lovely pictures of the cliffs on sunny days.

As they were leaving the café, Olivia bumped into Jean.

"Olivia?"

"Jean? What are you doing here?"

"I live here, remember?"

"No, I mean, are you back?"

"Yes, it's been a few months now. Glad to hear you're alive."

"Who told you?"

"Olivia, did you forget that I follow you on social media?"

"It's hard to forget, right, Jean!?" Olivia hated him even more now. She hadn't forgotten everything he'd done to her on social media, let alone what he'd done with her short story in the contest. Now all of this was even worse, as she added everything Fred had done to Catherine. She couldn't look at his face. She wanted to slap him. At that moment, Bella and Seoidín came out of the café.

When Jean saw Bella, he was startled. Suddenly he got serious and stared at her. He shook his head as if taking a sip of something he didn't like.

"Hello," Bella said, before giving the girls time to alert her about who he was.

"Hello, great to see you again Olivia. We'll certainly see each other a lot around here. Maybe we can meet for coffee some day. What do you think? I think we have a lot to talk about."

"I don't think we have anything to talk about, Jean. Bye."

Olivia turned her back and strode down the sidewalk, followed by her friends.

"Jean? Jean? Is that the manic Frenchman?"

"Yes, that's him," Seoidín said.

"What is he doing here? I had no idea he was back! Since when has he been in Limerick?"

"I don't know. It's been a while since I last saw him."

"His presence here worries me."

"Wow, I can't explain what I felt when I looked at him. I was disgusted by that guy."

"Don't forget that you killed him in a past life, Bella."

"You mean in your dream, right, Olivia?"

"Yeah, yeah, whatever you prefer. But seriously, I don't like knowing he's around."

"I think it shouldn't be a problem. It's been a long time since that all happened. You said he was having a crisis, right? He must have recovered and returned," said Seoidín.

"I hope he doesn't find out where I am. The last thing I want right now is to have to deal with him, especially with everything Fred did to Catherine so vividly in my memory."

"Don't worry. I'm sure he won't do anything."

They spent the next few days showing Bella around parts of Ireland. They didn't have much time left as the date of their return to Brazil was approaching. Olivia felt a mixture of sensations.

One day Seoidín came home with good news: she had managed to find out some things about Catherine.

"Well, I found some documents with details about Catherine. Since the day you told me about your dream, I've been doing some research, talking to some historians, some people I know who could give us some clues about the story. It's exactly as you said. She was the daughter of Eugene Crawford, married Fred Stafford, and died in childbirth. By all accounts, giving birth to Fred's legitimate son."

"And what happened to Fred?" Bella asked, visibly excited about the story.

"Well, there is no formal record of his death, only that he disappeared after losing his wife and child in childbirth. Apparently, some people believed he went crazy and couldn't bear the pain of losing his family in such a tragic way."

"Yeah, but we know it wasn't like that. He was to blame for everything bad that happened in Catherine's life and it was Emily who killed him."

"Speaking of which, what happened to Emily?" asked Bella.

"Wow, you're actually quite interested in what happened to Emily, aren't you Bella?"

"Of course, I identified with the character."

"Emily moved with Geoffrey to Amsterdam."

"Is that all you have on her?"

"Not really. I have something else to tell you."

"Then tell me, Seoidín."

"Be patient, Bella, I'll tell you. Well, I know a lot of people in Limerick, because my family always lived here, my grandparents... everyone. We know a lot of people and it wasn't difficult to find out who the current owners of the house are and get in touch with them."

"What do you mean? Catherine's parents' house?" asked Olivia.

"Yes. Do you want to go there?"

"Of course she does! When can we go?" replied Bella.

"Olivia, do you want to go?"

Olivia took a deep breath. She knew it would be quite difficult to go to that place, but she still wanted to go. After all, she also wanted to see how real her dream had been or if it was just a daydream she had while in a coma. That's what Bella told her it was all the time.

"I do. When can we go?" Olivia finally answered.

"If you want, we can go there tomorrow. I just need to call my friend and ask for the key. The house has been unoccupied for a long time and she told me that there is still a lot of stuff there that belonged to Eugene's family. After he died and Emily went to Holland, one of their brothers lived in the house for a while."

"And who owns the house now?"

"It's been a few years since the house was donated to the city. The idea was to set up a museum, but it never got off the ground. They have some projects in mind for the place, but for now, nothing has been done."

"Great! We'll go there tomorrow."

Olivia spent the night anxious. She didn't know how she was going to behave being in the place that she knew meant so much to Catherine once again. She remembered what she felt the first time she was in front of it. She even thought she knew what she would find when she opened the door. Was all this real? Would the house be exactly the way she remembered it in her dream? She wanted to believe so. Somehow she held on to the story she lived through while in a coma. She clung to the idea of having found her soulmate again and that, although they were not happy in this life, they would have other chances, possibly in other incarnations. Thinking about this brought a little comfort to her heart.

Olivia and Bella had been up since early in the morning. Olivia could see that her friend was as excited as she was about visiting the Crawfords' old home. She knew Bella very well, knew that she loved these kinds of stories and that she was dying to find out if this could be true or not. Olivia didn't know what would make Bella happier: proof that all of this could actually be true, or the certainty that her friend was wrong and that it had all been in her imagination. If that were the case, she knew that Bella would always bring the story up in a tone of, "Ah, Olivia in her past life." She loved her friend very much and even though Bella was always picking on her, she knew she did it to defend and protect her. Just as Emily had always done for Catherine.

They left for the house, and when they got there, the director's friend was waiting to hand them the key. They stood on the footpath, looking at the imposing building.

"So, this is the house..." said Bella.

"Exactly. This is where Catherine lived," Olivia replied.

"Olivia, I hope you don't get upset about what I'm going to tell you."

"If I got upset with what you say..." Olivia said laughing at her friend.

"So let's assume your dream is true, that everything you told us actually happened in the past, and that I was Emily. Why don't I remember anything? For example, when you were first here in Limerick, you felt like you belonged here. You identified with the city. I felt absolutely nothing when I arrived here. It was just another place I visited. Don't be offended; I loved Ireland and Limerick, but it's just a place I enjoyed visiting, nothing more."

"Bella, I don't know how to answer you. And yes, your question makes a lot of sense. I don't know why I felt that and you didn't, since we lived this whole story together, at least in my dream," completed Olivia, already lost in her thoughts. Bella's question was coherent and she didn't have an answer. It was at that moment of reflection that Seoidín began to speak.

"I also did some research on this. Like you, I had never delved into spiritualism, other lives or reincarnation. I was amazed when I saw how much material there is on this. I read some research from a professor at the University of Virginia who tries to reconcile this theme within science. He has been working in this line of research for many decades and collects stories like Olivia's."

"What do you mean, like Olivia's?"

"From people who, like Olivia, remember events from past lives in detail. I read a story of a three-year-old girl from India who told her father in detail about her past life, showing the house where she had lived, recognising her children, her brothers..."

"But were they still alive?" asked Olivia.

"From what I read, yes. But I've also read that the most common thing is that reincarnation happens many years later so that this doesn't happen, to find people from a past life in the present life."

"Well, actually, it would be a mess if everyone had the memory of what they were in past lives," said Bella.

"Yes. Besides, it could be very difficult for people to live knowing what they did in other incarnations. For example, how could someone who was a Nazi live today with the memories of all the atrocities he committed?

That's also why we shouldn't seek to know about past lives, because we might not like what we discover."

"I totally agree, Seoidín. For example, I didn't like knowing that I was a murderer in my past life. Nor did I feel anything when I saw that idiot, Jean, who was supposedly Fred."

"But I didn't go after those memories. They started to pop into my head from the first time I set foot in Limerick. And enough talk, let's go inside the house at once and find out if it was all my imagination or if there was something real in this whole story."

Seoidín handed the key to Olivia, who went ahead towards the door. She stopped, took a deep breath, and opened it, letting the sunlight in first. At first glance, she couldn't recognise anything. Everything was different from how she remembered it in the dream. There were some boxes cluttered right at the entrance. Olivia vividly remembered a painting hanging on the hallway wall, but it was no longer there—if it ever had been. It was Bella who boldly asked:

"So, is the house the way you remembered it?"

"No, it is quite different actually. I remember there was a painting on that wall," she said, pointing to the place.

Seoidín went to the wall and checked:

"Well, I would say there was a painting here one day. Look at those marks."

They approached and found that, in fact, there was once a painting hanging there.

"Oh, for God's sake, I have goosebumps. I don't know if I want to go in there."

"Bella, stop being ridiculous. Aren't you the one who's been telling me all the time that it was just my imagination? Be quiet and come with us."

When they entered the house Olivia noticed things were completely different from what she remembered, but somehow she felt it was the same house in the dream. She couldn't clearly identify the things she remembered, such as the large living room, the door that led to the kitchen, and the other door that led to where she believed Eugene's office was. Only the stairs leading to the bedrooms appeared to be the same. Olivia's breath accelerated.

"Is everything alright, Olivia?" asked Bella.

"Yes, it's okay. This is the house, but I have to confess that it's not exactly how I remember it in my dream." She then started describing: "That's the kitchen, there is Father's office, I mean Eugene's... upstairs are the bedrooms. Our bedroom was down here, through that door, come on."

Olivia took Bella by the hand and, accompanied by the director, they went to where the room was supposed to be. But it wasn't anything like what Olivia remembered.

"In my dream, this was our room. There was my bed and there was yours."

"You mean Catherine and Emily's bed."

"Yes, yes."

"But this doesn't look like a bedroom, Olivia. It's too big," Bella said, standing in the middle of the big room.

"Yeah, maybe you're wrong. Was it somewhere else?" asked Seoidín.

"No, it was here, I'm sure," Olivia said disappointed.

"Let's look for another place that might be the same," insisted the director. "Let's go to Eugene's office."

They went to the office but the room was empty and didn't look like an office. Olivia leaned against the door and stared into the empty room. Her face couldn't hide her disappointment; she was sure this was the same house she saw in her dream. How were things so different? Bella, seeing her friend's disappointment, started to walk around the house looking for something to get Olivia excited. She opened one of the doors and found what looked like an office, a library.

"Girls, come here, I think I found the office."

There were still some books there and Olivia quickly entered the room in order to find something that would remind her of the dream.

"Look, Eugene was a well-educated man. He had a lot of books and Catherine loved spending hours with them, reading and writing too."

"Is the office the way you remember it?" asked Seoidín.

"No, not really," Olivia said dejectedly.

They opened the window to get a better view. In the room, behind a table, there was a large bookcase, some armchairs, and a stain on the wall opposite the table, which suggested that there had also been a painting there. They were looking at the books and then the director called them.

"Look at this, Olivia."

The director had found an old notebook with many things written in it. Olivia took the notebook in her hands and said:

"This is one of Catherine's notebooks, see..." She turned to the front page and showed the name Catherine Crawford.

"She had a lot of notebooks like this, where she wrote about the history of Limerick, the Celts, and the Vikings."

"And is that the content of the notebook?" asked Bella.

"Do you think there are other notebooks here?" asked Olivia, heading towards the shelf where the director had taken that notebook.

"Apparently this is a diary or something like that."

"A diary? This is very interesting. Can we take it with us and then return it?"

"I think so, Olivia. I'll let my friend know."

"What is she saying?" asked Bella.

"I think it's from the time she got engaged to Fred. "

"Well, this notebook proves to us that you weren't Catherine," Bella concluded.

"What do you mean? It doesn't prove anything."

"Yes, look at her handwriting. It's beautiful, whereas yours looks like a child's who is just learning to write," said Bella to tease her friend.

"Oh, as if you have beautiful handwriting..."

"See this," said Seoidín, opening a book on Celtic tales and reading the dedication aloud:

"To my beloved daughter, Catherine, who never tires of learning more and more about her ancestors and making her father proud."

"Yes, I remember Eugene always bringing Catherine books. He used to travel all over the island and always brought presents for his daughters. The presents Catherine liked the most were these books."

"He seemed like a great father."

"He was, Bella, but he changed completely. It was in the office, but not exactly this one, that Catherine was beaten when her father thought she had lost her honour with Fred. He beat her so badly that she was in bed for days."

"What are you saying? You didn't tell us about this," said Seoidín.

"It was a horrible story. Fred turned Eugene against Emily, accusing her of dating Ian. Eugene took Emily into the office and Fred, like an animal, tried to rape Catherine."

"Rape?"

"Yes, Bella, he said it was about time to have sex with her."

"Gee, that man was disgusting."

"Catherine was a virgin. He didn't do it because one of the girls who worked in the house, and that was you, Seoidín, came in time to stop him. He beat the girl and when Eugene arrived, Fred said he had taken away his daughter's honour."

"So I was her in your dream?"

"Yes, you were her."

"What about Eugene? Did he let the man do that? And Catherine? Didn't she tell him that nothing had happened?" Bella asked in disbelief.

"In the religious and conservative society they lived in, she didn't even understand what had happened. He had tried to take her clothes off, put his hand under her skirt, but in fact, nothing had happened, but she couldn't tell."

"What do you mean she didn't know? She had to know," said Bella.

"Well, what I can say is that it was not uncommon for women to discover what sex was only on their wedding night. They didn't even know what men had between their legs," Seoidín clarified.

"Exactly. Catherine had no idea what that would be like... Things were very different. Sex was a big taboo, even more so for girls who were being raised by their fathers. They would never bring it up with them. So, when Fred said he had taken away her honour, she was horrified but believed him."

"And how did she find out?"

"Seoidín, in the other life, told her, Bella. She was suspicious because she didn't find any marks on her clothes. Marks of honour, the blood from the rupture of the hymen. Then she asked if Fred had put his 'gun' inside her."

"'Gun'? What do you mean, 'gun'?" said Bella, finding the expression funny.

"I don't know, I think it was the analogy the woman managed to draw. She was embarrassed to talk about it."

"And she got beaten up by her father, even though she didn't do anything?"

"Even worse... even if the intercourse had happened, she would have been raped and beaten for it," said Seoidín.

"Without a doubt, it was a more patriarchal society than it is today. And by then, Eugene no longer looked like this loving father who wrote sweet dedications to his daughters. He was about to go bankrupt and seemed to owe Fred his soul."

"To the devil, you mean, right? Because after everything you've told us, this Fred was nothing more than pure evil."

"I agree with you, Bella. What a terrible man."

"Yes, Seoidín, he was terrible. He seemed sick, sadistic; nowadays he would probably have some sort of diagnosis."

They went through the rooms and stayed a little longer in the house. Olivia didn't have many memories of the upper part, just small fragments mixed with other memories. This was definitely the house she'd dreamed about, but little was as she remembered.

Olivia thought it was good to have been there, but the visit didn't prove the dream had been real. She knew that Bella could be right, maybe it could all have been a figment of her imagination: a story that she had created using the information she had gleaned from those records of the past and mixing it with facts and people from real life. Maybe this whole past life story was really just soap opera stuff. Although Olivia rationally understood, it didn't keep her from being sad. She didn't want to give up this other life. She wished she could believe that her soul would still meet Matt's in the future. When they got home, she told her friends that she had a headache and was going to lie down for a while.

Both Seoidín and Bella knew she was very hopeful that the house would be the same, thus proving that the dream had been true. Seeing her sadness, they didn't say anything. Even Bella, who was just waiting for an opportunity to say Olivia was wrong, decided to shut up. It wasn't the time for that yet. Olivia had been sadder than they'd imagined.

Shortly after they returned, someone rang the doorbell. They were looking for Olivia. Seoidín went to the bedroom to call her.

"Olivia, a man who claims to be from a publishing house in Brazil wants to talk to you."

"From a publishing house? What is he doing here?"

"He said he wanted to talk to you about a book proposal that represents Continente Publishing."

"I don't think I want to talk to him, Seoidín."

"Oh, yes you do. You must talk to him, Olivia, please," said Bella, who was eavesdropping and came to see what it was all about.

"But I don't want to."

"Seoidín, Continente Publishing is simply the biggest publishing house in Brazil, and if they send someone here to talk to Olivia, she'll talk to him. She'll talk even if I have to drag her there."

"Stop it, Bella. I don't feel like talking to anyone."

"I don't mean to be nosy, but I think you should at least listen to what the man has to say. Then you can decide what to do."

"She will, Seoidín. It's decided."

"I will, but it's not because you decided, Bella. It's because Seoidín is right. It doesn't hurt to hear what he has to say."

"Fine. Come on. This could be the biggest opportunity of your life, Olivia. Tell me this coma didn't burn your neurons, please."

"Bella, please don't be so excited. We don't even know what he wants."

"Well, let's find out."

As soon as they got into the living room, they saw the man sitting on the couch. He was dressed in a business suit and grinned from ear to ear when he saw that Olivia had decided to talk to him.

"I am very happy to finally meet you. My name is Paulo Roberto Vasconcelos, and I represent Continente Publishing."

"Nice to meet you, Paulo. I'm Olivia, and these are my friends, Bella and Seoidín. How are things in Brazil?"

"I haven't come from Brazil, but as far as I know, things don't look good there. I work in London, and I flew to Ireland especially to meet you. Nobody from Brazil can enter Europe at the moment."

"And how did you find out I was here?"

"I did some detective work and managed to find the whereabouts of the most mentioned person on Brazilian social media in recent weeks."

Olivia was a little uncomfortable with the statement and decided that was enough. She wanted to get straight to the point.

"But Paulo, tell me, to what do I owe your visit?"

"We want to publish your story."

"What story?"

"The story of your coma. What it was like spending four months in a coma and waking up to a very different world from the one you left behind."

"But I don't know if I feel comfortable writing about it. I don't know if people would buy it, if people are interested in knowing about it."

"I can tell you that yes, people are interested. I'm sure you are receiving calls and emails from the press every day, wanting interviews and statements from you. I know that Globo Network and even European broadcasters are desperately after you."

"Well, so you also know that I'm not talking about this with anyone. I don't feel comfortable selling my personal story."

"But that's what you do for a living, isn't it? You sell stories."

"I'm a teacher."

"But you're also a writer. I read the manuscripts you sent us."

"Oh, you did? Up until now I wondered if they were lost or if they were so bad that they didn't deserve feedback from you," answered Olivia. She had sent all her books to Continente Publishing. She knew it was audacious, as this was the biggest publishing house in Brazil, probably the biggest in South America, but she wanted to try anyway. However, they had never responded to her emails.

"There's always time to make amends. Your books are really good. I know that you produced them independently, without a publisher, and that they were still a success. We would like to sign a contract with you that would guarantee new editions of your books published by us, with international release throughout South America, North America, and Europe."

"That would be great because Olivia has an unpublished book, and you can include it in the package," revealed Bella, and Olivia glared at her friend.

"Great, we're interested in whatever you write."

"But how can you be sure I would write a good book?"

"Anything you write will sell, Olivia."

"But I don't want to write just anything."

"But that's the way the industry works. Of course, good writers will always be good writers, but a story of the moment will likely sell far more than a book written by the best writer of all time. What sells is what's in fashion, what's in the media, and you're the next big thing. A young woman who spent four months in a coma and survived the coronavirus. When she woke up, she discovered that she had lost her great love."

"Wait a minute, do you want to use my pain to make money?"

"No, we just want to tell your story."

"I don't think we have anything else to talk about, Paulo."

"Olivia, I... I... I'm sorry. I didn't mean to offend you."

"Fine, but I have no interest in your proposal."

"But you haven't even finished listening to it."

"Excuse me," Olivia said, leaving Paulo Roberto with her friends. Bella told him:

"I'm sorry, but you have to understand that this whole story messed with her a lot. I've known her forever, and I've never seen her as involved with someone as she was with her boyfriend who died. Losing him was the worst part of everything that happened to her."

"But she shouldn't ignore this opportunity. It's the chance of a lifetime. Sorry to be corny, but this is literally an example of 'if life gives you lemons, make lemonade.'"

"I know, I know, but it's no use insisting now."

"Bella, your friend is very talented. I've read her books, and with the right publicity, they'll sell like hot cakes. Here, that's my contact. I'm staying in Limerick until the end of the day tomorrow, waiting for an answer. I hope it will be positive."

"I'll talk to her, but I can't guarantee you anything."

"This is her chance to become a well-known writer. Don't let her waste it."

The man left, and Bella and Seoidín didn't know what to do, although the two agreed that it was an excellent opportunity. Olivia had her whole life ahead of her and could have the life she always dreamed of if a publisher like Continente were willing to publish everything she wrote. Bella knew that this had always been her friend's dream: to live a quiet life and earn money by selling her books. That was always what she had wanted for the future.

Olivia never dreamed of having lots of money, but she always wanted a lot of people to read her books and get to know the characters she created.

"We need to talk to her."

"Don't you think that will make things worse? Maybe we should give her some time to think about it."

"No, let's go now. I know Olivia; she is probably regretting it already."

"Okay, but don't keep confronting her. I swear I'm afraid you two will fight at any moment. You argue a lot."

"Don't worry, we're just like that. But maybe it's good for you to talk to her; she listens to you. I know how grateful she is to you and how much she admires you."

"Then let's go."

The two entered the room but didn't find Olivia. The window was open.

"I can't believe it. Where is she? Did she go out the window?"

"Do you think so? Would she do that?"

"I can't believe it. My God!" Bella started looking all over the house for her friend, hoping she was there.

"She's not here. I think she has really left."

"Let's go after her. We can't leave her walking the streets alone. I don't know... something could happen. She's still pretty shaken up."

"I think she must have gone out to unwind. Nothing will happen, Bella."

"I think it's better if we go after her. I worry about her."

"Fine, I'll get a coat and we'll walk around the neighbourhood looking for her."

Olivia had gone out the window. She just wanted to get some fresh air and some time to think. She always enjoyed doing that, walking aimlessly, letting her thoughts fly freely. She was very confused; she needed some time alone even if it was to cry. She walked through O'Connell Street, with Georgian-era buildings witnessing her suffering and the tears she shed along the way. The fine drizzle that fell and the mask she wore disguised her crying, making it go unnoticed. She still couldn't believe what she was living through. It was hard to accept that she had lost her love, that she had been unconscious for four months, and that she had woken up in such a different world.

Borders were closed, and hugs weren't allowed. This damn virus had already made so many people suffer. She just wanted to sleep and wake up before this had all started, before everyone had lost control of their lives and found themselves at the mercy of a microscopic being that had changed everything in the world. She felt like she was about to have a panic attack; she was almost out of breath. She decided to go down near the River Shannon, sit on one of the benches and think and cry in peace.

It didn't take long for the Limerick Suicide Watch to show up. It was very common for people to take their lives by jumping into the deep, freezing waters of the Shannon. That's why every night a patrol, made up of volunteers, roamed the banks of the river to identify and help people who might be thinking about it.

Olivia had already talked to them a few times. She used to watch the sunset in the park near the Castle, the same place where, in her dream, Catherine and Ian had fallen in love while watching the same spectacle. Whenever she had gone there, even before she knew the story, she had felt a nostalgia, a longing for something she didn't remember having experienced. She often found herself staring at the horizon, looking out over the waters of the Shannon.

Someone from the Suicide Watch would occasionally go there to see if she was alright.

"How are you, miss? Can we help you?"

"I'm good, thanks."

"Are you in trouble? We can talk; you're not alone."

How was Olivia going to explain all her problems? How was she going to make them understand that neither they nor anyone else could help her at that moment? And it was at that moment she realised that one of her biggest problems could become the opportunity of her life - the opportunity to tell her story and to immortalise her love. She didn't know if she would be able to do it, and that doubt was staggering her.

"No, it's okay, you don't have to worry about me. I'm very sad, but I'm not planning on doing anything crazy. Don't worry."

"Fine, but if you need anything, you can count on us."

They said that and cautiously left her alone but remained a few feet away from her.

It didn't take long for her two friends to find her. She was sitting on the bench, hugging her legs and crying.

"Olivia, don't be like that," Bella said, hugging her friend.

"I don't want to write about it. I don't want to make money by exposing my pain to others."

"But isn't writing what you most enjoy doing in the world?" asked Seoidín.

"It used to be, but now I'm not sure."

"You once told me that you were born to write and that the perfect world would be one in which you would make money writing your books."

"Oh, that sounds like something I said in another life."

"But it wasn't. It was in this life. The same life you will continue to live for many, many years. You won't want to look back and realise you wasted that chance."

"But Seoidín, how am I going to write about something that is causing me so much suffering?"

"Olivia, one day you told me that Matt always encouraged you to write. I clearly remember you saying that you'd always wished that Cristiano admired you as a writer, rooted for you, and encouraged you, but he never did. Matt, on the other hand, was always supporting you, even though he'd never read your books because they weren't translated yet. He believed in you and I'm sure if he were here, he would encourage you."

"Bella, you definitely can't speak on his behalf."

"But is Bella wrong, Olivia? What do you think he would do if he were here?"

"If he were here, this story wouldn't sell."

"Still, if you were offered this opportunity, what would he tell you to do?"

"He would say that this is the opportunity of my life and that I need to learn to pull myself together and not make these sudden exits."

"And he would be completely right. You have to accept it, Olivia."

"But I don't want to make money from my pain."

"Don't think about the money, then. Think that this is the opportunity people will have to read what you write. This is the chance every writer wants to have. I know you don't want to hear this, but use all this publicity to your advantage to accomplish your dream of becoming a successful writer."

"And you, Bella, what do you have to tell me?"

"I don't think I need to say a single word, right? You know what I think and how I've been by your side every time you released a book. I've seen how hard you fought to get funding for each project. I know about pre-sales and sponsorships. I've followed your struggle, and more than anyone, I know your passion for writing. I think you'd be the dumbest person in the world if you gave it up, but I'm just your best friend and probably one of the people who know you the best. You don't have to take what I think seriously, but I'm sure you'll regret it if you don't accept it, and I won't comfort you because it will be your own fault."

"But I don't know if I can write again."

"How so?" asked Bella.

"It feels like I have writer's block."

"I had an idea. Why don't you write about your dream? Write down everything you've experienced. Tell us that story. I know you've already told us, but by putting it all down on paper, you could give us more details. Do it unpretentiously, just to get back to writing."

"I agree with Seoidín. I think that's a great idea."

"I don't know if I can, guys."

"You'll only find out if you try. Let's go home. Seriously, Olivia, you can do it."

"Yes, let's go home. You must be freezing to death."

"I don't feel sorry for her, Seoidín. It's good for her to learn. Who told you to escape through the window!?"

"Don't lecture me now, Bella. Please."

"Okay, I'll give you a second chance, but don't let it happen again."

Bella hugged her friend, and they headed home. Arriving there, Olivia went straight into the shower. When she came back, she found Bella in her room.

"Here, take it," she said, handing the computer to Olivia.

"Now?"

"Yes, now. Do you have anything better to do?" asked Seoidín, who was also in the room waiting for her to get out of the shower.

"I think... I won't be able to write anything now. I'm not ready."

"Oh, Olivia, cut the small talk. You have until tomorrow to answer the editor. Will you keep crying and wasting the biggest chance of your life, or go back to being the Olivia we know who will chase her dreams?"

"And do you think I can write with you two looking at me?"

"Don't sweat it. We'll prepare dinnerwhile you're here writing."

Olivia turned on her computer and stared at the blank page on word. She knew exactly how she wanted to tell that story; she just didn't know if she was prepared to. She was aware that her friends were right and that she couldn't let this opportunity go. Matt would never have allowed it.

She typed in the title 'Other Times' as if she had gone into automatic mode. She started typing.

She had been wrong; it didn't seem difficult at all. The words came to her mind much faster than her fingers could type. One page, two, ten, fifteen, twenty-three… she started to write lying on her bed, but it didn't take long for her to get up and go to her desk.

Olivia didn't want to stop for dinner. She went to the bedroom door and placed a note saying she was not to be disturbed. She wanted to keep writing; she wanted to make the most of all that inspiration she never suspected she might have.

When they found the note, her friends were worried. Had Olivia locked herself in her room and didn't want to see them anymore? Had she given in once more to crying? But they were relieved to hear the sound of her unstoppable fingers typing on the computer keyboard. It sounded like a gun, shooting letters and more letters, telling stories.

"I think she's typing."

"It seems so. But isn't she going to eat anything?"

"Don't worry, if she gets hungry, she'll go to the kitchen and eat something. I think we have to stop treating her like a child. It seems that our Olivia is little by little coming back," Bella said.

The two stayed awake for a few more hours, and before going to sleep, they went to Olivia's bedroom door once again. They could still hear her typing at full speed.

Olivia wrote all night. She could only sleep after she had told and reviewed the whole story. Her head was bubbling with more ideas to write. Before bed, she printed it all out and placed it on the kitchen table with a note:

"I hope you are satisfied. Your job is to read this while I sleep, and then we can talk to this guy, Paulo Roberto!"

When Bella got up, she found Seoidín sitting at the kitchen table, drinking her coffee as she got halfway through her reading.

"What's that?"

"It's called 'In Other Times' and it's absolutely fantastic and engaging."

"No! Did she write all this?"

"Yes, and it's really good!"

Bella sat down and immediately started reading the sheets Seoidín had already read. She was very happy that her friend had managed to write it all down and was even happier to see that Olivia was sharper than ever. The writing was as engaging as ever, but it felt like there was something more, something different in the way her friend expressed herself.

It wasn't long before they noticed Olivia standing in the kitchen doorway.

"I can't sleep."

"Olivia! You've written a lot and it's really good!"

"Have you finished yet?"

"I have, and Bella is almost there."

"Let's go talk to Paulo Roberto."

"Now?"

"Yes, I had an idea."

"What idea?"

"I'm going to tell my story, but I'm also going to tell Catherine's. I can merge the two stories, after all, they're already merged. I can use all the publicity he can provide and write something more literary."

"I think your idea is perfect and I think he'll like it too."

"This dream may not have been a vision of my past life, but it certainly inspired me to write about a time I didn't live through. I can put it all down on paper and make it all real."

"That's the magic the writer does, Olivia. I've always told you that."

"I agree with you, Bella. It looks like magic. Writers look like gods with the ability to create worlds, stories, change destinies, it's amazing!" said Seoidin.

"Well, the Goddess here doesn't feel that way, but certainly words give us power. I'm going to take a shower and when you finish reading we'll go and meet Paulo, okay?"

"Sure, do you want me to call to arrange the meeting?"

"Yes Bella, if you can do that I would appreciate it."

"He's staying at the Strand, we can meet there if he wants to," Seoidín said.

It didn't take long before everyone was ready to go talk to Paulo Roberto. Olivia asked her two friends to accompany her. She didn't want to risk letting that chance slip through her fingers again for lack of negotiation skills and knew neither of them would allow that to happen.

As they were leaving the house, Bella caught Olivia's attention:

"Olivia look, look at that man running over there?"

"What about him?" Olivia asked, watching the man who was running and was already turning the corner.

"I'm pretty sure it's that Frenchman."

"What do you mean? Jean?"

"Oh no, that can't be true! How did he find out you're here?"

"Well Seoidín, if even Paulo Roberto found out, that guy must have found out too."

"For God's sake, if there's one thing I don't want in my life right now it's having to deal with this mad guy. I already have my own crazy things to deal with."

"Which are considerable, right, Olivia?"

"Yes, Bella...yes, it's quite a lot..."

"But seriously, we have to keep an eye out. If that's him, we need to call the Gardaí. It's not the first time he's been around where you live," Seoidín recalled.

"Are you sure it was him, Bella?"

"I'm not so sure. Besides having killed him in another life, I've only seen him once," said Bella laughing at her friend.

"Blah, blah, blah. You're never going to stop, are you? But anyway, let's be careful."

"Yes, let's be careful. He's not an ordinary person, he can be dangerous."

Paulo Roberto couldn't have been happier to meet Olivia again. He had insisted on coming to Limerick, but he didn't have high hopes that the writer would agree to negotiate.

"I'm so glad you've changed your mind."

"Actually, it's not that I've completely changed my mind. Another idea has come up and I want to present it to you."

Olivia handed Paulo some sheets, explaining her idea in detail. She commented that she would talk about life before the coma, how the coronavirus had changed her life and the dream and sadness of waking up and realising that her boyfriend was no longer there.

He read the sheets Olivia had given him and mentally evaluated everything that was written. In the end, he said:

"I think this idea is fantastic, commercial and engaging, but I'm a little afraid of you getting into this field of past lives. It's a complex topic, it requires a lot of study. People spend their whole lives researching and studying about it and even still, they don't feel they have the right to write about it."

"I wouldn't write about other lifetimes per se. I would write about a dream that seems to have happened in another lifetime. Trust me, I'll write this out very clearly. I don't want to get criticised for writing about a subject I don't know much about."

"I believe that. And yes, I agree that it might work."

"If you are in agreement, I have this to show you."

Olivia took out of her bag the stack of sheets she'd written the night before — more than 40 pages long.

"What is this? Since when have you been writing?"

"She wrote all this after you left our house. You don't know her, Paulo Roberto; Olivia is very fast," said Bella.

"I'm only fast when there's a story worth telling."

"Without a doubt, we have a story here that deserves to be told."

"But Paulo Roberto, let's talk about Olivia's contract," said Bella.

Olivia wasn't good at thinking about such matters, but Bella was perfect. She knew how to negotiate and knew how to demand all that was fair. Olivia just looked at her friend and nodded to her to continue.

"Well, of course Olivia will receive a percentage of all books sold, as well as our commitment to re-release her previous books right away. If we close the deal today, I can message the publisher and get started working on it immediately. In addition, we will also sign a contract committing to release Olivia's next five books with massive publicity and everything our publisher is capable of."

"What about the initial payment? I don't know the terms used, but you know that any publisher will want to publish this book and it won't just be in Brazil. How much will you pay for the rights to publish the story?"

"Look, the publisher will bear all the costs and Olivia will receive a good percentage of every book sold."

"Of course, Paulo Roberto, I agree with you, but the publisher will make a big profit. After all, you are here precisely because you believe that. Other publishers must also have the same interest. Besides, you're wrong if you think that by relaunching Olivia's books you're doing her a favour. I'm sure that with the correct exposure, they will also become profitable material for the Continente."

"Olivia, where did you get this animal? I didn't know you had an agent."

"Bella has always fought for me, we've been in worse fights, believe me. And you better do what she says, otherwise, I'm sure that when we leave here she'll find a better proposal than yours," she said smiling, softening the threat in her tone.

"Of course, I can negotiate your percentage. But I need to make some calls first. I don't have the autonomy to make this decision myself. Do you have any other requirements?"

"Actually, we have one more. The contract will be for the release of five books. Olivia has already written two other books. It would be nice if they came out soon since you told us to take advantage of all this free publicity."

"And I want this book to be released in English as well," Olivia said.

"Of course, that's already our plan. And now it's my turn to make demands. The first of them: until I give you the answer, you won't contact any other publisher. I give you my word that it will be fast."

"Second, you need to get back to Brazil as soon as possible, start appearing on the shows you're being invited to and promoting your book."

"I believe I won't be able to return to Brazil within the next three weeks, at least. I have a lot of things to sort out here and as I know I won't be able to come back anytime soon, I need to sort everything out before I go."

"In this case, you can talk to the reporters by video call. I can contact one of our agents to arrange all this for you, help you with the interviews, organise your schedule, make your life easier and help you to promote your book."

"Fine, as you see fit."

"So, we have a deal?"

"We have a deal, but we don't have a contract yet, Paulo Roberto. We are waiting for your call to sign the contract with all the terms we mentioned."

"That's right Bella. As soon as I have an answer, I'll call you and we'll formalise the contract. Right, Olivia?"

"Yes, all good."

They walked to the car before celebrating. A contract with Continente was everything Olivia had ever dreamed of. In fact, it was more than she had ever dreamed of. She wanted a contract with any publisher and Continente was simply the best. She was sure that, with this publisher, if her books were really good, they would sell. This was the chance she needed.

Olivia was feeling an emptiness inside her chest, as her greatest desire was to be able to share this victory with her beloved. She was sure he would have been very happy to hear about this achievement. He knew how important this was and had encouraged her a lot. This book would be a tribute to Matt. If books are eternal, there was no better way to immortalise everything they had gone through together. All the love and also all the pain Olivia felt when she had learned that Matt was dead.

"He is dead."

Olivia repeated this to herself several times during the day. She needed to accept that sad truth, but her heart couldn't. She wanted to scream, to fight with everyone, to punch someone in the face to see if, somehow, she felt a little less of this pain that seemed to have taken away her will to live. She was doing everything she could to show Seoidín and Bella that she was okay. She wanted Bella to get to know the land she already considered a little bit her own. She didn't want the rest of her friend's time in Ireland to be only about her drama, but only she knew how difficult it was.

Before going to sleep, she cried every night. She would lie on the bedroom floor and, in tears, try to control her breathing. She often had panic attacks, but she didn't want to tell her friends who were doing everything they could to help her recover.

Despite missing her family a lot, she felt guilty because she didn't want to leave Limerick. Something still held her there. She used the fact that she needed to resolve the legal issues at the hospital before returning to Brazil as an excuse, but that was not the only reason. She didn't want to leave. It seemed like she just couldn't say goodbye.

They were barely home when the phone rang. It was Paulo Roberto bringing an initial offer for the book's production and sale. She put the phone on speaker and Bella nearly had a heart attack when he told her how much the editor was willing to pay. The speed with which he returned the call indicated that the book would indeed be a success. They closed the deal and felt they had a lot to celebrate.

"We need to open a sparkling wine!" Seoidín said, getting up to pick up the drink and glasses.

Olivia was really happy.

She had thought she had writer's block and wouldn't be able to write anything, but the idea of putting her story on paper and making it eternal somehow excited her. She felt full of energy and the desire to write. Olivia always surprised everyone with how quickly she wrote her books, but she was sure this one would be the fastest of them all. She didn't feel like eating, sleeping, drinking water, anything. She just wanted to put everything she was feeling down on paper.

Bella, like the good friend she had always been, was always around to ensure she ate and slept. She also handled all correspondence with the hospital, as she was very good at that. Bella also helped Olivia to organise the interviews she needed to give to various TV networks in Brazil and Europe.

Everyone wanted to know the face and story of the person who had spent four months 'dead' and woke up in a world changed by the coronavirus.

Olivia was nervous about her first interview. She would be interviewed by Fantástico, a TV Globo programme. It would be like a common video call, but that didn't make Olivia feel any more relaxed. Everyone she knew would probably watch the interview, and thinking about it made her whole body shake.

The reporter asked her to tell her a little about her life, what she was doing in Ireland, how she got infected with the virus, and what the lockdown was like in Ireland... Initial information to set the scene for the viewer. Then she moved on to more specific questions.

"What was it like waking up in a world so changed by the coronavirus?" she asked.

"I'm going to make a silly analogy, but when I was little I used to watch a movie on the Afternoon Session. The movie portrays a man frozen during one of the ice ages the Earth experienced, and his body is thawed in the 1980s or 90s; I don't remember exactly... Of course, he was frozen much longer than I was, but I woke up in such a different world that it felt like I had been frozen for years. I don't think any of us thought we would go through a situation like this. I remember that before I got sick, I felt like I was living in a parallel reality; the isolation and the way people started interacting didn't seem real. When I woke up from the coma, things were already much better around here. But I can see how much all this affected the economic and social structures, and honestly, I don't know if they will ever go back to the way they were before. I also know that in Brazil, the pandemic was approached very differently from how it was treated here in Ireland. I believe that here we were much more deprived of social interactions and services."

"Olivia, tell us, how do you feel about the mistake that made everyone think you were dead?"

"It was such an unfortunate mistake. Many people suffered a lot because of it, and their suffering deeply has affected me. I think a lot of things would have been different in my life if this mistake hadn't happened."

"Like what?"

"These are just assumptions, as we can't predict the future, but I believe that things would have been less painful for me," Olivia replied, referring to her boyfriend, but avoiding the subject.

"Many people have been curious about that. Who would go to my funeral? How would people react to my death? These are questions that have crossed some people's minds, and you had the chance to see them answered. Were you surprised?"

"Oh, I'll confess that it was a mixture of feelings. I saw many people I love mourning my 'death' so deeply that it was impossible not to get emotional. But in my city, we usually say that 'after you die, you become a saint', so I don't know if people were just being nice and polite, or if they really meant what they wrote about me."

"Olivia, when you say things could have been different, you mean still being with your boyfriend? He died tragically, right?"

Olivia felt her body falling into a bottomless pit when she heard the reporter's question. Yes, yes, yes, she believed so. Just as Matt's parents had replied to her in an email, it was her 'death' that caused his death. But she wasn't going to answer that for the reporter. She would opt for a more evasive answer, so she just replied:

"Yes, he might still be alive, who knows!? Sometimes an event causes a sequence of other actions. It's the butterfly effect. So perhaps he would still be alive."

"And what was it like waking up and realising you had lost the love of your life?"

"Many people will never find the love of their lives. I had found mine. Losing him caused such deep pain that I can't even find the words to describe it." Olivia's gaze was lost, and her eyes filled with tears.

"Sorry to bring up this subject, Olivia. Can I ask just one more question?"

"It's okay. It's still very difficult to talk about, but it's okay."

"Do you remember anything from while you were in a coma? What was that experience like?"

"I don't remember much. But I had a long dream during the coma."

"A dream?"

"I lived through a story during my coma."

"What do you mean? We need to know more about this."

Bella was close to Olivia and nodded to the girl as soon as she realised she had almost backed off from doing her merchandising.

"I'm writing a book to tell the story I lived through during the coma. Soon everyone will be able to know everything that happened to me during that time."

"Does the book have a name or a release date?"

"It will be called 'In Other Times' and should be released in less than two months."

"Oh Olivia, you need to tell us a little about this dream. What did you dream about?"

"It's actually a novel, and it tells a tragic love story that happened here in Limerick, in another time."

"Oh, you have to be a writer to create a story while in a coma," said the reporter, making Olivia let out a discreet smile.

The journalist asked a few more questions and requested Olivia to say a few more things, which would probably be used to fill in information in the editing process.

When the interview was over, Olivia went over to her friends.

"It was a disaster, wasn't it?"

"Of course not," Seoidín said.

"Well, it wasn't a disaster, but there were a few things you could have said differently," Bella said.

"How so?"

"First, where did you get the 'Encino Man' reference? That's the name of the movie you mentioned."

"'Encino Man,' that's right! Wow, I'm glad I didn't remember the name of the movie," Olivia said, laughing at herself.

"Second, when you referenced the 'Butterfly Effect,' another movie, people might think that you, I don't know, used some kind of narcotic, that you were high!"

"I know, I got lost in that part. But was it that bad?"

"No, I'm kidding, it turned out well. I only had these two comments because, as you know, I couldn't let it go unnoticed."

A few more interviews took place, and Olivia kept writing. The book writing was going pretty well. It was as if Olivia was in a trance in front of the computer. She didn't even need to think too much; her fingers moved at a dizzying speed.

As she wrote, Bella organised her schedule, sorted out bureaucratic and legal issues with the hospital, and took advantage of the extra time to get to know Limerick. It was easy for Bella to understand why the city had won her friend's heart.

On the appointed day, Paulo Roberto was in Limerick again, but this time he was accompanied by the editor, who was already reviewing the book. They were in the final stage, and soon the book would be ready to be sent to the printer. Paulo Roberto commented again that it was time for her to return to Brazil.

"But I don't need to go back now, do I?"

"You do. You won't be here forever, and it's essential for us that you are there for the book launch."

"But what difference will it make? How will a launch be possible if everything is closed there because of the pandemic?"

"But what difference will it make if you stay here? Olivia, we agreed on all the requirements you made, and we've fulfilled all our parts of our agreement. Your previous books are already on sale..."

"...and they are a success, very profitable for your publisher," Bella said, jumping into the conversation to defend her friend.

"Yes. We agreed that this would be our part, but Olivia also has her part. Do you intend to stay here forever, Olivia?"

"No, I don't intend to stay here forever because I have family in Brazil and many people I love there. I just don't know if I'm ready. I don't know. I think I should wait a little longer to come back."

"No, it's been long enough! You need to return this week. I'll send you the tickets for you and Bella. Is that okay, Bella?"

"I'll do whatever Olivia decides to do. If she wants to go, I will go. If she wants to stay, then I'll stay here with her."

Olivia didn't have an answer. She knew she had to go back; it was part of the contract, but she didn't feel ready to end her time in Limerick. It was as if her stay there was still incomplete.

"Olivia, that's your part of the deal. I'll send the tickets."

"I'm not ready to go back yet, Paulo Roberto. Besides, we need to talk about the book cover because I've had an idea."

"Oh yes, our graphics team has some suggestions. They're here; let me show you."

He opened the folder and took out three printed pages, displaying the cover options they had sent him. One of them showed two hands reaching for each other as if searching for eternity. The second option featured a Claddagh ring, also very beautiful, and the third was just an aged cover with the title in the centre.

"What do you think?"

"They're very pretty. I liked the first two, but I have another suggestion."

"What suggestion?"

"We could use a photo like the one that led me to Catherine's grave. What do you think?"

"What's the picture like? Can you show me?"

Olivia took out her cell phone and showed the photo to Paulo Roberto, who seemed to like it and showed it to the editor.

"Did you take this photo, Olivia?"

"Yes, this is one of the pictures I took."

"Great, I like the idea too. I need the publishers' approval, but I think they'll like it as well."

"Alright! I look forward to hearing from you."

"Yes, I'll get back to you as soon as possible. I'll send the tickets too."

Outside the hotel where the meeting took place, Bella asked Olivia,

"Don't you want to go back?"

"I want to, but I don't know if I'm ready to go back and end my time here."

"I didn't want to say this in front of Paulo Roberto, but I want to go back. I miss home, my family, and I think we're ready to return to Brazil. I came here to get you, and that's what I'd like to do. Let's go home, please."

Olivia considered the request of her friend, who had left everything in Brazil to be there with her. It would be fairer for her to return, especially to her family, who would also like to have her around. The longing she felt for her family seemed surreal; she even thought she avoided thinking about it so she wouldn't be suffocated by this feeling.

"Okay, we'll go back."

"Oh, thank God. I didn't want to have to argue with Paulo Roberto anymore."

"By the way, there's something I want to tell you, Bella. I think there is some tension between you and Paulo Roberto."

"What do you mean, Olivia? I think he hates me."

"You know that too much hate is also a sign of passion."

"Where did you get this idea, Olivia? Are you nuts!"

"He's handsome."

"Oh, stop talking nonsense. Let's go home and pack."

The two went back home, and Olivia couldn't believe it was time to say goodbye. She didn't want this to be a final goodbye. She would come back again as it would be hard to separate Limerick from her life.

As they were returning home, Bella said, "Look over there, Olivia, it's Jean."

"My God, Bella, it's him. What is he doing?"

"I don't know, he seems to be watching the house. He's looking this way. Oh no!"

"He's coming, let's run."

"No, no, wait. Let's see what he has to say."

He came over and started talking. He didn't look well; he actually looked a little disturbed.

"What a surprise to see you here!"

"I can say the same, what are you doing here, Jean?"

"I'm just…just walking. Why?"

"I don't want to get in trouble with you. If you start stalking me again, I'll call the Gardaí."

"Olivia, do you think the world revolves around you? Walking down a street is not a crime. You're being self-centred."

"Fine, if you say you were just passing by I'll believe it, but if it ever happens again, have no doubt I'll call the Gardaí."

Jean changed his tone and took Olivia's arm, saying, "You think you can boss me around? I'll do what I want. Are you trying to immortalise your love for that asshole in a book? It's our love you should be writing about!"

"Hey, let go of her, you psycho!"

"Get out of here, Jean. What love!? There's no such thing as 'our love'! You better go for treatment, I think you're out of control again!"

"Listen, Olivia! You're mine! You're mine! You're going to be mine!"

"I'm calling the police right now!" yelled Bella, picking up the phone, causing him to release her friend and stride away.

"Olivia, are you alright?"

"Yes, I am. Did you see that? He's out of control. Look here, I might get a bruise on my arm."

"Let's go to the police now, Olivia. He can't get away with this."

"Oh no, I don't want to deal with that guy again."

They went to the police station and filed a formal complaint against Jean. However, the police also stated that they couldn't do much. They couldn't stop him from walking down the same street where she lived. After all, there no restrictive measures had been put in place even after he'd been caught spying on Olivia the year before. They promised to keep an eye on him, but nothing could be done unless he committed a crime.

Olivia wasn't that worried because she would be leaving town in a few days and he wouldn't have time to do anything. After leaving the Garda station, one thing puzzled her. How did he know about the book and about it being a way to eternalise her love for Matt?

Okay, it would be easy for him to know that she was releasing a book that talked about her time in a coma, but he knew unpublished details... Was he hacking into her computer again? Suddenly, a certain tension took over her.

When they got home, Olivia had to deal with another tough situation: she would have to say goodbye not only to the people but also to the city she loved as her home.

It was difficult for Olivia to say goodbye to Seoidín. Even a thousand lives wouldn't be enough to thank her for all that she had done. She wasn't even referring to what Seoidín did after she came out of the coma, which had already been a lot, but everything she'd done before, since the first time she'd set foot in Ireland. Olivia was absolutely convinced that she had only been able to apply for the scholarship because of Seoidín. After the Brazilian group arrived, Seoidín was very helpful to everyone, showing them the best places in Limerick, taking them on tours to different places in Ireland, and being a true friend to everyone. It was hard to find someone in her position who was as available and as genuinely generous as the director.

Olivia's debt only increased after she came out of the coma. She treated her like family, taking care of her as Olivia's own family would. She welcomed her into her home and treated Bella as if she were her own best friend. Bella had also already grown to love the director.

Olivia didn't know how to thank her. She bought a bottle of wine and wrote an emotional letter. She couldn't wait to welcome her to Brazil, where she hoped to repay everything she had received.

Seoidín wouldn't be able to take them to Dublin because classes were about to start and there was a lot to be done. Olivia and Bella would go to Dublin by bus, but that was no problem.

They were going to catch the bus in the afternoon, and Olivia spent the whole day feeling nostalgic. Limerick had given her many joys. She had lived there for just over a year, and now she understood a phrase she heard a long time ago: "It wasn't a year in a lifetime, it was a lifetime in a year." Everything she'd lived there hadn't felt like it had happened in just one year. She had experienced so many challenges, met so many people, learned so much, found the great love of her life, got separated from him, spent months between life and death, had that dream so real that it seemed to have been true, and then experienced the loss of her great love. All these events were surreal, and she was sure many people live a lifetime without experiencing what she had in that one year in Limerick.

Bella knew it was difficult for Olivia and worried about her because she hadn't spoken half a dozen words all day. She understood that it was hard for Olivia to end this cycle, so she decided to suggest something different.

"Would you like to visit your grave?"

"Gee, what are you talking about?"

"You were supposedly buried. There's a grave with your name on it."

"What do you mean? Have you seen it?"

"Well, first Seoidín said there was a funeral for you, but they couldn't attend because of the coronavirus protocol. Then the grave was mentioned again in one of the hospital meetings. You know, I had several meetings you declined to attend…"

"Stop, Bella. I'm so grateful that you represented me and fought for me tooth and nail, but focus on the cemetery story."

"So, at one of these meetings, they confirmed that the grave is still there. I even know which cemetery, let me find it here."

Bella grabbed some papers and started looking for the address. She knew her friend would want to go to the cemetery, even as sad as she was at that moment. She would never pass up such an adventure.

"I found it, here's the address."

Olivia took the sheet from her friend's hands and looked at it.

"Um, well, it's close. Do you want to go?"

"Of course I do. The question is... Do you want to go?"

Olivia pondered. Of course, she wanted to. Who wouldn't want to see their 'own grave'?

"We can go, but it has to be right now."

"So let's go."

They called a taxi, and in less than 20 minutes, they were at the entrance to the cemetery. They didn't even know where to start.

"Do you have the exact location of my grave or do we have to look one by one?"

"I don't have the exact location, but I know there's a part of the cemetery designated for COVID-19 deaths. It shouldn't be hard to find. Come on."

They walked around the cemetery for a bit and soon arrived at the part that seemed like what they were looking for. It didn't take long for them to spot the name 'Olivia Walter Kalckmann'. However, the biggest surprise was when, on top of the tomb, covered by green grass, they found a rose with something written on a card.

"What is this, Bella?"

"I don't know, I've never been here. Someone must have left it for you. Let's take a picture of the grave."

Olivia bent down and took the flower in her hand. On the card, there was only one sentence: "The light that brightens my days." Olivia began to cry.

"What is it, Olivia?"

"Bella, this can only be a bad joke. Why are you doing this to me?"

"Doing what? What's written there?"

Bella took the card from Olivia's hand and didn't understand it either. The phrase was the same one Ian used to say to Catherine.

"Why did you do this?"

"Oh no, Olivia, do you really think I would do such a thing to you?"

"I don't know, first this story out of nowhere about going to the cemetery and then I come here and find this? What do you expect me to say?"

Olivia said that and walked out of the cemetery with the flower in her hand, leaving Bella standing there, not understanding anything. It was obvious that she hadn't put that flower there. Bella went after Olivia and found her crying beside the cemetery entrance. When she saw that Bella was approaching, she said:

"Sorry, I know you wouldn't do that to me. But how did that flower get there? Especially with that quote on it? I wasn't prepared to see this."

"I have no idea. But it must be Paulo Roberto's idea. Some publicity stunt for the book or something."

"It doesn't make any sense. That's what Ian used to say to Catherine."

"Yes, I know, it's in the book. Paulo Roberto knows it too. That's why I think he did it. Here..."

"What is it?"

"I took a picture of your grave," Bella said, trying to make her friend smile.

"Very funny. Wow, I expected more from my grave, huh? Please, if I die before you, make sure I'm cremated, I don't want a grave anymore."

"Stop talking nonsense. I can't bear to lose you again," Bella said, hugging her friend and walking her out of the cemetery.

Then Bella looked at her friend's hands and asked:

"What are you doing with that flower? For God's sake! Don't you know it's bad luck to take a flower from a cemetery?"

"This flower is for me."

"It's not for you. Did you forget there's someone else buried there?"

"How disrespectful! They didn't put her name, and mine is still there."

"Girl, they still haven't figured out her name. No name and no flower because you're taking the only thing she had."

"Stop, Bella. You know the flower is for me."

"Oh God, it's our last day here... I won't argue with you."

Olivia didn't know why, but she wanted to keep that flower, even if it had been Paulo Roberto's idea. That flower meant something, and she was going to take it home. The whole flower story had only made Olivia even more thoughtful and gave her a very strong feeling that she still had one thing to do before they left.

When they arrived at Seoidín's house, they didn't have much time left. Seoidín wasn't there as she had some meetings to attend. So, they just packed up and called another taxi. When Olivia closed the door to the place where she'd been living since she got back from the hospital, it was as if her heart had been squeezed. That was it; it was time to say goodbye to that house and that city.

Bella put her hand on her friend's shoulder. She knew that sometimes she just needed a bit of encouragement. They went downtown early because Bella wanted to buy some souvenirs before they left, and the stores were close to where they would take the bus.

They walked with their suitcases to the benches next to the river and, while Bella went shopping, Olivia stayed there, waiting with the suitcases. That way, she would have some time to be silent and say goodbye to the River Shannon.

The river was beautiful as always, with its waters painted by the orange tones of the sunset that, at this time of year, happened earlier and earlier, combined with the castle, the church, and the noise of the seabirds. That was the vivid image of Limerick she would carry with her forever. It was impossible to be there without remembering Catherine. That place had been the setting of her story. There Catherine had also lived through some of the happiest and saddest moments of her short life.

Olivia looked at the flower on top of her suitcase and decided to put it in her diary to dry. As she opened the diary to a random page, she read a quote she had jotted down before the pandemic began:

"Why think separately of this life than the next, when one is born from the last? Time is always too short for those who need it, but for those who love, it lasts forever."

The poem talked about longing and one soul needing another. The excerpt was from a poem called "Life and Death," written by Rumi, a 13th-century poet. Olivia had jotted down that snippet after seeing it quoted in the movie "Dracula Untold."

Her heart was once again taken by longing. She placed the flower on that page to dry, and as she was putting the diary away, one of the cover options suggested by Paulo Roberto fell to the floor. It was the cover with the image of a ring. More and more, Olivia was sure she needed to do something before she left. She couldn't leave without doing it.

Bella came running back. The bus was already there, and the driver placed the bags in the luggage compartment. The two crossed Arthur's Quay Square with long strides. Bella was afraid of missing the bus, but Olivia had other intentions.

Upon arriving at the bus, Olivia went to the driver and asked, "Please, can you tell me the time of the next bus?"

"The next bus to Dublin leaves in two hours."

"Do I need to buy another ticket?"

"No, you can change it through the website and board with the same ticket without any problems."

"What are you doing?" asked Bella, terrified.

"We're not going to board this bus."

"I understand that, I just don't understand why. Why don't we go now?"

"Because I can't leave without doing something first."

"What? What haven't you been able to do all this time we've been here that you need to do now? Just so we can miss the bus."

"Bella, calm down, please. Our flight is tomorrow night, so we have plenty of time to get to Dublin. I need to go to the cemetery."

"Again? What do you want to do there? Goddamn it! I shouldn't have taken you there."

"Are you going to board or not?" asked the driver.

"No, we'll take the next bus, thanks!"

"I can't believe it, Olivia. I can't believe it!" Bella said, sitting down on the bench at the bus stop.

"I'll explain..."

"You better have a very good explanation because I'm not enjoying your madness at all, Olivia."

"I promise you. We'll catch the bus in two hours."

"Okay. Which cemetery do you want to go to?"

"Well, ever since I found this flower back on 'my grave' with Ian's quote, I've had this fixed idea in my head."

"The flower that Paulo Roberto placed there?"

"It wasn't him. I texted him, and he said it wasn't his idea."

"So, who was it?"

"I don't know."

"And you want to stay to find out?"

"No, that's not it. I want to stay because of my dream, because of the story in the book."

"I'm not following..."

"I don't know how I never thought of this before, but there's a very simple way to find out if it was all a dream."

"Oh no, this story again? We already know it was a dream. The house wasn't the same. The notebook we found had nothing to do with what you said. Stop with the nonsense. Let's call a taxi to catch the bus. There's still time."

"I know this all didn't make sense, but there are explanations for it.

The house may have been modified, and we only found a notebook."

"Oh no, Olivia, I don't have the patience for this," Bella concluded, standing up and starting to pull her suitcase towards the taxis.

"Wait for me, Bella, let me tell you…"

"No, I'm leaving."

"I want to go to the cemetery and look for the headstone Catherine had made for Ian."

Bella stopped walking on hearing this.

"If it doesn't exist, I'll give up. I'll admit that my writer's brain works even when I'm in a coma."

"How did you not think of this before?" said Bella, turning to her friend.

"I don't know. There was so much pressure, especially from you, for me to believe it was just a dream. I was so sad that I had lost Matt, and I didn't want to think about it anymore. But as I wrote it down and put it all on paper, this feeling that it wasn't just a dream ignited inside me. Today, when I picked this flower, this idea came to my mind. The cemetery is right next door. In less than an hour, we can solve this mystery."

"Okay, but you know I'll talk about this and make fun of you forever, right? I'll call you stubborn from here to eternity. We won't find anything there. It was just a dream, Olivia."

"Okay, we have a deal. But now let's go."

The two left, dragging their bags through the crowded downtown streets. It was autumn, and the sun was starting to disappear very early, so the darkness of the night was already beginning to take over the scenery.

"Are you sure you want to enter the cemetery at night?"

"Are you scared, Bella?"

"Of course not, I just don't think it's the most appropriate time."

"That's new to me. You're scared of something? You're always the first to want to do things."

"I've never been to a cemetery at night."

"So today will be your first time."

They entered, and Olivia knew exactly where to go. She showed Bella where Catherine and the whole family's grave was. Bella was visibly uncomfortable. Olivia wanted to talk about each of them, but her friend didn't want to hear.

"Go straight to the place, Olivia. Where is he buried?"

"It's here. I mean, it was supposed to be here."

"Well, there's nothing there, let's go back to the bus stop."

"Stop, Bella. I'll look it up. Put your phone's flashlight here too."

The two illuminated the spot that Olivia had pointed out as the correct one, but they saw nothing, it was just grass. Olivia picked up a piece of wood she'd found on the floor and started digging.

"You'll be arrested if anyone sees you here digging in a cemetery. Digging in a cemetery! You've lost your mind for good!"

"Turn off the flashlight, Bella. Seriously, turn off the flashlight," Olivia whispered.

Bella complied with her friend's request. If they were arrested, then they wouldn't take that plane to Brazil. Olivia rummaged around in the dirt until she found something hard, like a rock.

"I think I found something. Help me dig."

"Ah..." Bella thought about refusing, but changed her mind. After all, the faster they finished, the sooner they would get out of there. She took a piece of wood and started removing the sand. To her surprise, it did look like a small headstone.

"Look at it. I was so sure about this."

"Calm down, Olivia. What if it's a tomb?"

"It's not a tomb. Let's find the initials."

It didn't take long for them to find the initials I.A.M.

Olivia started to cry. She knew this wasn't a dream. That story had been real. Bella couldn't believe that all of this had actually happened. She was shocked.

"Let's get someone to help us, Olivia."

"No, let's take it out on our own. Help me. If we call someone, we'll have to explain a lot, and it's going to take a long time. We have to sort this out now."

Olivia removed the headstone, which was slightly smaller than the dimensions of an A4 sheet.

"I remember, it's not too deep. Help me, Bella."

Even in the dark, Bella could see the sparkle in her friend's eyes. She was so excited that she decided to dig with her hands to be faster.

"You'll have to pay for my manicure in Brazil. Look here, my nails are full of dirt, and worse, graveyard dirt. Oh my God!!!" she said to tease her friend.

"I'll pay for everything. Just keep digging because I'm very close to finding it, and I don't want to risk being arrested," Olivia replied, admitting her fear of being caught.

"It looks like there's something here," Bella said.

Olivia helped her friend get the dirt off the little box. She knew what was in there.

"Oh my God, Olivia, I can't believe it!"

"See? I knew it wasn't just in my head," she said, crying and very emotional.

She opened the box and the ring was inside with the letter that Catherine had written to her great love. She gently took the ring that was wrapped in a piece of fabric. It was enough to lightly rub the cloth and the ring shone like the last time Olivia remembered seeing it. She cried nonstop. Then she took the letter in her hands.

"I'll read the letter to you, okay?"

"Read it," Bella confirmed, also crying while illuminating the letter with her phone's flashlight.

"My love,

The time we lived together might have been short, but it was enough for me to understand what true love means. The love that moves the world, inspires artists, songs, and poems. That overwhelming love that took over me from the first moment I saw you.

When I saw you, I knew my fate had changed forever. I was yours from the first look, or maybe even before that.

Being loved by you was the best thing that ever happened in my life. Even if I'll never be happy again, the time I spent with you was enough to make my life worth living.

I couldn't have lived my whole life without knowing what true love was, and you showed me that. I keep in my memory all the movements of your hands, your mouth, the sweetness of your eyes, the colour of your hair, your beard, and the tone of your voice. Even after you're gone, I still feel entirely yours. It's as if I only existed to find you and thus feel complete.

My greatest happiness is knowing that a little piece of you is inside me. This baby will bring me closer to you, and I'll talk to him every day about what an amazing father he had.

There isn't a single day that I don't dream of a different reality, that I don't dream of the life we would have had together.

I am absolutely sure that our souls have always been together and that we'll meet again. And then we'll live this great love forever.

I love you, my Ian. I will be yours forever.

You're the light that brightens my days.
Catherine Crawford McLeod."

When she finished reading, the two were in tears, very emotional, and Bella was almost sobbing. Olivia had her head down, staring at the ring she had already put on her finger. When she finished reading the letter, she spoke in a choked voice, "Poor Catherine, little did she know that in the next life everything would be repeated and she would be separated from her love once again."

"Calm down, Olivia, everything will be fine."

"No, nothing is going to be fine. This letter could have been written by me in this lifetime. Except for the fact that I don't have a son to remember my Matt. How I wish! That would be my only happiness. I don't complain all the time, but there isn't a moment when I'm not thinking of him or when my heart isn't mourning his death."

"I know, Olivia, I know. But your life isn't over. It has just begun."

Olivia sat on the floor and started crying again. That's when Bella's phone rang.

"It's Paulo Roberto. Hello."

"Hi, how are you? Are you close?"

"We're good, but we're still in Limerick."

"What?"

Bella looked at Olivia and signalled that she was going to get up to explain the story to him. Olivia started putting the dirt back into the hole they had dug. When she was almost done, she heard Bella's footsteps approaching.

"Yeah, I think we should go. Come on, we still have time to catch the bus to Dublin."

"I knew I wasn't wrong. I knew this had really happened."

"I still need a little more time to digest this whole story. It's all very surreal. Paulo Roberto was perplexed when I told him. He said that this will boost the publicity for the book. He thought it was fantastic!"

"He only thinks about money and publicity. Can you understand what I'm going through? What I'm experiencing? This is all very strong. It upsets me a lot. I don't even know what to think. Why did I have to relive this story? To feel this horrible pain twice?"

"I certainly can understand you, Olivia. Let's go home. I'm sure you'll feel better in Alfredo, surrounded by your family."

Olivia sat there silently, staring into space, as if trying to find a reason why this was happening. Then she opened her arms, asking her friend for a hug. Bella understood her request, hugged her, and caressed her while she cried on her shoulder. Olivia was very confused, but at the same time, she felt happy to have proved that she wasn't crazy, that her dream was real and not just a fantasy. She felt sad because an immeasurable pain took over her heart. All the suffering from the past had now been added to the pain she was experiencing in the present.

Bella tried to comfort her friend, and they walked back to the bus stop. They managed to catch the last bus to Dublin, which didn't take long to show up.

"Is everything okay, Olivia? Do you need anything?"

"No, it's okay. I just want to get to Brazil soon. Enough of all this here," she said, looking at Shannon through the window, trying to convince herself that she was doing the right thing by leaving Limerick. She said this while holding the ring she had found buried. That ring meant so much. It brought back so many memories, and it fit exactly on her finger. The same finger where the ring she'd given Matt and promised to take back had once been.

The bus started to move, and gradually Olivia began seeing things from afar, such as the Ferris wheel in the square and the modest harbour where the small boats and kayaks were docked. The bus turned just before the bridge Olivia loved. The street the bus followed ran parallel to The Locke Bar, with the river separating them. From the bus, she could also see the cathedral, which was about 100 meters away from the bar. It was then that Olivia shouted, "Stop the bus! Please, stop the bus!"

"What are you doing, Olivia?"

"It's him, I need to get off the bus!"

"Who?"

Olivia didn't answer her friend. She went to the front of the bus to talk to the driver while the other passengers asked her to sit down. The bus driver told her to sit down and kept driving. But Olivia insisted she needed to get off. Very reluctantly, he stopped the bus and opened the door.

Bella didn't know what to do and just watched her friend get off the bus and run down the street at full speed. Olivia ran to The Locke Bar and kept looking for the man she saw through the window but didn't find him. She looked around and entered the bar but couldn't find anyone. Was she going crazy? For a moment, she was sure the man she saw through the window was Matt. She then went to the corner and looked at the cathedral. She felt like she needed to go back there and visit the cemetery again.

When she got there, all the dirt she had put back in the hole was churned up as if someone had dug it up again in the same place. Olivia was very intrigued and, in an attempt to get an explanation, she looked for someone in the cemetery but found no one. Then, she spotted Bella walking down the street with her bags and an unfriendly expression.

"Patience has limits, and mine is gone."

"Bella, I thought I saw Matt."

"Olivia, he's dead. Dead. You left me there alone on the bus with a bunch of angry people and a driver breathing fire. I don't even know how I got our bags back. But I'm going to Dublin today. I'll call Paulo Roberto, rent a car, take a taxi... I'm leaving today even if I have to take a wagon. Whether you want to come or stay is not my problem. You're not a child anymore."

"Bella..."

"Don't 'Bella' me. I'm going to call Paulo Roberto now. Decide if you're coming or not."

Olivia knew her friend was right. It was irrational to get off the bus like that. Her friend was not sparing words to curse her; she was really angry. She was crestfallen, thinking about the scolding she had received. Getting off the bus like that had been reckless; Bella was absolutely right. But it looked so much like him; she really thought it was Matt passing by the pub. She was still very confused, thinking about what she had or hadn't seen, when she heard someone calling her name.

"Olivia?"

Her heart seemed to stop. She knew that voice, and it wasn't Bella's.

"Matt?" she said, turning around.

"Olivia, is that really you? I can't believe it."

The two stared at each other for a second and then hugged, although neither of them understood what was going on.

"Are you alive?"

"I can't believe it! They told me you were dead! What's going on? I can't believe you're alive. My God, I'm the happiest man alive!"

Olivia was speechless. She couldn't say a single word. She felt like she was going to faint. What was happening? She must be hallucinating.

"I think I'm going to faint.

She felt her body soften and fall against Matt's.

In the meantime, Bella returned.

"Holy Lord! Who are you?" Bella didn't know what to think. Was he a ghost?

"Help me! She passed out!"

"Who are you? What did you do to her?"

"I'm Matt, her boyfriend. I thought she was dead," said the man, crying.

"Let's get her closer to the light. I'll get her some water. She's breathing…"

Matt carried Olivia while Bella got the water. Gradually, Olivia's colour returned to normal, and she opened her eyes. The first thing she said was, "My love! Is this real? Bella, is this real?"

"It seems so."

"Can someone explain to me what's going on?" asked Matt, a mixture of joy and visible amazement in his voice.

"I just want to kiss you! I can't believe you're alive! You're alive, my love!"

"Calm down, calm down! Both of you, calm down! Everyone's alive. The one who won't be alive soon will be me if I can't understand what's happening. Matt, Olivia was in a coma for four months, and she was declared dead because of a mistake at the hospital. Everyone in Brazil thought she had died. It wasn't until she woke up that the mess was cleared up."

"Yes, I was told you were dead. It was the hardest time of my life. How did that happen? When did you wake up?"

"It's a long story, but it was about a month ago," explained Bella.

"And you didn't look for me?" Matt asked Olivia.

"Of course, I looked for you. I tried every resource I had, but you disappeared from all social media. And your parents emailed me, blaming me for your death."

"My parents? But why would they do that?"

"I don't know, but I have the email here. They told me you died in a car accident."

"My parents would never do that. When you died, my only wish was to disappear from the world and die too. I had no reason to live anymore. My parents knew that you being alive would be the greatest joy of my life. I bought a sailboat and left everything behind. I only came here because of a dream I have every night."

"What dream?"

"A dream in which we're living in another time. We die and then we meet again. I had to come here. Earlier, I stopped by the cemetery and left a flower on your grave."

"So, it was you? It was that flower that made me stay, that made me come here and find this. I was flying back to Brazil today."

"The ring! Did you find the ring?"

"Yes!"

Matt reached inside his shirt and pulled out a string with the ring Olivia had given him.

"Now you have two."

The two kissed passionately.

There were still many things to be explained, and Bella was already convinced that they wouldn't go to Dublin that day. They would miss the plane and who knows what else, but she couldn't contain her joy. This was all very impressive. She needed a Guinness.

"Does anyone else need a Guinness to process this story?"

Olivia looked at her friend and smiled.

"I'm afraid this is just a dream, that I'll wake up and go back to living that nightmare of a world without him."

"It's not a dream, Olivia. As surreal as all this may seem, it's real. He's alive."

The three crossed the street and went to The Locke Bar.

They sat at a table inside the bar and started talking, but the two could barely stop smiling or take their hands off each other. They had a lot to talk about, a lot to understand, but it was impossible to stop smiling.

"Tell me more about this e-mail from my parents."

"I have the email here, look."

Olivia showed Matt her phone. He read in disbelief everything his parents had supposedly written.

"I'm sure my parents didn't write this."

"So, who did?"

"I don't know. But it could have been that crazy guy."

"Who?"

"Right after you died, I mean, when you were presumed dead, all my accounts were hacked. My emails, my social media, my phone numbers. Even the accounts of some of my friends. We thought it was a random incident. But no, it seemed to be an attack directed at me. Then I got an email saying that they would continue to disturb my life forever because I had killed you."

"Did they say you killed me?"

"Yes, the person said I had caused your death by transmitting coronavirus to you."

"What do you mean? That doesn't make any sense!"

"I know it doesn't. But I was very upset. I didn't want to live anymore. So, I bought a boat and decided to travel without a destination. You know I've always wanted to do this with you by my side, so I don't know if it was a good idea, because I missed you all the time."

"I know exactly what you're talking about, Matt, because I felt the same."

"Patience, everyone, patience. You'll have the rest of your lives to make up for the lost time. Olivia, don't you think it was Jean who hacked Matt's accounts? Remember that time he ran into you at the café and made a comment about Matt's death?"

"Yes, remember I told you it was very strange?"

"Who is Jean?"

"Matt, Jean is that guy who hacked my accounts, who published my text in the paper and ended up disqualifying me from the contest."

"Yes, I think I vaguely remember."

"He's a sick and obsessive guy. He was chasing Olivia! He was admitted to a clinic, but now he's back in town. I have no doubt it was him," Bella said.

"I can't believe he was capable of such monstrosity!" commented Olivia, starting to cry again.

"It doesn't matter, my love. What matters now is that we're together and nothing will separate us again."

"Nothing at all. We'll be together forever."

"Well, I'll see what happened to our beer. I think it got lost along the way," said Bella.

The two stayed at the table, looking at each other without saying a word. It was as if they were trying to understand everything that was going on.

"I love you."

"I love you too, and I thought I couldn't live without you."

"I didn't want to live anymore."

"Neither did I. But now we're going to be together. I'm going to kidnap you with my boat and we're going to live forever together."

"I will not object."

Suddenly they heard a voice, yelling at them.

"You'll both die!" And the man started shooting, causing general panic.

"Stop, Jean! What are you doing?" He was completely disturbed and out of his mind, as if he was under the influence of some very strong drug.

"You bitch, if you're not mine, you won't be anyone else's!"

A man tried to stop Jean, but Jean shot him mercilessly, causing even more panic. Everyone started to run out of the bar, leaving only Olivia and Matt.

"This is no joke! I'm going to kill you both!" He started crying at that moment.

"No Jean, don't do this."

"You bitch! You slut!"

"Hey, who do you think you are?" Olivia took Matt's arm and held him. She nodded her head for him to shut up.

"Alright, alright. You can call me whatever you want."

"Sit down and shut up. I'm going to kill him first. And then you're going to be mine. We're going to get out of here and get married."

"Fine. I'll marry you. But put that gun down."

"Okay, but first I'm going to kill him."

Two shots rang out, making the window behind him break into several pieces.

"Nooo!!!"

"And now I'm going to kill you, you lying bitch."

Just as he pointed the gun at Olivia and was about to shoot, Bella threw a chair at him causing him to fall. Matt threw his body on top of Jean, punched him and made him drop the gun. The Gardaí were already arriving and soon entered the pub.

"Matt, Matt, are you okay?"

"Yes. I don't know if he hit me, I think that blood is just from the shards of glass. Are you okay?"

"Yeah, I think my wounds are just from the glass too."

"Olivia, Matt! Are you all okay?"

"Thank you, Bella, if it weren't for you…"

"Well, this time I didn't fail. Your sister Emily wasn't there to save you, but your sister Bella would never let Jean win again," said Bella hugging Olivia and crying.

"Thank you so much, Bella. Seriously, I thought I was going to lose Matt again."

"When I came out of the bathroom and saw this scene, I didn't think twice. My first impulse was to throw the chair at him, but it was reckless. If Matt hadn't been quick enough, this could have been a disaster."

"Don't worry, you did the right thing! You saved us."

"This story is so surreal, Olivia. I'm so happy! I think it's finally over now."

"Yes! And Bella, I need to tell you something."

"What? Sounds serious! What is it now?"

"You know the guy who was shot?"

"Yeah, what about him? He'll be fine!"

"He's Geoffrey!"

"You're kidding! My God!" said Bella, moving away from Olivia and heading towards the ambulance where the man was.

"What happened to her? Who's Geoffrey?" asked Matt, not understanding the story.

"Oh, we have a lot to talk about..."

That was a long night. They called Seoidín and it didn't take long for her to join them. The director had just returned from Cork and was in disbelief at the whole story she had just heard. They had to go to the hospital and then spent hours at the Garda station giving statements. At the end of the night, Bella went to Seoidín's house and Olivia went to the hotel where Matt was staying.

She just wanted to sleep being held by her love.

They were walking towards the hotel and the sun was already rising, illuminating the waters of the Shannon. They went to the bank of the river and watched the water that flowed lightly and the steam that rose from it as it began to be heated by the sun.

The River Shannon, as if eternal, had witnessed their love. Its waters had lulled the lovers on sunny afternoons and made them sigh with longing on lonely evenings. The same river that had been Ian's grave and received Catherine's tears, was now a witness to Matt and Olivia's reunion.

Olivia rose on tiptoe to wrap her hands around Matt's neck. She ran her hand through his red hair, stroked his beard and kissed his mouth.

He took her hand, which now had the two rings.

"Our love has overcome time, conquered the coronavirus, and will be eternal."

He knelt and said:

"Will you marry me?"

The End.

Carol Pereira, born in 1987 in Alfredo Wagner (SC, Brazil), is a multi-faceted author. Despite her passion for writing, she has a background in programming and is also a teacher. She holds a Master's degree in Education – Mentoring and Leadership in Schools from Mary Immaculate College, Ireland.

Recognized for her work, she was awarded the Professores do Brasil Prize by the Brazilian Ministry of Education (MEC) in 2013, 2014, and 2017. Additionally, she was a finalist in the Irish literary contest The Ogham Stone with her English short story Cailleach Aoife and the Crows of Ireland.

Carol is the author of several works, including As Aventuras de Eva Schneider, As Aventuras de Eva Schneider – Fronteiras entre o Amor e a Guerra, As Aventuras de Eva Schneider – O Livro Secreto dos Jesuítas, Conhecendo Alfredo Wagner, Histórias da Nossa Gente, Não se Distraia, and Limerick e o Tempo (Portuguese version).

She currently resides in Canada with her husband.

Other Books by the Author:

- As Aventuras de Eva Schneider (2017)

- Conhecendo Alfredo Wagner (2018)

- As Aventuras de Eva Schneider: Fronteiras entre o Amor e a Guerra (2019)

- As Aventuras de Eva Schneider: O Livro Secreto dos Jesuítas (2024)

- Limerick e o Tempo (2024)

- Não se distraia - A arte de ser eu (2025)

- As Aventuras de Eva Schneider: O Olho de Zyagba (Upcoming Release)

- The Adventures of Eva Schneider: Up and Down the Glens (Upcoming Release in English and Portuguese)

If you enjoyed this book, don't miss these other stories full of adventure, history, and culture!

Connect with the Author

Follow my work, news, and upcoming releases on social media:

Instagram: Carolpereiraaa@instagram.com
Facebook: facebook.com/carol.pereiraaa
Blog: carolpereiraa.blogspot.com
Podcast: pod_vagamundos3

I would love to hear your thoughts about this book! Leave a comment or tag me on social media. Your opinion is very important to me!